CLASSIC IN THE BARN

CLASSIC IN THE BARN

A Case for Jack Colby, the Car Detective

Amy Myers

This first world edition published 2011
in Great Britain and the USA by
SEVERN HOUSE PUBLISHERS LTD of
9–15 High Street, Sutton, Surrey, England, SM1 1DF.
Trade paperback edition first published
in Great Britain and the USA 2011 by
SEVERN HOUSE PUBLISHERS LTD.

British Library Cataloguing in Publication Data

Myers, Amy, 1938-
  Classic in the barn.
  1. Murder – Investigation – England – Kent – Fiction.
  2. Antique and classic cars – Conservation and
  restoration – Fiction. 3. Lagonda automobile – Fiction.
  4. Automobile dealers – Fiction. 5. Kent (England) –
  Fiction. 6. Detective and mystery stories.
  I. Title
  823.9'14-dc22

ISBN-13: 978-0-7278-8018-5 (cased)
ISBN-13: 978-1-84751-340-3 (trade paper)

All Severn House titles are printed on acid-free paper.

Severn House Publishers support The Forest Stewardship Council [FSC],
the leading international forest certification organisation. All our titles that
are printed on Greenpeace-approved FSC-certified paper carry the FSC logo.

Typeset by Palimpsest Book Production Ltd.,
Falkirk, Stirlingshire, Scotland.
Printed and bound in Great Britain by
MPG Books Ltd., Bodmin, Cornwall.

For Jim
car buff extraordinaire
with love

Author's Note

One thing is certain: this novel would not have been written if it hadn't been for the full-hearted cooperation of my husband James Myers. It was his lifelong enthusiasm and knowledge of classic cars that brought Jack Colby, his team and Frogs Hill Restorations into being, and he has plotted their route with me every mile of the way.

We are lucky enough to live near the North Downs not far from where this novel is set. Pluckley is a real and beautiful Kentish village, with the reputation of having a great many ghosts, but some other place names, including the village of Piper's Green, are fictitious, as are Jack Colby's home, business and cases. The cars, however, are very real and can be seen both in museums and at classic car meetings all over the country. I am particularly grateful to Tony Condon, a volunteer at the splendid Haynes Motor Museum in Sparkford, who showed and discussed with Jim and myself their magnificent 1937 drophead Lagonda and their 1965 Gordon Keeble with its memorable tortoise emblem. My thanks are, as always, due to my publishers Severn House and in particular to its publishing editor Amanda Stewart and to Rachel Simpson Hutchens, and to my friend and agent Dorothy Lumley of the Dorian Literary Agency; their expert hands on the steering wheel enabled Jack Colby to take the chequered flag in print.

For more information on Jack Colby and his cases, he has own page on amymyers.net and his own blog at jackcolby. co.uk/classiccars.

ONE

There had to be something weird going on. What sort of maniac leaves a classic Lagonda rotting in a barn in the middle of the Kent countryside? I clambered over the ditch and undergrowth bordering the public bridleway to see if I could get a closer look. The ragstone outbuilding was on the far side of a hedge about six foot high, so although I'm a reasonably tall man, I needed a gap to peer through. I found one by an oak tree – and caught my breath: there she was in all her glory, waiting like a beautiful woman crying out to be loved. I could almost hear her whispering to me:

'Jack . . . Jack . . .'

The voice of the siren was summoning me. Fanciful? Not really. Len and Zoe tell me I have a nose for such classic car treasures – as well as a nose for trouble. They have to work with me, so they should know! Trouble is, I also lack a nose for storing up money, which at that moment was not so much *on* my mind as eating it up. And here, with luck, might be salvation.

This time it looked as if all three noses could be in cahoots, including the one I lacked. Either this car had been abandoned when the property changed hands and left to rot by the uncaring new owner – or, as I said, it was owned by someone very weird indeed. '*By the pricking of my thumbs, something wicked this way comes,*' I said softly to myself, every antenna on the alert. To the average person riding or walking along this remote track, it would be just another old wreck of a car mouldering its final days away. But in the classic car world, it's a crime to see such prizes lost to the world through man's neglect; it's like storing a Leonardo in a damp cellar. And Leonardos, so nose number three reminded me, bring in large amounts of cash. If the owner could be persuaded to part with this one, my luck might be in.

No question about it: I had to know more about that car. Like *now*. Len and Zoe jokingly call me the car detective, and right now my nose was twitching like a water-diviner's dream. I had been walking along this bridleway to Charden, where the great Harry Prince lives. It was a Thursday and a bright May day, but I was in a far from happy mood. I'll explain later, but for now let's just say Harry Prince had seemed the only way out of my problem. The worst possible scenario. Now lovely, kind, fate had thrown out a glimmer of hope.

This path is several miles from where I live, but I'd strolled along it several times before and could swear I'd never once seen the doors of that barn open. They looked in none too good shape, and we'd had a bad storm two nights ago; it could be that they'd blown apart then, revealing the Lagonda in all her nude decaying glory – the swine who owned her hadn't even had the decency to put a tarpaulin over her.

First, whose farm was this? No, make that second. First was to take a closer look at the object of my lust. Dad always told me I never know when to give up, and I guess he was right. I used to be a geologist for a big oil company before I came to my senses; there you learn not only to sniff oil, but also to have the determination to believe you're right when every idiot in the business is telling you otherwise. It's the same principle whether it's oil or a dark-blue 1938 or '39 V12 drophead coupé Lagonda with – if the sun would only stop getting in my eyes – what looked like tan leather upholstery. No number plate, and the headlights were surely wrong, but even so she was a beauty. I could only see a glimpse of the interior through the dust-covered windscreen, although the temptress was only a tantalizing six feet from me. I could imagine the purr of her engine though.

This was a lady who needed someone at her wheel, not to die of old age alone and unloved in a field. Even a Kentish field. She needed a knight on a white charger to rescue her.

OK, Jack, I told myself as I persuaded a thin part of the hedge to become a gap, a forty-eight-year-old classic-car sleuth in a silver Alfa Romeo Sportwagon (and with a Gordon Keeble at home under wraps) would do nicely as a knight to rescue a princess like this. Trouble ahead? I had left the oil business, but I still knew how to play tough-guy – and in any branch of the car business this can come in handy. Right now my accelerator pedal was saying:

'*Go*.'

Result: I turned off the competing tiny warning signal that was saying: '*Stay right where you are,*'and found myself on the other side of the hedge, only a few leaves and twigs the worse for wear.

And there she was. My beauty.

I managed to take my eyes off my quarry for long enough to look around me for spies. To my left, back the way I had come, was a large meadow; in front and to my right were apple trees, stretching as far as I could see. The pathway running along beside the hedge looked nicely deserted, at least as far as the bend some way ahead, and so I turned my attention to the lady in question, to explore the most beautiful body I'd seen in a long while.

She was looking at me in appeal – or was that the headlights? They were post-war, and this was definitely a pre-war lady. Not a big blemish; only a purist would object to slightly undersized breasts on an otherwise perfect Venus. In all other respects she looked in grand nick. Uncared for, certainly, but not so decayed as I'd feared. For some reason, her nether regions were packed in hay, which must have tickled her blue paint here and there.

I decided to have a squint. No number plates, but they might be lying around; was the chassis rusting away? So far as I could see, neither was the case, and nor was there any sign of a tax disc. The concrete floor was mucky, but the car wasn't jacked up, so I had to lie on my stomach to peer underneath her. There I could see the underside of a lady who needed attention, although she certainly wasn't rusting away.

I scrambled up with the help of the driver's door handle – and, glory be, it moved. The lady was unlocked and invitingly lay open before me. I had no choice. I slid on to the seat and had a few moments of make-believe vroom-vroom, gazing at that slinky bonnet spread out before me and wishing I could just drive her out here and now.

Even I knew that wasn't on the cards. I didn't even know the owner's name. I rummaged in the glove compartments, but they were empty of clues. No logbook either. My eye fell on some pieces of paper stuffed down in the door map-compartment, so I fished them out, hoping they might give me a clue to the reprobate who owned this vehicle.

They didn't. Merely a garage receipt, and one for a couple of cappuccinos dated way back. Could the car be stolen? It would explain the lack of number plates, but not what she was doing here. If stolen, she'd have rapidly sold on, so she was probably pukka – which meant I needed to meet the owner.

Which was sooner than I'd have wished.

'I don't recall asking for an MOT.'

A cool frosty voice from outside had me scrambling in disarray out of the car, still clutching the bits of paper. Cool frosty eyes met mine as she held out her hand for them. I meekly handed them over, feeling like a naughty schoolboy as I tried to regain as much sangfroid as I could. This wasn't a lot, faced by the original model for Ice Queen. Moreover, she looked vaguely familiar, though I could have sworn we had never met. I'd have remembered.

In her forties, slim, well-dressed in jacket, sweater and trousers, stylish haircut, boots, just what *Vogue* would recommend for a rural weekend. Her face didn't look as if she was enjoying it much, however, although given encouragement I could see those frosty eyes dancing with the joys of life – and I bet I knew what one of those was.

I apologized and grinned sheepishly, hoping that the eyes would relent, but there was no response. She simply unravelled the bits of paper, stared at them and scrunched them up. I had a feeling her mind was on something else. So was mine. Money.

'Jack Colby,' I continued desperately, seeing my hope of a warm discussion over the sale of an unwanted Lagonda disappearing fast. 'I live at Frogs Hill Farm near the Piper's Green to Egerton Road. I'm a classic car enthusiast, so—'

'Hardly a reason for vandalizing mine, Mr Colby.' The voice was even frostier than the eyes.

'I wasn't.' It came out as a yelp. 'I run –' almost true – 'Frogs Hill Classic Car Restorations from the farm,' I continued, getting my sangfroid together again and foreseeing Len's delight if I brought this beauty home to roost (the Lagonda, of course, not the lady, though that wouldn't be a bad idea either). 'We specialize in classics, of course. Stupid of me to jump the gun, but I wanted to be sure of what I was seeing, before I approached you with an offer to see if you'd be interested in letting me restore and sell it for you. On consignment, of course.' That meant she'd get the cash only when I'd sold it.

'It's not for sale.' The anger was vanishing from her voice, but there was no doubt she meant what she said. The odd thing was that she still seemed abstracted, concentrating now on the car rather than on what I was saying. She looked pale and not at all happy, I thought. Naturally, I supposed.

'I could come back—'

'*It's not for sale.*' She wasn't distracted now, and her attention was fully on me. Anger flashed from her eyes, and there was a red flush on the pale cheeks. She even seemed to be trembling. She surely couldn't be that furious? 'Do you understand, Mr Colby? Not for sale.'

I was so taken aback that I didn't see her tame Rottweiler approach – this being in the form of Guy Williams, whom I knew by sight from a local pub. He was a fruit farmer, and I was probably on his land.

'Trouble, Pol?' he growled, his eyes narrowed, as in all the best thrillers. That might be stereotyping, but Guy Williams seemed to step right on to page one of the Heavies for Rent Directory. He wasn't much taller than his wife – I presumed he had that honour – perhaps five eight, but his solid figure and square-jawed face made it seem as if he was dominating her. In corduroys and check lumber shirt, he looked what he was: a farmer doing his work and highly annoyed at strangers intruding on his patch.

'Yes. Get rid of him, Guy.'

I wasn't too happy about this, not knowing whether 'get rid of' meant permanently or merely off her turf. 'Sorry.' I tried to look penitent again. 'I inherited this passion for classics from my father, Tony Colby. Did you know him?'

I'd caught him off guard for he looked somewhat less aggressive. 'Yes. Car collector over Egerton way.'

This was like calling the Tower of London an old prison, or St Paul's a parish church. The Glory Boot, as the farmhouse extension holding Dad's collection is called, has every sort of classic car book, sales brochures, technical manuals, badges, and even a copy of one of the Peking to Paris rally route maps of 1907. And it was the contents of the Glory Boot that the great Harry Prince particularly wanted to prise from my possession – as well the entire farm and business, which would mean rubbing my nose in the dirt even harder.

'He was,' I replied to Guy, 'and unfortunately he passed the passion on to me. Hence my intrusion. Sorry again.'

I wasn't that sorry. I'd remembered where I'd seen Polly – where *everybody* had seen her. I'd only been back in Kent about three and a half years, but I'd heard about Mike and Polly Davis. They'd moved here twelve years ago, well after I had left on my travels in the oil business, and so I had never actually met them. Polly Davis was once better known as Polly Beaumont, a TV presenter and everyone's luvvy. I hadn't seen her on the screen since I came back to England, so she must have given it up when she and Mike moved here, or perhaps it gave her up because of advancing years. She looked all the better for them.

When I returned to Kent, Polly was a recent widow. Mike, who had run a chiefly Internet car business, had been found dead in his car in a station car park. He'd had a heart attack. I'd been sorry to hear that, as Dad had had a soft spot for Mike. He'd referred to him as 'an old rascal', although Mike must have been about twenty years Dad's junior. I think I'd even met Mike once; he'd been the affable sort, who'd pinch your last penny but then make sure you didn't starve. Since Mike's death, Guy might well have moved his heavy boots under the table, and maybe even married her, although she didn't look that stupid. My guess was that she was still Mrs Davis.

They were both surveying me, from the top of my crew-cut brown hair to my less than posh jeans and trainers. It was a question of which of us emerged from our corner for the next round first. I made it me, with one last try at saving the situation.

'I've made a real pig's-dinner of this, and I don't wonder you're annoyed, but could I call on you properly, appointment and all, Mrs – er – Davis, isn't it?' I threw in a smile in case it helped. I'd like to add that women have been known to swoon at my smile, but it wouldn't be the truth. I have to work a lot harder than that, or so I'm told by those who should know. They must be right, because my smile at Polly seemed to have fallen short in the success stakes.

'There would be no point. It's not for sale,' Polly replied, more patiently this time, which might be a good sign, although I could still see knuckles white with tension closed over those bits of paper.

I could also see my only hope of staving Harry Prince off receding rapidly, especially as good old Guy decided to up the stakes. 'The word's no, Colby, no matter who your dad was.' His fists were clenched, and I backed off. Lesson one in the oil trade: don't do fists until you have the advantage of surprise. All the same, the whites of Guy's eyes were getting unpleasantly close.

I tried reason. 'It's a rare car,' I said. 'Especially the drop-head version. If you don't want to sell it for your own sake, Mrs Davis . . .' I looked from one to the other, but there was no sign that Guy was going to take ownership either of her or the car. 'My fault. I understand now; maybe it belonged to your late husband?'

I broke off as Guy marched even closer, but that wasn't the reason I stopped. It was Polly. She was no longer kneading scraps of paper, but was looking directly at the car with an expression not of anger but almost, I thought, near to tears. Fool that I was, I realized this must have been the car Mike died in.

When Guy reached me, he simply spun me round and pushed me headlong into the hedge.

'Crash back through your hole, mister,' he suggested, 'and stay there.'

You get to know how to look after yourself in the oil trade, and I could have floored him so quickly that he wouldn't be able to enjoy his fruit trees – or Polly, if that was the relation-ship – for some time. But that wouldn't have achieved anything except momentary satisfaction. Instead, I said sincerely to Polly, 'I'm sorry, Mrs Davis, if I brought back sad memories.'

I don't think she even heard me. She was still looking at the Lagonda, with a grief that humbled me. No one would ever look at me like that. A woman like this . . . I dragged my thoughts away from a vision of Polly in bed and concen-trated on the lovely Lagonda. Polly had known the car was there, so why this intensity now? Why did she keep it at all, if it was so upsetting? There had to be some story attached to it. People keep old cars for all sorts of reasons. To be buried in them, for sentiment's sake, for lack of money to restore them, or just because it's too much trouble to get rid of them, or too expensive to run them.

Nothing about Polly Davis suggested any of these explanations worked, however. The very opposite. She looked the kind of woman who would relish being seen in a classic car – unlike dear old Guy. I was back to my first explanation: this was the car Mike had died in. And yet that didn't fully satisfy me either. There was something weird about this situation – and about the Lagonda itself. Everything I had seen suggested that apart from the headlights it was a beauty of a car, and yet something didn't quite add up. Two of my noses, for precious cars and for trouble, were pushing me forwards, towards my own, my very own, black hole.

TWO

To sum up my situation as I stalked back to Pluckley where I'd left my car: it was the Lagonda or Harry Prince. I preferred to pursue the former, since the latter brought to the fore the nose I lacked, the one for storing money.

'Any time, Jack, any time.' Last time I had seen Harry, he had chuckled in joyful anticipation of getting his hands on Dad's collection of automobilia, with or without Classic Car Restorations and Frogs Hill Farm itself. It had been the first time he had made an offer to me without getting dirt straight back in his personal fuel line. He's a car dealer, is Prince, and sees himself as King and Emperor of the car trade in this part of Kent. So far I'd refused his deal every time. I don't like the way he does things, I don't like the way he treats people, and I don't like Harry. I do like his wife, but that's not much help.

My major problem was money. Not an unusual one, I grant you, but crucial to me at that moment. When Dad died, just after I'd returned to Kent, he was greatly mourned by all who loved him and classic cars. Especially his family. Having returned to Kent merely to sort things out, somehow I never left again. A man can only take the oil trade for so long.

There was no question of selling Frogs Hill Farm, even if I was forced to because of the debts Dad had left. The moving costs would outweigh the sale profits. The Greeks believed that we all have fatal flaws that lead to our ruin, but I had searched in vain for Dad's when he was alive. After his death, however, it had emerged that his world famous Glory Boot had got that way because he'd never let cost stand in the way of a new acquisition. Result: first class collection of automobilia – but mortgages galore on Frogs Hill Farm which Croesus would have had a job paying off, let alone me. So I had settled down with Classic Car Restorations, blithely hoping that I could make it pay. It was a struggle, and now it had reached crunch point.

I'd set out along the bridle path this sunny day just to talk over prices with Harry, and we would both know this meant it was getting serious. Fortunately, he didn't know I was coming, as I'd wanted the advantage of surprise. The happy surprise had been mine – the Lagonda. It might give me a lifeline to pay my debts for a couple of months – even if Polly and Mr Rottweiler were standing in the way. I didn't yet know quite how I was going to get hold of that elegant lady – and perhaps even Polly into the bargain, which was an increasingly nice thought. Something, I told myself, would turn up.

With this optimistic outlook, I decided Harry Prince could wait until I had exhausted every other avenue. I'd head straight back to Frogs Hill Farm to begin my Lagonda campaign.

Frogs Hill Farm is so tucked away that it's surprising any customers find their way there. They generally arrive at the large modern barn that houses the restoration business with a great air of triumph, as if they've just solved the enigma of perpetual motion. Len likes it this way. We are high up on the Lower Greensand stratum with fine views of the Kentish Weald beneath us in the distance, and if one squints between the trees in roughly the opposite direction we also have brief glimpses of the chalk North Downs.

What road are we on, customers naturally ask. Road? The way to Frogs Hill Farm is along a mere track, though a lane leads grudgingly off from Piper's Green village on the Pluckley to Egerton road and runs somewhere near the farm. After that, it's a slog up our long drive – or pleasant motoring, according to how many potholes need to be filled in. Len Vickers, who is in charge of restorations with Zoe Grant's help, believes in making customers work to find us, whereas I take a duller view. I prefer not to be sued for damage to classic and fragile beauties.

By the time I reached the farm again that morning, I was full of renewed hope and vigour. Guy Williams' aggression had receded in my mind and so had my gut feeling of something nasty in the woodshed. All I could think of was that beautiful Lagonda, which had my name written on it as surely as my passport. And if by any happy chance its owner was part of the deal, Shangri-La appeared to be just over my horizon.

I went straight to the petrolhead zone of operations, where Len and Zoe were working on a 1934 Riley 12/4 Kestrel saloon. This little gem needed some serious suspension, braking and electrical work if it was ever to see another MOT certificate, so I was up against stiff competition if I expected eager interest in my concerns.

'Lagonda, V12,' I announced for openers as I marched into the Pits, as we call the barn workshop.

Silence. Not even a grunt.

Then Zoe's hand did briefly wave above the grease pit and a spiel of stuff about various chassis and engine lubrication systems followed. Push-button grease jobs and full-flow oil conversions are now delights of the past, but for their devoted admirers they are subjects of never-ending joy.

Len and Zoe make a good team – but a strange mix. Len must have reached sixty now, although I've never dared ask him. I'd get a crusty put-down. Any words not devoted to the inner workings of, say, a Cotal preselector gearbox are wasted, in his view. His father was a World War Two engineer in the RAF, but Len took to cars. He was big in the racing scene in the fifties and sixties, then opted for a quieter life tinkering with classic cars off circuit. At one point he got in with a bad crowd and made the mistake of believing that a good classic must have a good owner. He went even quieter after that, but he brought a car to show Dad one day, and somehow – neither of us knew quite how – he moved into the barn and never moved out, thus beginning Frogs Hill Classic Car Restorations.

Because Len is good at his job – very good – business is brisk. Unfortunately, he is also slow, so the briskness is all on one side: cars coming, but not so often leaving. Len is a perfectionist, but the result is that there's no reliable monthly income to pay off those delightful mortgages on the farm, even with my input.

The only way the business works at all is because of Zoe, Len's saving grace and mine. With her spiky orange hair, surmounted by a baseball cap, she and Len make an odd couple, but a great team. She must be about twenty-three now, having dropped out of university and into classic cars, preferring getting her hands dirty over wheel bearings and half-shafts to engineering courses. Clad in jeans, sweatshirt and baseball hat, she worked happily (and more speedily) with Len for a couple of years until Dad died and the cuckoo in their comfortable nest arrived. Correction: two cuckoos. Firstly, me. I squawk around them anxious to help, but my knowledge of classic cars is mostly in my head, not my hands. Secondly, her boyfriend – lover, perhaps, who knows? – Rob Lane, who is trouble with a grin on its face.

'Ever seen a drophead round here?' I yelled at Len and Zoe, trying for more decibels than Classic FM, which was apparently essential for their work, as it slowed them down, Len claimed . . . No comment.

'Yup. A thirty-eight V12,' Len shouted back, and then returned to his work. This time, a Laycock de Normanville overdrive unit seemed to be the object of his affection.

'I saw one in an old barn—'

Off went the radio, up came Zoe from behind the tool chest, interrupting with a bawled-out:

'There's a car in my barn,
'Dear Jack, dear Ja – ack.
'Oh what is it doing there,
'Dear Zoe, dear Zoe . . .' And on and on. Even Len was trying not to laugh.

I eyed them with scorn. 'If neither of you has the imagination to think beyond idle jests—'

'I have, I have,' she pleaded. 'Please do tell us *all* about this barn, dear Jack.'

'On the bridleway from Pluckley to Charden.'

'Greensand Farm, Polly Davis's place. Yup. That's where I saw the drophead. Years ago, it was. Serviced it once.' This was a long speech for Len. Talking takes too much time away from what's really important in life, such as Roots-type super-chargers or the superiority of desmodromic valve systems. 'Guy Williams rents the orchards,' he added.

'You know Polly Davis?' The adrenalin began to rise. This could be a breakthrough. Casually but smartly dressed in a Ted Lapidus blazer and slacks, I could stroll up to her at a drinks party – and who knows? Problem: I don't do drinks parties, or rather I'm not in the right set to do them.

'Nope. Met her though.' Len grew positively chatty. 'Mike ran that classics to order business. Before your time.'

'Yes, but was it a good 'un?' By which I meant: was it strictly legit? I'd hate to think of that Lagonda being part of a non legit set-up, i.e. stolen.

Len considered this for so long I had to fight to control impatience, which never works with Len. 'Seemed to be. I wouldn't have touched it.'

Helpful, I thought. I could not recall Dad ever mentioning meeting Mike Davis, but he wasn't exactly one for the social life. Mum had done her best to winkle him out of his mental garage, but after she died, its doors rarely opened. He ruled over the Glory Boot and waited for people to come to him, when he proved the best and most affable of hosts.

'Polly's OK,' Zoe volunteered.

'She wasn't OK today,' I said ruefully.

'I was at school with Bea; she's her daughter,' Zoe continued undeterred. 'She's just come back from working abroad. Got a job in Canterbury. Polly runs a picture framing business at the farm.'

'Any hope of getting me an introduction as a respectable citizen?'

A snort. 'No way. Long queue.' A wave, and Zoe was back in the real world of nuts and bolts.

Len was still ruminating though. 'That Lagonda,' he said. A long pause, spanner in hand.

'I presume it was Mike's, perhaps the one he died in,' I said. 'Hers, not his,' he said to my surprise. 'Belonged to her dad.'

That was a relief. My foot hadn't been quite as big as I thought. Of course, it could still be the car Mike died in.

'So why is she letting it go to rack and ruin in the barn? Has she got no soul?' Surely such a face must have a soul somewhere.

'Used to drive it,' Len informed me. 'Pride and joy.'

'I could restore it for her and sell it,' I said plaintively, 'but she won't hear of it.'

'Takes all sorts,' was Len's final offering, and then he too went back to his real world and left me to worry about mortgages.

As may be apparent, I don't have any capital stashed away for rainy days. I had thrown up my oil job, confident that, with my early and brief marriage well in the past and my daughter in her early twenties, I was a lily of the field and could take my time over choosing how to toil and spin. One sight of the massive debts of Frogs Hill had cured me of that quaint notion. Fortunately, I'm not totally dependent on Len's and Zoe's contribution for income. I'd become a car detective in earnest.

One day Zoe had had enough of my incompetent technical abilities. 'Stop poking your nose in, Jack,' she had yelled in exasperation. 'Poke it *out*.'

So, with their help – Len on the knowledge side, Zoe on the 'let's go for it' side – I had begun working with the police and insurance companies on routine jobs and then added the hunting down of rare cars on commission for individuals, or anything anyone would pay me for. Zoe and Len eye me warily now, as though my detective work might tempt their cuckoo to migrate to foreign parts again and leave a devastated nest behind him. He won't, of course. This cuckoo is here to stay, but *not* in a nest run by Harry Prince.

That Lagonda was, therefore, my next mission. Strictly speaking, I should have been returning a call from DCI Dave Jennings, who operates the Kent Police Car Crime Unit, but the Lagonda called more loudly. First step: meet Polly Davis under more favourable circumstances. In order to do that, I needed to know more about this Lagonda. A few facts and especially figures might come in very useful. Attractive though Polly was, the Lagonda had to be my main target.

Was that true? I had a moment's doubt because classics and their owners are joined at the hubcap; you can't have one without understanding the other. The thought of being joined at the hip with Polly – although what I had in mind might be somewhat difficult if we were – was a highly pleasurable one.

We'd got off to a bad start, but there was surely something I could do about that.

I thought out a rapid plan of action. 'Fancy the Wheatsheaf on Sunday week?' I threw out to the two heads that were all there was to be seen of my colleagues, who were back at their far more interesting jobs. These included, I knew, making an elaborate exhaust system for a 'blower' Bentley, and therefore I naturally only received a couple of 'ums' in reply.

Every third Sunday in the month the Wheatsheaf pub, a few miles from Piper's Green, hosts a classic car get-together. I'd seen a Lagonda there once or twice, and if I struck lucky I might have a chance to find out how rare my barn discovery was, and whether it was well known to the buffs. Given the noses of the usual suspects at this gathering, there was a pretty good chance someone would know something, even if the Lagonda I'd seen there previously failed to show.

The classic car world is a knowledgeable one, and a friendly one – usually – and a lot of my sleuthing work is done at car shows both here and in continental Europe. Len had implied that Mike Davis wasn't squeaky clean in his car doings, and if so I might pick up some vibes on that.

Then, on a whim, I changed my plan of action completely. Although the logical thing was to do my homework first, what I *wanted* to do was see Polly Davis again. I thought of Zoe's throwaway 'a queue at her door'. A whole lot of trouble might lie ahead, but hey – when had that ever stopped me?

Or stopped Zoe, come to that. There was, after all, Rob Lane in her life.

Rob Lane, the big drawback to Zoe. 'He means well,' had been her less than wholehearted excuse for Rob last time he had turned up at Frogs Hill. He hadn't exactly covered himself with glory when he'd put a fingerprint on a freshly lacquered Bugatti firewall. Or the time he'd backed his old banger into a customer's priceless Mercedes 540K Cabrio.

I'd spent ages of avuncular time trying to warn Zoe off Rob. Warn her off? You'd think I'd urged her to make a bid for the best catch in Europe. Somehow, however, fate has a way of choosing unlikely messengers, and this time I'd had to grit my teeth. It seemed my path to Polly could be through Rob.

'What?' I asked dangerously, 'are you doing here?'

I had come to the Pits the next morning, my head still full
of Polly and Lagondas, to find Rob sitting on the bonnet of
an MGB, and even Len wasn't yelling at him to get the hell
off. If I'd done that, it would have been a different matter. I
was only the boss.

Zoe had run into Rob at university and made the mistake
of not instantly running in the opposite direction. Was it love?
Was it sex? Was it some fatal attraction for catastrophe? Don't
ask me. I'm a car detective, not a psychologist. All I know is
that Zoe eyes him as fondly as if he were Clarence, that
messenger sent from the heavens in the old James Stewart
weepie *It's a Wonderful Life*. Not with Rob around it isn't.

'I came,' he said plaintively, moving off the bonnet, 'to ask
Zoe if she'd like to go to Hurst Manor tonight.' He looked
injured, every inch the victim.

'Do you, Zoe?' I asked politely. Typical Rob invitation. He
is, as they say, of good family, and every inch of his confident
face and neatly trimmed designer stubble betrays it. Bored
charm is Rob's speciality. He's waiting for the big opportunity
that fate will drop in his path tomorrow. But even if tomorrow
should happen to come, he would have to be coaxed into
taking up the offer. That's where Zoe comes in. I don't think
they live or even sleep together, but how would I know? Zoe
keeps her private life to herself.

'Private view,' Rob condescended to explain. 'Local art
show. Everyone will be there. Fancy it, Zoe? Bea's going.'

Full alert! All the antennae waving together. 'Bea Davis?'
I asked, unable to believe my luck.

Zoe grinned. 'The very same.'

'And her mother?' Could this be manna dropping from
heaven? Rob's presence usually suggests the other place, so
it seemed too good to be true. Lagondas temporarily receded
in my mind.

He regarded me as a simpleton who has to have allowances
made for him.

'Of course.'

'I'll come,' I said.

'Will you?' The eyes glittered as the two rams locked mental
horns, and Zoe got unconcernedly on with her rebuilding of
a Scintilla Vertex magneto. 'I invited Zoe.'

'As an exception, I'm prepared to forget the errant fingerprint and the scraped bumper episodes if you'll let me come with you both.'

I endeavoured to look menacingly formidable, but without success. Rob is some eight inches shorter than I am, boasting a slighter frame and featuring cocky charm. No, delete the cocky. Rob was merely assured. Although, I had to be generous today, I could see no quarter being given in those triumphant eyes.

Nor could Zoe, so she entered the fight. 'Rob, lighten up.'

Rob could obviously see his free dinners and sympathy flying out of his reach, because he promptly grinned. 'Sure,' he said languidly. 'Lorna likes beefy guys.'

I'd get my own back later. Beefy is not a word I'm comfortable with – it smacks of Arnie and *The Terminator* – but there was too much riding on this to take revenge now. 'Lorna?' I queried.

'Lorna Stack. Sex bomb lady of the manor – or thinks she is. Wife of Rupert Stack, who's the leader of the "second homes" brigade.'

I'd heard of him, a London businessman. The second homes folk tend to keep themselves to themselves, so I only met them if they were bringing their classics to me. We don't frequent the same watering holes and troughs. They're rather like expats. We locals are here for amusement and service. Unfair? Of course. Some of them are good fun and do their bit for the village, but on the whole it's like the grain and the grape: we don't mix.

Today, however, I felt able to take on the world. First, I rang Dave Jennings. Result: there was a job tracking down a Merc for which he might have to call me in, and a missing Rolls he needed my help on more or less right away. So I would have to give Polly, the Lagonda and the art show full throttle. They might present dangerous curves to be approached with caution, but I was up for it.

THREE

Hurst Manor was on the far side of Piper's Green, towards Egerton, and, anxious as I was to meet Polly again, I did spare a thought for the May greenery and blossom as I turned into the drive that Friday evening. Kent is a beautiful county, and the North Downs could be seen in all their glory on the one side, while on the other the fertile Weald lay beneath the Greensand Ridge. Spring gives an edge to the beauties of nature, and, full of its joys, I was looking forward to the evening.

The manor is tucked away in its own grounds. I had a vague memory of going there donkeys years ago, when the Squire, as my father quaintly referred to him, still lived there. But such feudal situations had passed, and the Squire's descendants now lived in a modern semi somewhere in Lenham.

For Hurst Manor to be merely a second home seemed to me sad, but perhaps that was just jealousy. All the money in the world thrown into the upkeep of a house and gardens such as these won't compensate for lack of the atmosphere of a house that is empty much of the time. It had been a family house once. This building had come into being in the early nineteenth century, but was on the site of several predecessors over the centuries, beginning with the first one in early medieval times built for one of the children of the family living in the nearby Chilston Park estate. Hurst can hardly have been in the same class in size or importance as Chilston, and certainly wasn't now, but it was charming all the same. Not, of course, that we hoi polloi were going into the house itself. Nothing so grand.

'Over there,' called Rob from the back seat of my Alfa Sportwagon, where he relaxed in aristocratic hauteur, with one of his arms casually round Zoe. Zoe wasn't even objecting, though she's hardly the type of girl that needs cosseting. She's more the tigress variety, liking to leap out at unexpected moments – except, of course, where Rob's concerned.

We'd negotiated hard over Rob's terms for agreeing to let me come – by hard, I mean Rob stated his terms and I agreed. 'Transport,' he'd drawled. 'You drive, Zoe and I drink.'

'Fair enough,' I'd promptly conceded. Anyway, I needed my wits about me, if I was to catch Polly in my toils. Silly phrase that: what was there to toil over where Polly was concerned? Then I remembered that toil used to mean trap, and it struck me that if traps were on the menu then it was more than likely that she had trapped me rather than the other way around. I let my imagination play . . . a drive in that handsome Lagonda on a summer's day; an old-fashioned picnic basket strapped on the back, stuffed with foie gras and a bottle of champagne; a blanket spread upon the ground by a stream – and Polly. Or maybe the back seat of the Lagonda . . . Back, Colby, back to reality. Work to be done, I realized. Harry Prince to be staved off one more time.

'Tell me about this queue at Polly's door,' I said to Zoe as our incongruous threesome made its way towards the converted stables where the show was being held. 'What's the competition?'

Zoe grinned. 'Best in Show, Best Watercolour, Best Oil . . .'

'Most amusing,' I agreed sourly.

Already, I did not fancy the Stacks. The public were directed to park in a field behind the stables. The Stacks' own cars were spoiling the look of the gracious red-brick house. One can tell a lot about people from the car they own – or I tell myself that I can. The Bentley Mulsanne Turbo and BMW convertible outside the manor said anonymous grey-suited businessman and spoiled wife respectively. Some detective I would be, however, if I believed first impressions. Often they were right, but sometimes they were very, very wrong, such as the time I dismissed a chap as a *poseur* for arriving at a car show in a tarted-up Triumph Stag, only to find out that he also owned a Ferrari 250 GTO. I concentrated on the job in hand, however, as I marched dutifully behind whippersnapper Rob to the stables' entrance.

Two elderly ladies at the reception table duly fell for his charms, and I was in. One of them had looked rather doubtful as she checked me up and down, but must have decided I was an eccentric artist rather than a heavy mob villain, because she suddenly awarded me a smile and told me the programme was a pound. She held out three – I bought them.

Rob took two from me and graciously handed one to Zoe as though he'd just forked out for it himself. A good trick that, and I'd remember it.

'We'll leave you to it,' Rob then announced, making no secret that I was no longer wanted. That suited me down to the ground. 'See you for dinner,' he added.

'That's included in the entry price?' I asked, surprised but imagining some enormous buffet to be laid on courtesy of the Stacks.

'It is for us.' Rob smirked. 'You're paying. I thought we'd go to the Green Dragon.'

The most expensive restaurant in Piper's Green, of course. Zoe, I noticed, was looking the other way.

'Naturally,' I agreed graciously. I'd think about the mortgage tomorrow. What was a mere hundred quid or two with a Lagonda and Polly at stake?

The stables had been modernized to make one long building, which was currently so packed with people that I despaired of ever spotting Polly. Movement wasn't helped by the fact that temporary display partitions had been erected to divide one artist's work from another's, so there was nothing for it but to force my way round from one to the other.

I'm no judge of amateur art – or any art, come to that – but this show, which according to the programme notes presented both professional and amateur artists, looked of high standard. It was varied in subject matter, with landscapes, portraits and abstracts, and incomprehensible mixes of all of these. I tried hard to absorb enough to chat sensibly to Polly once I'd tracked her down, which meant forcing myself between eager groups eating canapés and miniature sausage rolls. I was beginning to despair when Zoe, as so often, galloped to my rescue by seizing my arm. No sign of Rob, luckily.

'Jack, come and meet Bea.'

Bea? Bless you, Zoe, I thought fervently. Bea was with a young man, maybe a year or two older than her, who stared at me suspiciously.

'Big Boss Man at Frogs Hill,' Zoe introduced me airily. 'Jack Colby.'

'Hi, Jack,' Bea greeted me, then giggled. 'Sorry, no pun intended.'

I tried to reply wittily, but all I could think of was Polly and that this was her daughter. I liked the look of Bea. She was no Polly in the beauty stakes, that was for sure. She was shorter, rounder and with a much warmer, eager face. Unfortunately, her companion looked the sort to take full advantage of such openness. From his accent as he continued to talk pointedly only to Bea and Zoe, he was Polish, I guessed, especially when Bea introduced him as Tomas Kasek. His arm slid round Bea in case I had any idea of making off with her.

Just as I was wondering how to break up this cosy twosome, Zoe did it for me.

'Jack's fallen in love with your mum's Lagonda, Bea,' she said brightly.

'What Lagonda?' Bea looked genuinely puzzled.

'In one of your barns,' I said casually.

Bea looked even more puzzled. 'Not to my knowledge. She and Dad had one. It might still be around, but I don't see why it should be. All the cars got sold off to Andy Wells.' She turned to lover lad. 'Tomas, you've met Andy, and you like cars. Did Andy ever mention it?'

Tomas's square chin grew even squarer for some reason. 'Never.'

'Very odd.' Bea frowned. 'Do you know Mum, Jack?'

'I've met her.' The way this came out made it sound as if it had been love at first sight. Perhaps it had been, on my side at least.

Tomas must have seen his opportunity. 'Mrs Davis is here somewhere,' he said pointedly, to hasten my departure.

'Off you go, Jack,' Zoe said unhelpfully.

'Don't tell her you've met us.' Bea grinned.

'Why not?' I asked. After all, what other opening would I have?

'She doesn't approve.' Bea pulled a face.

'Of you?'

'Of *me*, I think,' Tomas told me casually.

So Polly had good taste, I thought. Bea deserved better than Tomas.

'Tomas is farm manager for Guy Williams, and Mum *does* approve of Guy,' Bea told me.

'Is he here?' I asked warily. A punch-up was not going to improve my status.

'Sure to be. Fighting off the competition,' Bea told me blithely.

I decided to enquire no further. This might be a case where ignorance was bliss, and in any case it was high time I located Polly.

The display units might have been efficient for concentrating the mind on one artist's work, but it didn't work as well for anyone intent on coming casually upon friends – or upon Polly Davis – and I was getting more and more frustrated.

And then I found her. She was talking in one of the units to someone I recognized from local classic car shows. I go to so many that I can't carry all the owners' names in my head, but by Jupiter I remember the cars. And this man's face said Maserati Mexico to me. I thought his name was Dan or Don. What better introduction could I have asked for? Polly was dressed in a flimsy floating lemon-coloured affair and made my heart and various other organs ache in admiration. Then she caught sight of me, and what had been a beautiful normal woman switched back into ice-queen mode. Unfortunately for her, she could not move, as I had carefully hemmed her into a corner between Dan (or Don) and myself, and she couldn't very well tell me to get lost – chiefly because I got my oar in first, and not with her.

'Maserati Mexico,' I said to Dan (or Don). He was a good-looking man, and I seemed to recall he had been, or still was, in motor racing at some level. He certainly had the looks that went with wasting a bottle of the best champagne. Not that he himself looked a waste of space. Far from it; I remembered liking him from previous encounters. I reckoned he looked more like a Dan than a Don, and I needed to be right, especially if he was in the famous queue for Polly's favours. They had been standing very close together and talking very earnestly. About art? I don't think so.

'And it's Dan – er . . . ?' I finished enquiringly.

'Right. Dan Burgess. And you're Jack Colby of Frogs Hill Classic Car Restorations. Related to Glory Boot Colby, I imagine.'

We were off, and short of pushing us both out of the way Polly was temporarily stuck with me. My opportunity was right here, and I took it.

'I have to apologize to you again,' I said ruefully. 'We didn't meet under the best circumstances last week. I don't usually do wilful damage to hedges. Blame your good taste.'

She managed a sick grin. I decided not to enlighten the obviously curious Dan – he might want a slice of the Lagonda action – so I quickly added, 'I've just met your daughter Bea. She's a friend of my mechanic, Zoe Grant.'

A little colour came into those pale cheeks, and the goddess spoke. 'I like Zoe. She's great fun, isn't she?'

'The best,' I agreed. Wow, a real conversation. This was

progress. 'It isn't always a barrel of laughs at the farm, but we all get along fine.'

We rambled on, and Dan informed me he was a painter by profession – and had his own pictures hung here, even though he wasn't a member of the society. 'Right here,' he emphasized, glancing at the walls with the glow of pride shining all over his Superman features.

'Cars, I see,' I said fatuously, taking in the subject matter of the pictures around me for the first time and wondering whether I was expected to buy one to impress Polly. This was a man who adored cars. His cars had stately homes and impossibly beautiful landscapes plonked down around them, but the cars themselves were painted with a love and skill not evident in the backgrounds. No Lagondas though. Thoughts of the blanket I had shared in my fantasies with the lady standing next to me flashed through my mind all too uncomfortably.

'I take commissions,' Dan told me, when I'd duly admired them. 'I go round and paint cars for their loving owners. So next time you want a paint job to hang on the wall, call me.' We joked around for a minute or two, but then an announcement that the speeches were about to begin threw me off track. I momentarily turned my head, and with a light touch on my arm, Polly slipped past me to freedom.

Once away, she did pause long enough to murmur, 'I'm sorry about the other day, Jack. I really am. Come up to the farm one day, but no talk about Lagondas. Deal?' She smiled at me, and the world spun out of control.

I was so stunned I could only nod my head. 'Better than nothing,' I blurted out – hardly a phrase calculated to woo a lady to my bed, but she didn't seem to take offence. That smile lit up her face like the cracking of a glacier, and my dreams began to flow once more. Lyrical? Believe me, I felt lyrical as I watched Polly disappear into the mob.

'Quite something, isn't she?' There seemed to be some wistfulness in Dan's expression. He only looked in his thirties – much too young for her, I thought, but then beauty such as Polly's had no relation to age.

I agreed with him. She *was* quite something. My car detective nose was reminding me that whatever mystery hung over that Lagonda V12, Polly must be involved in it up to her beautiful swanlike neck, but I didn't care. I was on my way to Shangri-La as she and the Lagonda floated through my mind.

I remained in a daze throughout the speeches, squashed between a chap who looked so scruffy he could only be one of the artists, and a lady of such flowing curves that Rubens would have been inspired. Every so often I caught a glimpse of Polly, who was in charge of the raffle – to which, I realized guiltily, I had not contributed. Black mark, if Polly realized it too. The MC seemed to be Simon Todd, the leader of the art group, who was presiding over the awards of the prizes. Next to him was a quiet man with spectacles and dull fair hair – perhaps once straw-coloured – wearing an exquisitely tailored suit. He looked in his mid forties, and when I heard Todd address him as Rupert, I deduced he was the manor's owner.

I recognized Simon – he'd brought a mid-fifties Austin Metropolitan in to Frogs Hill last year. Normally, Len would have turned up his nose at a yellow and white Custard Torpedo, as this Anglo-American hybrid was charmingly nicknamed, but I persuaded him otherwise, with dull old thoughts of mortgages in my mind. I hadn't taken to Simon, even though he was a prissy sort of chap and, in my appraisal of his sexual leanings, was hardly likely to be in the running for Polly's affections. Nevertheless, they seemed pretty chummy from his arm possessively round her as she picked out the raffle tickets.

I decided to rest content with my progress and not seek Polly out again, so after the speeches I began to wander round the show once more. By mistake, I found myself among Lorna Stack's work – the lady who apparently liked beefy guys. I was jammed in there, so I had no choice but to study her work with close intent. She had, after all, won one of the prizes – though that, I thought, was hardly surprising.

'What do you think?' came a husky voice from behind me, and I leapt sky high at being unexpectedly addressed. Had Lorna Stack been stalking me? No, it was Polly, to my amazement.

'Daren't say,' I replied briefly.

I'm no art critic, but I do know what I *don't* like. I don't like fussy neat landscapes of gardens and parks that tell me less than a photograph would convey.

She laughed. Polly? Oh the joys to come if she could laugh

so seductively. There was a warmth between us now. 'Very
wise of you, Jack. Especially as the artist is right behind you.'

Alarmed, I turned round, but there was no one there who
could possibly be Lorna Stack.

My turn to laugh. 'I may not call,' I threatened her.

'I may not answer.'

No mistake. There was sex in that voice, and surely, surely
sex in the air. And yet she was holding back. Something seemed
not to be resolved. It was as if what Polly wanted, Polly wasn't
sure if she should have. I'd seen that look too often on wistful
would-be buyers faced with the classic car of their dreams. If
I was right about my diagnosis, I could surely change all that.

But at that moment Lorna Stack *did* arrive. Fate seemed to
be saying that my luck might be in, but I couldn't be given
too much of it. Sharp dark eyes in a sexy face switched from
Polly to me and rapidly summed the situation up.

'Darling, how nice,' she cooed at Polly. 'I thought I'd find
you with Rupert. You so often are. But here you are with a
new admirer. How do you manage it?' Her voice sounded
flattering; her eyes revealed she had a bitchier motive in mind.

'Easily, Lorna.' In a trice Polly had turned into the ice queen
again as she delivered this cool shot. 'As for Rupert, he brings
pictures to be framed every now and then.'

'Whenever he puts a deal to bed, I expect,' Lorna fired back.
Her eyes turned to me. I was next for the rack. I felt their
power, but they left me inexplicably cold. Her sex appeal could
batter itself against me all it liked, but it would be in vain.
Sharp eyes incandescent with promise, but I wouldn't be taking
up their offer, even though Polly pointedly excused herself to
leave us together.

'I've seen you in the village.' Lorna made it sound like the
sexiest rendezvous imaginable.

'That or the pub maybe. I've seen your Bentley around.' I
hadn't, except on their forecourt, but it made the point that
cars, not black-eyed witches, were my thing.

'Not the pub. We never have the time. Rupert brings work
home with him, and I'm an artist.'

I gulped. 'And a talented one too.' I indicated the ghastly
pictures. What else could I do? She looked pleased anyway.

'There's not much to do round here, so painting fills in the
time I don't spend at the gym.'

Not much to do? When there were walks over the downs and in the fields and woods, drives around the lanes, country pubs, birds, animals, history lurking in every corner of this wonderful county? And yet she drew pictures of flower beds. I smiled, and she must have read it as an invitation.

'You must make your own entertainment, and I'm sure you do it beautifully. You're the –' she broke off, and I nearly finished 'beefy sort' for her, but she found her own word – 'innovative sort.'

'Too busy to be innovative,' I said hastily. 'I'm in classic cars.'

'I'm sure there's a lot of mileage in you.' Her gaze swept appraisingly over me, until I felt like a stud gigolo.

Fortunately, my honour was saved by the bell. Her husband arrived, took a look at me, blinked, smiled, chatted and then to my relief removed his wife from my presence. I prefer to eat dinner, not be eaten for it.

I told myself I had achieved what I had come for more or less. Fifty per cent, anyway. The Lagonda mystery was no further forward, but at the very least I was on talking terms with Polly. I even met Guy Williams on my next promenade, with a woman at his side who was presumably his wife. Thankfully, it wasn't Polly. He glared at me suspiciously, as if I was about to make a dash to pinch his Volvo. I grinned at him in return. The grin wasn't so much for him as for the fact that I had just spotted Polly again. She was talking to both the Stacks now, though Rupert left them as I came sauntering up. It was pushing my luck to talk to Polly again, but that's the trouble with lucky dice. One's tempted to keep on throwing and throwing.

I was just in time to hear Lorna say viciously to Polly: 'Just keep away in future, darling. Rupert's mine, remember, and *only* mine. You really must remember that, because I'd hate a pretty face like yours to be rearranged. Why not stick to that new bloke of yours? He's a hunky softie.'

I never did hear Polly's reply.

As usual, Rob had arrived at the wrong time. 'We're ready for the Green Dragon, Jack,' he told me, clapping me heartily on the back. I gave in gracefully. After all, I'd got halfway to Paradise this evening, and if Paradise could have a Lagonda thrown in so much the better. Whatever its story, it was

probably something quite innocent. Something to do with Polly
and Mike, perhaps, not the car itself. How could there be
anything odd about something so sleek and handsome? I
thought of that old never-ending song: 'You'll never get to
heaven in an old Ford car,' which my Dad used to sing
non-stop.

No, but I could in a Lagonda V12. Especially with Polly in
it too.

FOUR

I felt like a kid again at a prospect of a first date. When to
make the move? It shouldn't be too soon or she might back
off. Not too long, either. What 'reason' should I give for
calling? Come out for a drink? Come out to the Ritz? A casual
'I was just passing and I fancy you'? Fancy was hardly the
right word where Polly was concerned, but I'm not sure that
the English language, subtle and beautiful though it is, includes
a word for halfway between fancy and love when potential
hovers in the air. I suppose Blake's poem got nearest with
'catching the joy as it flies' – and I had a suspicion that Polly
might fly out of my reach at any moment, so I had to get this
dilemma sorted. None of the above approaches pushed the
right buttons, but I couldn't just turn up on the doorstep
grinning fatuously; I needed some cover story, however
transparent.

On Monday morning I was prowling around the Pits,
where Zoe and Len were still grappling with the Bugatti
firewall, and trying to pretend I had a mission in hand. Not
very well, as I knew Zoe's sardonic eye was on me, whenever she could spare it from the far sexier firewall. Today
not even the Bugatti was tempting me to stay. I had other
wheels to spin.

'Take her a picture to frame,' she threw at me offhandedly.

'Good idea.' I meant it. It was a brilliant idea, even though
it raised another dilemma. 'But I don't think she'd be over-
whelmed with the job of framing a print of Canterbury
Cathedral.' I'd inherited a house whose walls were full more

of family memories than artistic jewels. 'Have you any lying around? I'd pay.'

'Nope. Haven't seen any Rembrandts I fancy recently.' Zoe relented and gave my problem all the attention that she normally reserved for work (or Rob). 'You've got some yourself.'

'I have?'

She regarded me pityingly. 'The Glory Boot.' She might justly have added, 'dumbbell'. She'd be within her rights.

Glory be, I exulted, the Glory Boot. I went over to give her a hug and got a whiff of that indescribable smell which is the mix of petrol, grease and a bit of the wild outdoors that adds up to Zoe – and occasionally Len, but I rarely rush over to hug him. I sometimes wonder whether Zoe keeps a bottle of that smell at home so that she isn't parted from it in the evenings. The wild outdoors in her case comes from her love of long walks, especially in the rain. Don't ask – I don't know.

Of course the answer to my problem lay in the Glory Boot. One of my father's 'finds', of which there were many, had been a car artist called Giovanni Berazzi, who was struggling away in a garret in Milan painting out his vision of cars. He did very few on commission because classic car owners who pay up front tend to expect every loving detail of their Lancia or Lamborghini captured in paint, and Giovanni doesn't paint that way. He's more of an impressionist, so he likes to paint the cars in somewhat ethereal settings, thus blending the cars into particularly magical and mystical landscapes that would be in harmony with the subject car. Imagine a red Ferrari Testa Rossa on a misty Venetian canal, a Porsche floating through clouds, a Lotus in the midst of a Monet flower garden.

Dad had fallen in love with Giovanni's work, which was unfortunate because it led to a tussle between them. Giovanni wanted to be sure that his beloved paintings were going to a good home, and what Dad told him of the set-up at Frogs Hill did not appeal to him. He had to be wooed, he had to be convinced, and the tears of sorrow at parting with his treasures had to be wiped from his eyes after he eventually agreed to sell Dad eight unframed.

That's one of the reasons Harry Prince is hanging around for the happy day when I really can't pay the mortgage. But I have news for him. Giovanni got the hang of what it was

like to have money in his pocket and came to a compromise
with an Italian dealer. The result? I'd have to sell everything
I have to afford to buy just one more of them now, although
occasionally Giovanni allows me to drool over them in his
studio. Even I can see he's a terrific painter.

So why didn't I frame one and put it up for auction? Because
I could almost hear Dad breathing down my neck in fury at
the very idea. He'd made me promise never to part with them.
Never? I'd queried dubiously. He'd glared at me. Never – unless
you're starving. I wasn't yet starving, and, though Harry Prince
didn't know this yet, even if the worst came to the worst and
I had to sell up, I'd be lugging those Giovannis into my one-
roomed garret to gaze upon their glory, ignoring my hunger
pains. So no auction room would be seeing them yet awhile.
Framing one was a different matter, however. 'Bless you, Zoe,'
I added fervently.

'Pay me instead.'

Guilt consumed me at the mock stricken look of the girl in
front of me. True, she had her usual grin on her face, but I
had broken my strictest rule. I hadn't paid either her or Len
on Friday, and it was now Monday. Polly and Lagondas had
temporarily sent me insane. While I was busy writing the
cheques, Len decided to put his oar in. He came over to me,
wiping his hands on a greasy rag. In his case, I think he does
it to increase the smell, not get it off. He can't bear to be out
of reach of the heady scent of petrol.

'That Lagonda you saw . . .' A pause. 'Drivetrain problems
with that model. Wouldn't mind checking it over.'

'Fat chance,' I said. 'The lady won't let anyone near it.'

A longer pause. More hand-wiping while he thought about
this. 'Something dodgy about that. Steer clear of it. If a
woman's got in her mind she's not selling, she won't be
budged.'

'Len, I'm an expert at budging.'

He considered this. 'Number plates?'

'Off, but could be lying around.'

'Chassis number?'

'No time. I was pounced on.'

'Get back there.'

'Give me time,' I pleaded. I wanted to be 'in' with Polly
before risking another run-in with Guy the Gorilla. I think I

had some vision of sauntering down to look at the Lagonda hand in hand with her.

'Harry Prince won't,' Zoe piped up.

I winced. 'Look, how about I get on with the police job to keep the wolf from the barn door, and tackle the Lagonda step by step?' Both 'police jobs' involved the theft to order of prestigious cars; the Rolls was a left-hand drive, and these were disappearing to the continent so fast that they were sometimes across the Channel before their owners knew they'd been stolen. This one belonged to a retired army officer living near Sandwich. The Merc was owned by a chap called Peter Winter, who lived in Holtham near Maidstone.

I get on well with Dave Jennings, especially as he's a bit of a car buff himself and rather begrudges the fact that he has to farm out interesting cases to me because of pressure of other work. In fact, he looks more car buff than policeman, which is often an asset. He's got a face like an eager wolfhound, sharp nose, fine features, hair sort of streamed back, as if the wind's blowing a Force 10 gale, which makes him look as ready to take off as the Rolls Royce Silver Lady, Spirit of Ecstasy. He had rated the Rolls the more urgent job, since he thought the Merc a lost cause. Reported missing in April, it had disappeared without trace, even though Dave's men had covered the usual channels themselves. So my job would be to think of any *un*usual ones that might be worth checking.

By the time I rang Dave, however, the Rolls had been traced, and I was to hold off on the Merc. So the wolf was back at my door, howling with a vengeance. On the other hand, Dave needed me at HQ to run through overdue paperwork with his team, which left me champing at the bit as to when I could call on Polly 'casually'. I'd had a pretty full week booked anyway, with some spare-parts runs, visits to potential customers and a couple of car pick-ups and delivery (no, you won't see me on the motorway entrance ramp with trade plates!). On Wednesday or Thursday I'd ring Polly and tell her I'd be dropping in shortly with my masterpiece – I would check which of the paintings seemed most likely to impress Polly and dig it out. Luckily, Giovanni hadn't then got round to a Lagonda, because it might have been a tad obvious if I'd turned up in my Alfa with that.

I decided I'd leave the great day until after the weekend,

partly so that I wouldn't have to rush off anywhere if there was a chance of spending more time with Polly, and partly because Sunday was the classic car meeting at the Wheatsheaf, where I might pick up some interesting information about the Lagonda.

The Wheatsheaf was a fun pub, and its owner, Bill Mount, didn't mind too much whether one partook of his cuisine or not. He was only too happy to see a couple of dozen classics improving the look of his establishment, while his staff (usually Mrs Mount) slaved over the Sunday roasts. For me this kind of event is the fair face of the classic car world. The auctions present a tougher one, for one needs to be wary of to whom one's talking, and dealers are dealers, not just someone you're having a pint with. Not-so-honest traders might be hovering around like sparrowhawks.

At the Wheatsheaf I could kill two cars with one stone. I'd seen Andy Wells there once or twice, although we're not on close terms. He was just the sort of chap who could be useful for my police work, and he would also have been well in with the Davises as he'd taken over Mike's business. If the day went well, then a mention of Polly's Lagonda might conceivably bring forth fruit.

Pushing it? Maybe, but if I didn't push I would get precisely nowhere, and somehow I felt my passion for Polly was inextricably linked with that wonderful car. I'd still feel the same about either if that link were snapped, but at present it was going strong.

There was another reason that I could never resist the Wheatsheaf meetings. It was a chance to show off my beloved and venerable 1965 GT Gordon Keeble. I've never flown a Spitfire, but I'm told that glorious experience is only comparable to sex. For Spitfire, read Gordon Keeble in my case. Over the years I'd had some great times with it – and some great companions in it. Now merely driving in it reminds me of happy days and former loves. Such is life.

'What do I do?' Zoe asked plaintively.

It was a rare concession for her to agree to accompany me to the Wheatsheaf, and this fake helplessness was one way of showing it. She's enthusiastic about her car detective role, but her methods and mine differ. She likes snooping around on her own, not arriving in state in a Gordon Keeble with the boss at her side – even if the boss is only me. Nevertheless, she had condescended to abandon her usual jeans for a posh mini skirt and matching cream jacket that went rather well with the orange spikes of her hair.

I took my revenge when I answered her. 'Just look beautiful, my lovely.'

A scathing look as we drew up outside the pub, where a dozen or so cars had preceded us. My practised eye passed over several, but then the sight of Maserati Mexico cheered me up. Dan would be somewhere around, which could be good. He would be amiable company, without being inquisitive as to my doings. I wish I could record that there was a breathless stunned silence of admiration for the Gordon Keeble as it came to a standstill, but, as they say, it doesn't work like that. It didn't this time. I was going to have to fight for my admiration.

Zoe immediately marched off into the pub, so I raced after her to provide her with a glass of wine (as befitted the feminine outfit) and myself with a modest half of shandy. She immediately began work by buttering up someone I didn't recognize – or maybe it wasn't work, but mere pleasure. Who knows with Zoe? Anyway, I dutifully returned outside to start work myself. To my pleasure a Lagonda had now driven up, the one I'd seen here before. Post-war, but it was good news: a very rare 1950 DB 2.6, a car of considerable charm. The even better news was that Andy Wells was standing by it, talking to Dan Burgess.

'Hi, Dan. Good to see you again. Hi, Andy. Nice.' I gave a nonchalant nod of approval at the Lagonda, hoping to flatter him by assuming him to be the proud possessor, although it was clear neither of them was.

Andy did not reply.

'Quite a lady,' Dan agreed. 'Not my cup of tea though. Make mine a Maser any day.'

I could see his point. His dashing dark handsome hero looks made him good Maserati material. I pressed on: 'Always wanted one of these. Way above my price range though. I saw one advertised well into six figures.' True enough, I'd been doing my homework on the Internet. 'Lagondas are your cup of tea too, aren't they, Andy?'

A nod. Andy, like Dan, is only in his thirties, but has even
fewer words to spare than Len. He's OK, but keeps himself
so tightly spannered in that I doubt if even his wife can turn
the right nuts and bolts. In the village he's referred to as 'good
old Andy', because he runs an efficient good garage out on
the Pluckley Road and can be relied upon to help out – or,
rather, his stooge Jimmy can. Andy's most financially rewarding
activity, however, must be online classics dealing – the business he bought from Mike – although quite a few classic
beauties actually turn up in his forecourt, which sometimes
allows me the odd drool as I drive by.

I've never quite hit it off with Andy, and that isn't solely
down to the fact that he is no Gordon Keeble fan.

'I heard Mike Davis was a Lagonda aficionado,' I tried again.
Nothing like pushing the boat out before you've tried the water.
I sank.

'You didn't hear it from me,' was Andy's reply.

'Must have heard wrong. Perhaps it was Polly.'

Andy didn't deign to reply, so I tried Dan. 'Mike was a
good chap. You know Polly, of course, Dan. Mike too?'

'Sure,' Dan agreed. 'Everyone knew Mike. Not well – I
painted a couple of their classics.'

I was in like a flash. 'The Lagonda V12?'

Engines have their own way of telling drivers they're not
happy, and so did my audience. There was an atmosphere that
indicated that I'd landed on the hard shoulder without meaning
to. Total breakdown. The way Andy was looking at me
signalled all lights should be flashing, whereas Dan, a simpler
soul, merely looked bewildered.

'Wouldn't know about that,' Dan replied. 'I remember doing
an Alfa 1750 and a Porsche 356. Same time as I did paintings
for a couple of others in Piper's Green. Lorna Stack, for one.'
He caught me looking, well, let's say quizzical, and grinned.
'It was a commission.'

For him or the picture? I wondered. Both, probably: art and
artist in one haul. Fortunately, that grin of his suggested he
was no dumb toy boy and could look after himself.

'Give me Polly any day,' I murmured. I meant it as a light
aside, but Dan replied seriously.

'You won't hear Lorna saying that. There's no love lost
between them.'

'I'll stick to Polly then.'

A rare guffaw from Andy. 'Don't get your hopes up, Colby. The lady's not for sale.'

He might as well have added, 'And nor's her Lagonda.'

The bull terrier in the back of Andy's car (which was the Aston Martin DB5 next to the Lagonda) had been slumbering peacefully, until he picked up his master's voice, decided he had been mistaken about my intentions and woke up snarling. It was time for me to depart. As I made my way into the pub to touch base with Zoe again, I was aware that Andy was staring after me in a thoughtful kind of way.

I was thoughtful too. If Andy knew all about the Lagonda, why was he so cagey about it? Fair enough, he could rightly have assumed that I was making plans for it, but he wasn't in the restoration business himself, and if Polly did decide to sell it, he was in a much better position to make an offer than I was. A fact that, thanks to Harry Prince, must be no secret.

I found Zoe still chatting to the same chap, who was pleasant-looking and in his mid-fifties. He didn't exactly look the normal ball of fire that Zoe sought out. She noted my arrival and smiled graciously upon me, indicating that I could approach. I was impressed at this new Zoe. She was doing well with whoever her companion was, and presumably there was a reason for it.

'Peter's the lucky owner of a beautiful Lagonda,' she cooed to me.

I picked up on my cue. 'Not that gorgeous DB 2.6 outside?' I gasped.

I'd hooked him. I listened patiently to his blow by blow account of how and when and in what condition he had acquired his beloved, and empathized with his obvious pride in owning one of only 510 ever produced.

'Peter lives at Holtham,' Zoe informed me as he handed me his card.

Great! It was Peter Winter himself, the missing-Merc man, though I wouldn't mention that now. He seemed a nice fellow, and with the Lagonda being his classic-in-the-garage, he might have known the Davises. Holtham wasn't that far away.

'I heard there was a drophead V12 still around in the Pluckley area,' I remarked cautiously. 'Someone told me it belonged to Polly Davis.'

Peter looked surprised, but was cooperative, bless him. 'That's right. She and Mike went everywhere in it. It was her father's. Tim Beaumont, Spitfire pilot. A 'thirty-eight, one of the last cars produced before the wartime hammer fell on civilian car production. Beaumont and that drophead went through the Battle of Britain at Biggin Hill.'

'He flew it?' I asked. Mistake. Don't make jokes about classic cars unless you know your audience.

'No,' Peter replied with a puzzled look. 'He used to pinch petrol and drive the lads to the pub in it.'

Zoe was eyeing me as if I should take off right now, though not in the Spitfire sense. She clearly saw another line of approach in which I would be hindrance not help, so I meekly murmured my excuse and left her with her prey. No problem. I'd be seeing Peter Winter again shortly, and, besides, I could see some interesting prey for myself sitting in the window seat, although where Liz Potter was concerned prey was not the right word.

FIVE

L iz runs the local garden centre in Piper's Green, and her other claim to fame is that for nearly a year after I returned to Kent she was the woman in my life. Inevitably, we split up, being far too alike in temperament for easy permanent togetherness.

Unfortunately, our now platonic friendship comes with a price – the dreaded Colin, a forensic scientist in a chemical lab, whom she married a year or so ago. A train enthusiast, his eyes only gleam when he sees the Flying Scotsman or anyone attempting to approach Liz. He's anti-cars and anti-Colby. Especially the latter.

Liz just laughs, as fortunately she has a mind of her own and is quite capable of telling him to stuff it – or, alternatively, giving me the same message. Liz is intelligent, alert and attractive. When we met she had been going through the dreary process of a marriage break-up, something I knew about. I was well over my bout, however. Now I chiefly remember

wedlock (what a descriptive word!) because of my lovely
daughter Cara, who lives and works in London. She's twenty-
four now, older than her parents were when they so foolishly
and tempestuously hurled themselves into marriage. Both Cara
and I have lost track of Eva, my former wife. Cara was brought
up by my beautiful Spanish werewolf until the age of twelve,
when Eva promptly dumped her with her own parents and ran
off to some remote Pacific Island with a Mexican bandleader.
Occasionally, she has turned up roaring and bumping through
Cara's and my lives like a Formula 1 car on a grass track, but
we've been left in peace for many a year now.

'Here to car-spot, are you?' I asked as I joined Liz, having
made sure that Colin was safely at the bar.

'You must be joking.' Liz's idea of a car is something that
gets her from A to B without too much breaking down. She
drives a Hyundai for choice.

'Would I joke about cars?'

She grinned at me, and just for the moment I wondered
what was so special about Polly. Then I remembered, and the
world tipped back to normal. Just as well: the last time Liz
and I were on lover terms, there was china and, as I recall, a
large teddy bear and his family flying all around me.

'Polly Davis,' I began. 'Know her?'

'Of course. That why you were talking to Peter Winter? He
was a chum of the Davises. I wasn't.'

'You don't like Polly?'

'I might if I could get near her.' She glanced at me sideways.
'Don't fall for her, Jack. Seriously.'

'Too late.'

She sighed. 'Ever fancied yourself as a lemming?'

'No. I like to see where I'm going. Did you know Mike?'

'I met him a few times. He was a rough diamond. Polly is
too, underneath that "don't touch me" stuff. She adored him.
He complemented her in some ways, and they suited each
other like a pair of gloves in others. After his death she retreated
into icicle mode, and it would take more than you to chip it
away.'

'You underestimate me, Liz.' She was probably right though.

'No, I don't. But when Mike died, so did Polly.'

'Wrong, Liz.'

'I hope so for your sake, Jack. I really do.'

I believed her, because Liz is like that. Unfortunately, my time was up, as stentorian tones rang out behind me:

'Colby!'

'Colin,' I greeted him heartily. 'Good to see you. Here to drool over the classics, are you?'

He stared at me as though analysing a particularly noxious larva at a crime scene. 'No. We picked the wrong day to come.'

That ended that conversation, and I made a graceful exit – followed, I'm sure, by a suspicious scientific eye on me. My luck was out again, because I promptly bumped into Harry Prince. Like Colin, I'd picked the wrong day to come. He was just getting out of his monster canary-coloured American hardtop coupé. Just right for him. Big, showy and guzzles too much. I could have done without this reminder that the day of reckoning could not be far off unless I cheered up Frogs Hill profits.

Nevertheless, on a good day I can take Harry, and this, I supposed, could be reckoned a good opportunity. I'd been hoping for the low-down on a few subjects, and you can't get much lower than Harry. He was all smiles. Oily, how-soon-can-I-get-my-hands-on-what-I-want smiles. Confident smiles. I had a fleeting thought of punching that smile right off his plump rosy face, but suppressed it. Harry's a car dealer, but not just of classics – all cars, any cars, anything that spells money. He has a chain of garages, but that's not enough for him. He's always hankering to go upmarket and deal with the crème de la crème. He had that in mind when he married Teresa Clare, who is definitely a cut above him. As Polly with husband Mike, I can't see what Terry gets out of marriage with Harry, but they seem contented enough.

'Just the man I wanted to see, Harry,' I said as cordially as I could.

A chortle. 'Heard you had a run in with old Guy the other day. Poking your nose into other people's business, as usual.'

'Other people's barns, actually.'

'Barns?' He looked blank. Oh hell, I'd wrongly assumed he knew all about Polly's Lagonda, as everyone else seemed to.

'Bars,' I speedily recapped. 'You know, bar for drinks. It was a joke.'

He looked at me oddly, but I seemed to have got away with it. 'Polly Davis, you see,' I added. 'I met her at the art show.'

'Ah. Now I'm with you, old chap. You can't afford to keep
that lady going, I can tell you. Ready to talk turkey yet?' He
poked me in the chest, and I wondered whether to poke him
back a little more forcefully, but I would do myself no favours
that way.

'Not even the parson's nose, Harry.' I sounded more
confident that I felt.

'I can wait. You'll be along some day. We can do a deal.
How about you running the old place for me? Prince's
Restorations at Frogs Hill Barn. No breathing down your neck.'

As the bishop said to the actress. 'I'll give it some thought,'
was all I replied. Why not lie through my teeth? He does.
'You were a neighbour of the Davises, weren't you?' I added.

It might have been my imagination, but I thought his face
paled a little. 'Near enough. What about it?'

'What sort of chap was he?'

'What's that to you?'

'Got an early Bentley in the shop that had been through his
hands once,' I lied. 'Something smells wrong.'

'Often did.' Harry was playing for time, and he tried to
make a getaway by strolling into the pub.

No chance. I strolled right after him. 'Was his business
legit?' I hissed in his ear.

Harry's a cunning man, but it's a focused cunning. On
money. He's not too good on the finer shades of psychological
perception. He leaves that to his wife Terry – whom I like a
lot, incidentally.

He stopped in his tracks, whirling round so suddenly that
we were practically chest to chest. 'Andy Wells is around here
somewhere,' he told me, looking very defensive. 'Ask him.
He's running it now.'

'Come off it, Harry. You can do better than that. Let's put
it another way. What was Mike's illegit line?'

He decided to give me full eye contact – suspicious in itself.
'What illegit line?'

He had told me enough. Now I knew there must have been
an illegit side to Mike – simply because Harry hadn't denied
it – so Mike's classics to order business had probably included
stolen to order. No proof, of course, but I didn't need it. After
all, I knew the Lagonda was probably legit. Not stolen, anyway;
I'd double-checked.

Harry was looking shifty now, obviously wondering whether to speak or not. In the end he gave a nervous cackle. 'Look here, Jack, there are some odd people around, so my advice is to shut it. I'd rather buy the Glory Boot and Frogs Hill farm off *you*, not off your executors. See what I mean?'

I did, and it took me down a notch or two.

'Take care where Mike Davis is concerned,' he added conspiratorially. 'Hate you to step into a minefield. You might forget you promised the Glory Boot to me. And forget where that Bentley had been, get rid of it fast.'

'Bentley?' I asked blankly, then remembered. 'Sure, I'll do that, Harry. Thanks for the warning.'

The day suddenly had an extremely nasty edge to it, and I decided I'd think about pleasant things – such as Polly. Even the Lagonda was beginning to have a very dark shadow over it.

I picked out one of Giovanni's paintings, which could have been a Van Gogh except for the Lamborghini speeding past the haystack. The day had come. Not too soon, not too late. I wasn't going to tell Zoe where I was going, but she guessed. I was wearing my best bib and tucker. Zoe had done some sterling work with Peter after my departure and had won a Lagonda friend for life, it seemed. It had transpired that he, too, had fallen in love with Polly's inheritance from her father and had offered several times to buy it during Mike's lifetime. Each time the offer had been refused. After Mike's death he had tried again, only for Polly to tell him it had been written off after an accident. He would have taken this at face-value, but various rumours about it made him follow up this state-ment. It had been without success. However, as far as the Swansea Driver & Vehicle Licensing Agency was concerned, the car was alive and well and living in Kent. I should know – I'd checked.

'Is that gear for the Lagonda or Polly?' Zoe called over to me, having spotted my unusually smart attire.

'Both.' I tried to sound casual.

'Want company?'

She'd got me. 'No,' I yelled, at which she and Len both guffawed.

That made me feel even more like a schoolboy. When I had telephoned Polly, I discovered I'd scored an own goal by telling her I was intending to ask her to frame my Giovanni. I would have to wait an extra day as she did not open her office on a Monday, in compensation for working on Saturdays. The amusement in her voice told me she knew exactly why I was coming to Greensand Farm in company with Giovanni. The office was, however, open on Tuesdays, and I nursed a vision of her breathlessly waiting for me.

When I drove up the drive to Greensand Farm, the antici-pation was making my mouth dry. The farmhouse itself was an old red-brick building from, I guessed, the early nineteenth century, and once I had reached the forecourt it was easy to see where Polly worked. In front of me was the house, to one side were what must have been the stables, now clearly a garage, and on the other was a barn, converted into what looked like an office and showroom. I strolled over to them, not wanting to seem in too much of a hurry in case she was peering out. I need not have bothered. Both doors were firmly locked, and there was no note to suggest where Polly might be.

I hung around for three quarters of an hour, and then went over to the house. No answer there either. Had she forgotten? With some people that might have been all too likely, but with Polly that couldn't have been the case. A deliberate no show? That, too, seemed unlikely. She had seemed friendly on the phone.

I was going to give up, but then the Lagonda loomed up in my mind. If for some reason Polly had gone out without remembering our date, or had been delayed, then the Lagonda and barn would be unguarded. The perfect opportunity for a snoop. I seized a car blanket in case it helped, left my Alfa where it was in order to provide a legitimate presence, and walked back down the drive to the bridle path bordering the Lagonda barn.

Being May, the path looked even more overgrown, but I was glad of its leafy cover. Ten to one, after my first visit, Polly had locked the barn up securely, or even – a nasty thought this – taken the car away.

What the hell did I think I was doing? I wondered as I set off. I wasn't sure. I'd checked through a police chum that the Lagonda had duly been registered to a Tim Beaumont until 1994, and then to Polly. Still was. Fair enough. But it was off-road, so why take the plates off? Maybe they'd just fallen

off, along with the tax disc. Weird. And yet Polly had been
anxious about the car itself, which hadn't looked as if it had
been used since her husband's death. There must be something
I'd missed. At the very least I wanted to check the VIN number
and have a hunt for the missing plates.

Every step made me more and more certain that I wasn't
going to turn back. Nevertheless, even though I could legiti-
mately say I had business with Polly, I felt like a criminal,
and I cursed my luck when I passed a dog walker. To her, I
probably looked like a mad long-distance walker, except for
my trainers, which weren't exactly Wainwright 'Coast to Coast'
path standard. They passed muster with her Alsatian, anyway.

At first I thought the barn had vanished along with the car.
Surely, Polly couldn't have taken things that far? Then I realized I wasn't far enough along the bridleway. One clump of
trees can look remarkably like another to a man in a hurry.

At last I saw the oak tree I'd stopped by before. Never since
Charles II has anyone been more grateful to see one. I was
sure it was the right one, even though the gap in the hedge
had been filled in with fence posts. Fine. I'd scramble over
the top this time. There through the leaves of the tree I could
see the ivy-covered roof and glimpse the ragstone walls of the
barn. I slithered across the ditch in preparation, stopped by
the hedge to take my posh jacket off, and hoisted myself up
the tree to decide my point of entry. Only then, from my
elevated position, did I let my eyes go to the barn doors.

They were indeed closed, but I had more to think about
than that. My eyes were riveted on what lay at their foot. A
body lay sprawled on its back, covered in blood and with the
face half blown away. I had no trouble in identifying whose
it was.

It was Polly's, and she was dead.

SIX

I know crime scenes. I've seen several before, but this one
was different. I'd had ten minutes or so after my call to
prepare myself for the first PCs to arrive. Prepare? How?

I'd thrown up several times and tried to get my mind into some kind of shape. I hadn't succeeded. My head seemed to be full of bees humming away to their hearts' content while I stared helplessly at Polly's body.

'Don't contaminate the scene,' I told myself.

I repeated the words over and over again like a mantra, but they were meaningless. How could I contaminate a scene already so ghastly? Half of me wanted to run like blazes and pretend it wasn't happening, and the other half was telling me I should stay put. I had forced myself as far away as I could and perched on the low branch of a tree, sufficiently near for me to be visible to the police when they arrived.

After I'd related my story to the two PCs, they kept a firm eye on me until the whole caboodle came marching in. That was the worst. I had told the PCs the truth, included my method of entry over the hedge, but they patently hadn't believed me. So we just waited. I tried to concentrate on who could have done this to my Polly, but my mind kept sliding past the issue.

Had there been a gun lying at Polly's side? I couldn't remember. Suicide? Not Polly. Oh, surely not. I hadn't stayed by that terrible sight long enough to look for powder burns, exit wounds and any of the other signs that would give any indication of murder or otherwise. She had been lying partly on her side, partly on her back. Would she have fallen that way if she'd shot herself? I didn't know, and I most certainly didn't want to think about it. I just wanted to get on with the whole ghastly police crime procedure that had to take place. After the SOCOs arrived and the cordon tape was up, it was slightly easier, as the tape seemed to distance me from the body. Think of it that way, I told myself: as a body, not as Polly. There was only one entrance to the crime scene now, and a grim-looking PC held an entry log to repel all strangers. That suited me. My trainers had been taken away from me – with my permission, it has to be said, but I knew they'd have been taken anyway. A pair of scene shoes had grudgingly been given to me in exchange.

It was like looking at an old sci-fi film seeing all those scene-suited SOCOs going about their slow methodical business, but it was one I didn't want to watch. Who would tell Bea? I wondered. I thought of her, I thought of Polly, and then I thought of myself. Happy dreams had been just that.

The fantasies that fate had first encouraged me to entertain and then torn away had left a gaping hole. Had Polly and I been soulmates? We had surely been on the brink of being so. I couldn't have been mistaken about that.

The senior officer in charge of this lot was DI Brandon of North Downs Area. I recognized him, as we had passed like ships in the night at police HQ in Charing near Ashford from time to time when I'd been there with DCI Dave Jennings. Brandon wasn't like Dave. Brandon got his man by being a bully. Not an obvious one. Too clever for that. But he bore down on you with such heavy determination that it was clear one's fate had already been decided – at least in his mind.

I was left in peace for some time – although peace was hardly the word in these circumstances – but that was about to end. Brandon was coming towards me, his sidekick (a weedy youth half his girth) a few steps behind him. I began to tell him I'd touched nothing – I couldn't have done – but he cut me short.

'PC Cartwright tells me you jumped over the hedge. Care to tell me why?'

First on the scene, natural suspect, I calmed myself, but my mode of entry – which the first crime scene search would have revealed anyway – didn't look good. I contemplated saying I'd spotted the body and leapt over the quickest way to investigate, but decided against it. I'd have to have a reason for clambering up to peer over the hedge. No, stick to the truth. After all, no one ever got slung inside if they were innocent, did they? Grim joke. Anyway, I told Brandon I had recently met Polly, that I knew she had a classic car in the barn, that we had a date for this morning at her picture framing office, that my car was in front of it complete with painting to prove it, and that as she wasn't in the office or farmhouse I thought she might be down here.

'Why come down the bridleway and over the hedge? Why not walk through the farm?'

Sinking in quicksand immediately. 'Wasn't sure whose land this was. A neighbour objected to my looking at the car a few days ago.'

Weak, but Brandon was too clever to push it now. 'Thought it was her you came to see, not the car,' he said amiably.

'Both.'

Not too good, but not too bad, I suppose. But then Guy
Williams came storming along . . .

An hour or so later I was being questioned at Charing Police
HQ. I suppose having one's DNA taken is some kind of
distinction, but it was the last straw for me. I understood that
I had to be checked for scratches – luckily there was only one
from my encounter with the bushes – but I was still in a state
of shock, and although my brain might have been trying to
tell me this was all routine, the message wasn't getting through.

'Mr Williams seems to think you were on bad terms with
Mrs Davis. She objected to your previous mountaineering
practice with her hedge,' Brandon shot at me.

'That's true,' I admitted. 'Then I met her again – with
witnesses – and apologized. So I was on good terms with her,
and I decided to bring her some business.'

'Names of these witnesses?'

I thought of Zoe and Len – only my word for it. Rob might
oblige. Then I remembered Dan Burgess. He'd seen me chatting with her at least, so I offered Brandon his name. Good
old Guy had obviously given the police every last lurid detail
of that first meeting, including a few additions of his own,
such as how he'd thrown me bodily back over the hedge
while I was effing and blinding about vengeance. Luckily,
he had come over as the blusterer he was, but even so Brandon
could hardly have ignored the clear implication that I had
returned for exactly that purpose.

'Quick change on Mrs Davis's part, wasn't it?' Bulldog
Brandon asked. He sounded merely politely interested, but I
could see a hammer patiently knocking nails in one by one.

'Yes. I got the impression it wasn't *me* she had objected to
so much as being reminded of the car.'

That went down like a lead balloon. Brandon didn't pick
up on the car angle, and I wasn't sure whether I was glad or
sorry about that. I didn't want the police examining it before
I could. 'She might have been holding back what she *really*
thought of you because there were others present. Used to
that, I'm sure. TV presenter once, wasn't she?'

'Yes. But Polly wouldn't have invited me to her home if
she hadn't meant it.'

'Home? You said it was business. Picture framing.'

'True again,' I said patiently. 'I thought if I took her some work it would help my apology ring true. Her office is next to the farmhouse.'

'Keen to see her again, eh?' The words 'cover story' were written all over his face. 'You left this painting in the car, arranged to meet her at the barn to discuss the Lagonda and killed her. Let's consider that, just for the sake of argument.'

'Let's not,' I said, trying to stay cool and failing. 'Why the hell should I kill her?' My brain decided it had better take a more active part in the proceedings. 'I'd only just met her. If I wanted to steal the car, it would be a pretty stupid move to have killed her.'

'Heat of the moment, Mr Colby. All sorts of things can happen.' He was now watching me more like a hawk his prey than a bulldog.

'With a gun I just happened to have with me and must have buried with a spade that I also happened to bring along?'

Brandon managed a nod, as if to cede victory on this one.

'*Was* there a gun at the scene?' I still had no idea.

'No.'

'So Polly didn't kill herself.' That at least was a relief. I remembered that heartbroken look she had given the Lagonda on that first occasion we'd met. Something inside me tied itself in aching knots. That look hadn't been for me, and now it never would.

'You're not off the hook yet, Colby. Move anything, did you? Such as a gun?'

'No.'

'Then it's unlikely to be suicide unless you're lying. Anyway, the blood spatters don't tie in. Sorry about that.'

That did it. I exploded. 'Sorry? You think I'd want Polly to have been so unhappy that she killed herself?'

He gave me an odd look. 'That's one way of looking at it. Right. You can go now, Mr Colby, but don't leave town, eh?'

So much for a friendly chat. DNA results take time to come through, however. Brandon had probably been winding me up in preparation for the next time, hoping they'd find a gun with some nice DNA on it – like mine – or trace evidence on Polly's clothes. I suppose I should be grateful that I'd been left with my own. Brandon kindly refrained from pointing out that for a lady I had only just met, I seemed very concerned for her welfare, and I was taken by surprise at my quick release. Dave Jennings might have put in a good word for my overall credibility, but that wouldn't exclude me from a murder charge. I was only temporarily off the hook.

It was gone six o'clock by the time I reached Frogs Hill, and never had I been so glad to see it. I'd even been allowed to pick up my car and, thankfully, my Giovanni painting. Pasta would be flying if he heard one of his precious creations was in police custody for the foreseeable future. Normally both Len and Zoe would have departed by then, but although there were no signs of Len, Zoe was still there. For once she was not in the Pits, however, but in the farmhouse itself, to which she and Len had house keys. She came to the door to meet me as I drew up, looking anxious – which was unusual for her.

'Bea's here,' she said without preamble.

Both of them must therefore have heard the news, and I suppose it was a sign of confidence that I was clearly expected to be able to cope with this situation. I wasn't sure I was up to it. Apart from anything else, the etiquette books don't cover what a suspect says to the bereaved family of his alleged victim. Putting that aside, I didn't know Bea well enough even to guess what she was going through. In the event it proved easy.

'Hello, Jack.'

Bea was sitting in Dad's old armchair, clutching the arms as though it was giving her his moral support. The poor girl was hardly the rosy-cheeked lass I'd met at the art show, although she was doing well. That's a stupid word to use in such circumstances, I realized. Her exterior self was coping, that was all. She was dry-eyed, though her voice was wobbly, but her comparative composure put me on the right track.

'What can I do?' I asked gently and, remembering my situation, added, 'You heard it was me who found her.'

'Yes. The police told me. They fetched me from Canterbury. That's where I work. Guy told me about you too.'

He would. 'I just barged in at the wrong time. I had nothing to do with this—' I stopped. No words could sum up Polly's death for me.

'I wouldn't be here if I believed you did.'

'Then back to my first question. What can I do?'

She looked so young, with her white T-shirt and skirt, and her hands clasped round her knees. Younger than Cara, and I felt as fatherly towards her as if Polly and I had created her. Stupid though it might seem, I felt I had a duty of care.

She and Cara were both robust and normally able to cope, but when the unexpected strikes, hand in hand with tragedy, it could be a different matter.

Bea's words shot out like bullets: 'Find out who did it.'

I'd half expected this, as why else would she have come to see me? The word 'detective' was obviously a rock for her to cling to, no matter that a car detective like me might not have the same powers in a situation such as this. Half forewarned and half prepared, I switched gears as smoothly as an automatic.

'So the police do think suicide is ruled out. They wouldn't come clean with me. I'm glad about that, Bea. How could she have been so unhappy, with you at her side?'

She winced. 'I made them tell me the truth. They tried the usual stuff. Awaiting the path report, but –' she gulped – 'the blood and angle of the . . .'

I jumped in to help her. 'Had her body been moved?'

'They don't think so. Not even by you.' Brave Bea managed to summon up a smile. 'Or so I gathered.'

'You really think I can help? It's cars I specialize in.'

'Same stuff needed,' Zoe said firmly with one of her looks which dared me to let Bea down.

Was it? I thought about the qualities that made me useful to Dave Jennings' crime unit. It's hard to be objective about one's own attributes, but I suppose mine might include obstinacy, devotion to the hunt, eye for detail, an ability to see the whole picture and instinct. The mere whiff of a recent paint job can set me off on the right (or sometimes the wrong) track. And last of all, though it should perhaps have been top of the list, comes knowledge. Knowledge of past, and present and possibly future cars, together with the experience of mankind's spectrum of attitudes to them and consequent behaviour. Nevertheless, knowledge of relationships between human beings was what was needed in this case, and much as I would be flooring the accelerator to put Polly's killer behind bars, I was a relative amateur in this field. For my car detective work, I have a link to the crime world through a chap called Brian

Woollerton, who runs a team of informants, but for human relationships I've only myself and bruising experience.

'I don't know enough about Polly,' I said simply. 'I'd need help.'

Bea understood. 'Nobody ever knows more than a part of someone else. I reckon that's true of mother and daughter as well as you and Mum.'

I was taken aback. 'Did I make it that obvious?'

'We're not babes and sucklings, Jack,' Zoe said gently for her.

'Suckers though,' Bea commented ruefully. 'The police are after Tomas, as suspect number one. They were asking me just what our relationship was, and when I told them the truth, I could hear their little brains clicking away: Tomas thought he was on to a good thing in me and decided to hurry along the day when he'd be married to the heiress of an English farm. Heiress! That's a joke.'

'Oh Bea. But you don't think he's guilty, do you?' Zoe asked. And when Bea didn't answer, she sighed. 'You always were easy prey for romantic foreigners.'

'I don't know what to think. I *can't* bloody think. Tomas wasn't on good terms with Mum and that's for sure.'

'Did Guy have a hand in this? After all, he's Tomas's employer – although I guess Brandon would favour me over Tomas for the high jump.'

'Preferably,' Bea answered flatly. 'After all, you were there. But why on earth should you want to kill her?'

'My thoughts exactly,' I said gratefully.

'Tomas had been threatening Mum,' Bea said. 'He didn't mean anything by it, though.'

'Threatening her with what exactly?' I asked.

'They had a major row. Tomas got stroppy when Mum told him to get off the gravy train, as she expressed it. I objected. I'm nearly twenty-three, for heaven's sake. But even Guy admits Tomas got drunk one night and shouted the odds in the pub, about marrying me and getting his own back on my mother.' Bea's face was twisted with pain. 'I'm only telling you this because the police know it, Jack. Otherwise you wouldn't get a peep out of me about Tomas. I don't think he's a murderer, but I have a feeling the police have more on him than just threats. There was some kind of scene at Guy's place too, one day, when Mum came storming in to protest. I wasn't there, but I heard all about it from everyone concerned.'

'Has he been arrested?'

'He's being questioned.' Bea burst into tears, and Zoe, not normally the most demonstrative of girls, put her arms round her.

'A drink,' I said hastily.

'I'm driving,' Bea hiccuped.

'*I'm* driving,' Zoe told her. 'You're staying with me tonight.'

'That's cowardly.' Another hiccup.

'That's sensible, not cowardly.'

'No.' Bea was very white. 'I must go back to Greensand Farm. I want to make sure the barn door is locked.'

The Lagonda. How could I have forgotten it? Easily, I thought, when its late owner was still stuffing every corner of my mind with the waste and horror of her death.

'It's in the crime scene,' I explained to Bea. 'The police will keep a twenty-four-hour guard on it until they've finished their work there. And, indeed, the farmhouse too. What worries you about the car? That someone might steal it?'

'No. Because it meant a lot to my mother.'

'You said she'd never mentioned it to you.'

'That's how I know it meant so much.'

I was humbled. It all came back to knowledge. For all Bea had said, I might not have sufficient about Polly to help her daughter. 'You're going to have enough to do without involving yourself in what is the police's job.'

She brushed this aside. 'I have to feel I'm helping *her*. I know there'll be mountains of routine work, notifying people and dealing with everyone from the window cleaner to Great Aunt Maud, but I want to be sure. I don't mean I'm going to stalk the hunt, I just want to think it through and work out why it happened, to be sure that the police are on the right track. Do you see?'

'I do,' Zoe said promptly, and the laser beam from her eyes turned on me. 'And so do you, don't you, Jack?'

The laser wasn't needed. 'Yes.'

Bea relaxed a little. 'I want you to do it, Jack. I just couldn't bear to talk to people while wondering all the time: was it you? Or was it you?'

I was with her one hundred per cent. This was going to

have to replace my lost future with Polly, even if that had never existed except in my mind.

But the mind is the most important place in the world. It can, as the poet said, make a hell of heaven or a heaven of hell. I was going to do my best to make hell at least a little more bearable. The poet, I recalled, was John Milton, and the poem *Paradise Lost*. Never had a title seemed more fitting for what lay ahead of me.

SEVEN

Bea had taken compassionate leave from work, and I'd arranged to go up to Greensand Farm the next morning. Before I left, however, I went to the Pits – I needed to speak to Zoe. She had arranged to stay at the farm overnight with Bea, and when she reported to work she looked as if she'd had little sleep – and no wonder. 'Bea's OK,' she said, 'but don't come down heavy on her.'

As if I would have. I don't think I was capable of 'heavy' that day, particularly where Bea was concerned. 'Tell me, Zoe. She's your chum, but if I'm to help I need to be sure I know where I am.'

She looked amused. 'Where's your nose, Jack? You boast that you can tell if a classic's good or not, regardless of the paint job.'

'But Bea—'

'She's a classic, Jack. Like that blessed Lagonda, she needs to be on the road again. OK?'

Standing there with spanner in hand, orange spiked hair standing up fiercely in defence of her friend, Zoe was in fighting mode, and I told her so. 'You'll make a great foot-soldier for the team, Zoe.'

That sounded patronizing, but it wasn't meant that way. Zoe and I knew where we were, from long experience. 'Go for the flag, Jack. We'll win,' was all she said.

When I reached the farm on that Wednesday morning, Bea was in businesslike form. 'I can't face Mum's sanctum yet, so you'll have to make do with the conservatory.'

The interior of the farmhouse was a surprise to me as we walked through. With Polly's cool, calm approach to life, I had somehow expected a cross between minimalist and show-case for art and antiques. I was wrong. This was a home, not a museum. Bookcases, threadbare but good carpets, a mix of old and new furniture, and walls displaying a higgledy-piggledy collection of paintings and photographs.

Bea must have noticed my surprise and divined the possible cause. 'Mum didn't touch a thing in this house after Dad died, except to clear out his personal belongings. She wasn't into shrines, but the rooms themselves are the same, down to Dad's beer mat collection and his precious photos of greyhounds, racing and rescued. He was an East Ender, and his grandparents and their kids were blitzed out of their house in 1940. Everything that got rescued eventually made its way down here with Dad and Mum.'

The farmhouse was larger than it looked, and my heart went out to Bea, who seemed to be wandering forlornly through it. Even though it had been her home for so long, it was no longer, and to have it thrust upon her so tragically must be an added burden. It would doubtless now be hers if she was an only child, and the responsibility for it, after her probably snug little flat in Canterbury, couldn't have been easy to contemplate. Not that she'd have had much time for that.

'Is Zoe staying on with you for a while?'

She pulled a face. 'I hope so. All the world and his wife in the way of obscure relations are threatening to descend on me.'

'Could you cope with that?'

'No way. That's why I want Zoe here, so that I don't have to have everyone else.'

'Company can help.'

'Too much of it can hide the problem. *Not* a help.'

I switched tack as we sat down in the comfortable conservatory. It looked out on the garden – which looked as if it had been Polly's pride and joy, but I didn't say so. Bea sat with her back to it, which might be confirmation enough. 'Any news of Tomas?'

'Not yet. He'd be right here if he'd been released, so I think they must have kept him in all night.'

'I'd like to know what evidence they have to do so.' I could try Dave Jennings on this in due course, but it would be useful to know now.

'I'll ask Guy. He may have heard.'

'Look, do you still want me to go ahead with this? If so, I'll do it.'

'Yes, but I'll cope with Guy. You're not his favourite person.'

There was no doubt that she was committed to this course, for tears filled her eyes, so it was going to be tough. On us both, I thought, but on her mostly.

'Did Polly own a gun?' I asked, getting down to the nitty gritty. 'Do you mind my calling her Polly?'

She shook her head. 'I like it. It makes life seem more normal. Mum hated shooting. Dad used to go sometimes, but only to be chummy with the local nobs, as he called them. The hoity-toity "let's go out and bag some game" gang, Dad used to joke. Never brought any booty home because Mum wouldn't stand for it. They'd argue like crazy. Just to provoke her, he would say there was no difference between shooting-parties and butchers, and they'd be off again.'

'Happy marriage though?'

'Are you joking? Of course it was. They were joined at the hip, were Mum and Dad. I couldn't fight my way in most of the time.'

'That figures. Was it an only marriage for both of them?'

'Yes. Dad was five years older than Mum, but he used to say that he was waiting for her to catch up.'

How could I put this? 'So after his death . . .'

'A string of lovers?' Bea picked up immediately. 'I've heard the odd rumour. Nonsense, all of them.'

I could hardly ask Bea whether sex and love might be two different things in Polly's case, and she didn't volunteer any more on this subject. Which meant I had no choice but to make the running.

'At that art show, Lorna Stack was crying to all and sundry that Polly was after her husband. Rupert . . . ?'

'Yes. Henpecked little Rupert. Lorna does that for show. She bowls men over like skittles and doesn't stop to pick up the pieces. She enjoys shifting the focus to poor old Rupert. Mum was used to it.'

'She was threatening to kill her if she got too near Rupert again. Is that par for the course?'

Bea looked uneasy. 'Not usually.'

Right. Progress at last, I thought. 'Was Rupert Polly's type?'

'No. Rupert wouldn't have the guts to have an affair anyway,' Bea replied simply. 'Not with Lorna following his every move. As a couple, they were friends both of Mum and Dad, but I don't think that close. Rupert runs this arty-farty gallery in London, Mum used to do most of his framing, and Lorna added two to two and made ten as usual. After Dad's death, she took a fancy to Guy, but I'm pretty sure he would have declined the honour though. He might have hoped Mum would look his way. As if. Lorna did her best to skittle Dad over too.'

'Did she succeed?'

'I doubt it, though I might have been too young to realize if anything was going on. I was away a lot at college that last year or so and only had time to think about the Great Me, not my parents. Dad used to laugh at Lorna and talk about her tarty line, but that doesn't mean he didn't fall for a quick one. The odds are against it though. They really are. What with cars and Mum, he had his hands too full. Lorna wouldn't have liked being turned down.'

That applied to me too. 'Enough to take revenge?'

'Lorna wouldn't do it herself. Might hire a hit man, but it's unlikely four years later.'

'They had a big row at the show.'

'I heard about it.'

Cooperative as Bea was, I felt I might not be getting the whole truth here, probably because she didn't know it. I'd no option but to let it go. 'How did Polly come to framing after her TV career? A big switch, wasn't it?'

'Not really. She'd always painted a lot of her own stuff. She just expanded it sideways into framing. Said she was never going to be a Leonardo, so why not frame them instead? It was something to do after Dad died. She used to spend all her time helping Dad when he was alive, and a lot of the time they were doing car shows here, there and everywhere, either in the UK or somewhere else in Europe.'

'She helped him in the classic car business?'

'Right. She didn't want to go back into TV. Too proud. Said she didn't want to join the ladder downwards as her looks went.'

She'd had no need to fear that, so far as I could see.

'Anyway,' Bea continued, 'she was used to working at home with Dad, so the framing was only a short step away. Maybe Rupert suggested it. He gave her plenty of work.'

'Or Dan Burgess?'

Bea grinned. 'No way. Don't see Mr Heart-throb soiling his hands with his own framing.'

'Heart-throb . . . Polly was keen on him?'

'I think she liked him; no sex though. He was a protégé of Dad's, really. Like Andy Wells.'

'Would either of them have any reason to hate Polly enough to want her out of the way?'

Bea lifted her hands helplessly. 'Not to my knowledge, but I suppose it's possible. She never talked business to me. Not Dad's, anyway. I have a feeling she didn't like Andy much.'

'He seems amiable enough.'

'I expect Jack the Ripper did on his good days.'

Bea was trying to be upbeat, but failed miserably.

'Coffee,' I said briskly. 'I'll do it.'

I went into Polly's kitchen to leave Bea to cry for a bit unhindered. The kitchen was easy – I found some instant, a fridge with milk, and two mugs and a kettle. No doubt Polly did things more elegantly, although how would I know? The lady had been a mystery. All I knew was that I hadn't been mistaken that there had been a future with a golden sunrise, and that someone had taken it away. For me, and for Bea, I was going to find out who – unless the police preceded me, in which case I'd be cheering from the public gallery when he was found guilty. He – or she. Guns aren't choosy as to who pulls their triggers.

Len and Zoe seemed concerned about me. For a start they left me alone without the usual banter, which allowed me to mooch in and out of the Pits where they were working on a Triumph Stag. The clincher was that not a word was spoken about Polly, although I knew the village was full of the story. Postman Bill Paget had come into the local pub, the Half Moon, where I'd made the mistake of going in for a late lunch, and despite my no doubt stony face he'd insisted on telling me – and no doubt the press – the current gossip. It wasn't much different, I imagined, from what they'd been chewing over on Tuesday

night too. This ranged from suicide to 'it was one of them
pickers' (which wouldn't go down well with Guy the Gorilla
Williams) and to a theoretical serial sex attacker, who might
or might not have been the no-doubt harmless walker who'd
dropped in for a pint the day before yesterday. Alternatively,
the said serial murderer might have been the someone in Mrs
Pope's general stores who had looked at her oddly, news that
had already been imparted to the nation via press and TV.

Bill had left the pub with a cheery wave, leaving me all the
more depressed.

Finally, by the end of the day, I could stand no more and
rang Dave Jennings. I needed to get the suicide option sorted
once and for all, and I was fairly sure that he either knew about
the case or could find out for me. It turned out to be the latter,
but Dave is a good sort, and he did indeed ring me back, as
he'd promised. He is the opposite of me in some ways, and
we coincide in others. We're both determined individuals once
our engines are revving, but Dave is more organized and
methodical than I am. That's good news for the Kent Police
Car Crime Unit.

'No gun yet, Jack,' Dave told me. 'Nothing interesting in
the way of prints anywhere in or on the car or barn except
– sorry, mate – yours, and a few of the lady's. No DNA results
yet, of course.'

'Professional job then?'

'Tired of detecting cars, Jack? Switching to CID?'

'Nope. All yours, Dave. I'm only nosing into this case to
avoid being part of it.' I hesitated. 'Am I off the hook, or are
your lips sealed?'

'Temporarily off, it seems. They've arrested that Polish chap
and given him pre-charge bail.'

Mingled relief and compassion for Bea. True, she didn't
exactly seem committed to Tomas, but we had only been
talking theoretically then. She might well find it hard to come
to terms with the fact that he was definitely in the frame,
especially if he was back in this area. There'd be more interviews for her, more statements and undoubtedly more
heartbreak.

'Between us and this open phone line, Jack,' Dave continued,
'Brandon implied they could have a strong case. Not only has
the guy been making no secret of his threats to the victim,

but he also seems to have a keen interest in cars, old and new. He's also got a brother in Poland whose name keeps popping up on the international buzz line. May be a receiver, and so his kid brother Tomas could well be a spotter.'

Highly possible, I supposed. Organized car crime depends on a freelance team staking out potential prey.

'Ever heard of a chap called Trent?' Dave rattled on. 'Mason Trent?'

It rang a faint bell, but I couldn't place him. 'Tell me.'

'Nasty piece of work. Used to be in the car cloning business big time, working with a chap you wouldn't want to run into on a dark night, Barry Pole of Baypole Cars. That was clean, but he also ran a car theft gang. Mason Trent did time, but Pole carried on. Keeps his head down, but he's around. Mason Trent came out a year ago, then fell off the radar, and it's he the Met's interested in. The word is he's back in the cloning business, but he changes name and premises so often it's like the crazy mirror show at the fair. Now you see him, now you don't. Know what I mean?'

I did. Mason Trent wasn't the only one in that game. 'What interest do you have in him?'

'Name's in Kasek's mobile, that's all. Still, Andy Wells is in it too, and so's the local pub.'

'No proof of murder then.'

'True, but if a villain says he's going to steal a car and then the car disappears, you'd be the first to say check him out seriously. That's what Brandon's doing. But the Trent mobile number's dead. Anyway, it's my guess that possible spotting is not all Brandon has on Kasek.'

'But your lips are sealed?' I asked when he stopped.

'They only open on cars for you, Jack. Talking of which . . .'

He went on to tell me I could now move on Peter Winter's missing Mercedes S500, which would normally have had me growling in anticipation of another mortgage payment or two being covered. My heart wasn't in the Merc today, however, despite it meaning money at the end of the trail. I went through the motions of discussing the case with Dave – which chiefly came down to my putting out feelers. It was routine stuff. The probable fate of Winter's Merc was that it had been stolen, cloned with an innocent identity and shipped on either abroad or to a series of dealers in the UK. If the former, it was possible that Dave's team had missed it and it was gone for good. If the latter, I supposed there was a faint chance it was still around, though it seemed pretty unlikely, and the hidden message of what Dave was telling me was to go through the motions of trying to find it to satisfy the insurance company and, if he was still interested, the rightful owner.

I couldn't afford not to take the case. Harry Prince would soon come sniffing around if I missed a repayment date. I sometimes think he has a direct line to my bank and imagine him rubbing his fat little paws together in glee at the first hint I'm on the ropes. I had news for him this time. I was still in the ring, merely reeling from the shock and grieving over Polly's death. It seemed strange, even to me, that a woman I had only met on a couple of occasions could affect me so, but she had and did. I would find her murderer for my own sake, as well as for Bea's.

Then I realized I was missing a trick. I'd had the impression that Peter Winter had known them only as a couple, rather than having been close to Polly recently, but nevertheless it was odds-on that anything he thought would help find her killer he would want to share with me. Suddenly, the stolen Merc was the most interesting car in the world.

'You want me in on this right away? I can ring Peter now.'

'Yup. I take it you know him then?'

'I met him once.' But that was going to be quickly remedied. I had to bear in mind, however, that even if he could point me in the right direction where Polly was concerned, the police seemed already to have made up their minds who was guilty. Tomas was the obvious suspect, and who was I to say the police were wrong? I'd no evidence either way, and the fact that my nose was telling me something different was hardly going to weigh heavily on DI Brandon's mind.

And what was it that my nose was imparting to me? Almost with a sinking heart, I had a stupid feeling that somehow Polly's death was tied up with the Lagonda. How could that be? I argued. Apart from the fact that the Lagonda had been in the barn while Polly's body had lain outside, there seemed nothing to connect them, and it was probably pure coincidence that she had been there when she'd met her death.

Or was it? I remembered the way she had suddenly appeared on that first occasion when we had met – with Guy Williams suspiciously popping up shortly afterwards. I'd assumed they'd been together, perhaps walking from his farm back to hers, or perhaps it had been their rendezvous point for either business or pleasure. But that didn't add up. If the Lagonda caused her so much grief she'd have avoided the barn, not sought it out.

Had Polly perhaps been considering selling the Lagonda to him? I thought this over carefully, but although it coincided with my preference I had to rule it out. Polly had been white-hot with fury at my even looking at her precious car. That suggested a strong emotional attachment, which in turn suggested that she would not have sold it to anyone. After all, if Guy Williams had made an offer for it, she would not have been quite so vehement about my also being interested in it, as the mere *idea* of selling would not have been repugnant to her. She could hardly have taken against me so strongly on personal grounds that selling it to me, as opposed to Guy, was ruled out. No, she hadn't wanted *anyone* touching that car. Her own daughter hadn't known she still had it.

Nevertheless, the idea that her murder had anything to do with that beauty of a Lagonda was a far cry from a tenable theory, or so I told my nose. My nose patiently pointed out again that that was where she had been killed. What had she been doing there? I came back to the only answer there seemed to be: to meet someone or to look for something. But what about her appointment with me? Had she forgotten it? Or had she been dead some time? I forced myself to think about that. I hadn't touched her body. Concentrate on the blood, I told myself. My forensic knowledge is limited to cars, but having seen her body my layman's guess was that the blood had clotted, but she hadn't been dead that long. That tallied with my eleven o'clock appointment with her: a time she'd suggested, not me. I'd seen that as a subtle indication that business might extend to lunch. Instead I'd seen her dead body in all its stark goriness. So for some reason she had gone to the barn earlier that morning. Why? On a whim or to meet someone? Either way, the Lagonda might have played its part.

EIGHT

So far so good. Next: the word had been going round, partly thanks to me, about this car. Andy Wells' interest had been keen enough, and even heart-throb Dan's. But if either of them had wanted to buy it, why hadn't she just delivered the same message to them? Push off, not for sale. Could Andy have had some hold over her where the Lagonda was concerned? I began to speculate. Suppose he'd had a contract to buy all Mike's classic cars and had only just found out he had been baulked of this Lagonda. That was a possibility. Or Dan? Or, it occurred to me, even Harry Prince. Had he become interested enough to follow up on the Lagonda himself?

I knew it was pointless to try to go further on these lines. I'd only had a couple of days to reconnoitre this problem, and I could well be seeing it from a completely lopsided angle. However, I did agree with my nose that I should see that Lagonda again. There did not seem much rhyme or reason to this, but I became fixed on the idea. After all, painters gaze at their models for inspiration. Perhaps the Lagonda would do the same for me, and Peter Winter might be persuaded to talk about this. Back to his missing Merc for openers.

The Mercedes S500 was just the sort of car I would have envisaged him driving: expensive but not too expensive; showy but not overdone, fast but not too fast. It was an *affable* car, just right for an affable sort of chap like Peter, who was clearly making his pile. I gathered from Dave that he ran some antiques-brokering business near West Malling – successfully judging by the Merc and his pride and joy, the Lagonda he'd brought to the Wheatsheaf. Unfortunately for him, the Merc S500 can be attractive to the less scrupulous members of society, hence Peter's car disappearing to order – which was probably what had happened, and the chances, as Dave said, looked slim of his ever seeing it again.

'It's not fair,' he told me plaintively when I arrived at his home, spot on the time he had designated on Saturday morning. He showed me the empty garage – well, empty of the Merc. There was an Audi convertible in there – his wife's, he explained – and the Lagonda. Together with a luxury Range Rover parked in the forecourt, it suggested he wouldn't be waiting for the daily bus to take him to work. He lived some way out of the village, in a red-brick Georgian house that, like Peter, was gracious and pleasant, rather than boastful of its heritage.

'No, it's not fair,' I agreed. I didn't weep too much for him though, even though he told me the Range Rover was the Merc's temporary replacement, thanks to the insurance company. Dave had given me the background on the phone so there wasn't much for me to ask him about the Merc, except whether there were any special details to help identify it. He shook his head, and I was free to go ahead on what I most wanted to talk about: Polly. I was a bit surprised that Dave had even asked me to do a follow-up, as the Merc was such an open and shut case. I suppose he had to go the extra mile though, and I was the one to hoof along it.

I was just about to subtly switch to the Davises when he saved me the trouble. 'You found poor Polly's body, didn't you, Jack?'

'Yes. Right by the Lagonda. Remember we talked about it at the Wheatsheaf?'

He nodded. 'That seems to be coincidence, though. I heard they'd arrested some Polish farmhand.'

'A bad time for you. The Davises were friends of yours, you said.'

'Good friends.' He hesitated. 'I hadn't seen much of Polly since Mike's death though. Busy lady, that.'

I took the plunge. 'And a lively one. I heard a few rumours . . .' This was a risky ploy, as Peter was hardly likely to open up on Polly's sex life, and it could well rebound on my head, with him telling me to go to hell.

Luckily, he took it in his stride. 'There always are, especially with someone of Polly's character and background. Don't believe them. She was a very attractive woman and had had a high-profile TV career. Rumours attach themselves automatically in such cases, just like leeches. Mike knew that. She knew it.'

'Sorry, just the car crime detective in me,' I said. 'If I hear something, I feel bound to follow it up. Could there be any unfinished business left over from Mike's death that could have led to Polly's? That's if it wasn't this Polish chap. He sounds as if he could be a bad ''un.'

He considered this carefully. 'Perhaps. Mike sailed near the wind on occasion. He used to tease me about being an old fuddy-duddy where business was concerned.'

'By "sailing near the wind" you're implying some of his classics weren't exactly legit?'

'There were rumours, especially when he died. But nothing came of them. There was even a rumour that Polly didn't seem to have inherited quite as much as Mike would have left, if you see what I mean.'

I did. 'Illegit cash?'

'Quite. For months there were stories that he had it stashed away somewhere.'

'Swiss bank account?'

'Possibly, but knowing Mike I think it would have been more tangible than that.'

'Polly didn't seem to me to have an extravagant lifestyle. Indeed, the very fact she needed to start a picture framing business seemed odd to me.'

A pause, and I could see something weighing on his mind. 'Now about my Merc, Jack . . .'

At that point his wife made her appearance and was introduced as Jill. From the Audi convertible, I'd set her down as perhaps a trophy second or maybe third wife, but no such thing. Whether wife number one, two or three, she was about the same age as Peter and had gardener written all over her – literally, as she was wearing one of those huge aprons doled out in the Christmas-present catalogues, emblazoned with 'Gardener at Work'.

All talk of Polly and Mike Davis stopped as we returned to the subject of the Merc. As I drove away, however, I kept coming back to the Lagonda. These rumours of Mike's money – could it be stashed inside some secret pocket? It was possible, I supposed, but unlikely. All the same, the niggle remained, and I became more and more determined to take another look at it.

At that point fate played into my hands. Once back at Frogs Hill, I had a call from Zoe as soon as I walked in the door of the farmhouse. 'I've had Bea on the phone,' she said almost accusingly. 'I came home yesterday because she said she could cope, but she's heard the bad news about Tomas being out on bail and wants me to go back for a few days. I'm going over there now to see how things are.'

'Sure. Can I come?'

She considered this rather too long for politeness. 'Don't see why not. She wants you as her private eye, after all. I'll get my stuff and see you there.' She rang off, and I thought I should give Bea a ring to ensure my welcome.

There was no doubt of that, however. Her first words on the phone were: 'You've heard the news then. I still can't believe he's guilty, but I can't stand the idea of his being out, wandering around.'

'Do you know what the evidence is against him?'

'They won't tell me, but they seem to think he was at the barn sometime that morning.'

Footprints? I wondered. It had been dry, so that was unlikely. DNA? Too early for results on that, I'd have thought. Witnesses? Email evidence? No, why should he be on email terms with Polly?

'I'm not sure I can take this,' she added flatly. 'His row with Mum really turned me off him.'

'Was it that bad?'

'Yes it was. It was on the Sunday afternoon after the art show opening. I was staying here, not in my Canterbury flat. I thought Mum was out all day, but she came home early. She found Tomas here –' a slight hesitation – 'well, in bed with me, actually. She raised the roof, and I couldn't blame her. She didn't like him, and this is her house. Was,' she corrected herself dolefully. 'They had a real set to, with him cursing and effing. He was saying – oh, awful things about her, which turned me off. He said he'd be back. And there was something else.'

A long pause now.

'He said,' she began again, 'he'd make sure the Lagonda was done for too. I'd only just heard about it, of course, and I don't know why he should have picked on that. I should have told the police about it, shouldn't I, Jack?'

'Yes. Any idea why he thought that was relevant?'

Bea had no answer to that, and I hung up, after saying I'd be right over and would see her in fifteen minutes or so.

Zoe's and my arrivals at the farm coincided, and we stepped gracefully out of our respective cars at the same moment. I'd had time to ponder Tomas's interest in the Lagonda, but had come to no conclusion, save that it could fit in with the spotter theory. On the other hand, it could also have been because he had heard about my interest in the car, and Polly's love of it, and had decided to attack her in a weak spot.

Yet that did not satisfy me. In fact, nothing did about Tomas. The motive of wanting to marry Bea just didn't add up to me as cause enough for murder. If he had taken a gun with him to the barn, it could hardly have been an unpremeditated crime on his part – or anyone else's. Or could it be that Polly herself had taken a gun, and her murderer had torn it away from her, killed her and then buried it to avoid the risk of trace evidence? No, that was nonsense. Polly was too calm to think of a gun as the way out of her problems.

Bea was at the door waiting for us and actually managed a giggle at our dramatic joint entrance. 'I feel better now you're both here,' she told us. 'It's daft, but I keep feeling I'm being watched. It's creepy and all the worse now I know Tomas has got bail. I'm afraid if I go out for a minute or two he'll nip in and burn the house down.'

'Not while I'm here,' Zoe promised her.

I didn't like the sound of this. There was no chance of a police guard without a specific threat once the crime scene was finished with, and the idea of Tomas creeping around either the farmhouse or the Lagonda barn was not a pleasant one for me, let alone for Bea.

'I'll stay over too,' I told her, and Bea looked pleased. So did Zoe, in fact, but I doubted whether Rob would be. 'What about the Lagonda, if he was making threats about it?'

'The crime scene's lifted now, so I should check. I waited for you,' Bea said diffidently, which made me realize just how bad she was feeling despite the stiff upper lip. 'I expect Tomas was only throwing out idle threats about it, though. He thinks there's a mystery over it because I told him Mum had never mentioned it to me.'

'Let's go see,' I said, trying not to sound too eager.

'It's a kind of test for me,' Bea admitted. 'I haven't been down to the barn since it happened. So it would be good if we could go now.'

'Fine with me,' I said graciously. Aware of Zoe's cynical eye on me, I was hardly able to believe my luck in getting to see it right away.

And so for the third time I walked down to the barn, only on this occasion we took the orthodox route, through the farmhouse, garden and fields, not over the fence. I could see Bea was having trouble as we drew nearer, and without a word Zoe and I positioned ourselves on either side of her. Physically, it provided little protection, but emotionally I hope she felt we were shoulder to shoulder with her.

We walked through two meadows, which I guessed were still attached to Polly's farm, then through a kissing gate by the bridle path, which also had broad padlocked gates for farm traffic, and then the apple orchards, which judging by the number of birds around were being sized up for their harvesting potential in the autumn.

'The barn is officially on the land that Guy rents,' Bea told us, 'but I doubt if he'll turn us off.'

I wasn't so sure and was glad Bea was with us. As Tomas had been given bail, he could well be back there at any time he liked, and I didn't fancy the idea of that. As the barn hove into sight, we all became quiet, as though Polly's death had marked the place for ever. As indeed it had for Bea and myself. I had to school myself not to run to it, to make sure that it held no corpse now – and that it did hold a Lagonda. The former crime scene was much trampled, with plenty of signs of former activity. It had a desolate look to it, with chalk marks still visible.

Bea stopped short. 'I can't do it, Jack. You go across and see the old banger's all right.' Zoe stayed with her (nobly in the circumstances) and, carefully skirting the area where I remembered Polly's body had lain, I unlocked the padlock – to which Bea had given me the key – and pulled open the door.

There she was, still beautiful even in her uncared for state, and so innocent looking that it was hard to pull myself together enough to contemplate how she could possibly have had a role in Polly's death.

'OK inside?' Bea called.

I pulled the door wide open so that she could glimpse the car from where she was standing.

She sighed. 'I can't think why this was so important to Mum.'

'Because of her family connections,' I said. 'It was your grandfather's, after all, and she and your father had a lot of good times in it. It seems very natural it meant a lot to her.'

Bea didn't look convinced. 'If I'm to keep it,' she announced, 'I'll do the thing properly and have it fixed up.'

A week ago I'd have been right there with my sales pitch for selling it on commission, but not now. 'Keep it, Bea; for the moment, at any rate.'

'Would you restore it for me, or whatever you do to old cars? Would it start? Are the keys there?'

I went into it, feeling like a trespasser, and ferreted deeper into the glove compartment than I had on my first ill-starred visit. I felt like an intruder into Polly's past life.

'No, but that's a problem we can deal with easily. I don't know if it would start – or even if that would be a good idea. We've got a low-loader if you don't mind it trundling through the farm.'

'So you'll do it?'

'Love to,' I said promptly.

'As soon as you like then.'

'There's no hurry,' I forced myself to say, thinking of all she had on her mind and plate.

'There is,' Bea contradicted, to my relief. 'I need to feel I can advance something. Actually get something accomplished, not something like paperwork and probate and whatever that goes on for ever. Look, I've had enough of this place,' she added abruptly. 'I'm going back to the house. Do you want another look, Jack?'

'Yes, please.' I accepted gratefully and said I'd be along in five minutes. She and Zoe (who clearly had a tug of loyalties here) turned round to walk back to the farm, and I went back into the barn to see if I could recaptured the fleeting thought I'd had that something was strange about this Lagonda – apart from the headlights.

I went to where the princess lay still and quiet, waiting to be awoken from her long sleep. Unlike Polly, who would never wake. A sharp jab of physical pain hit me at the thought. I gave her an overall look, but nothing came to me. Another one, with the same lack of result. All seemed as it should for a classic '38 drophead. We could ask Brian Woollerton about those head-lights. Not only did he run that useful team of informants, but

he was a chum of long standing, long memory and a long
storehouse full of every spare classic part imaginable. Oh the
pleasure and joy at the thought of what Len, Zoe and I could
achieve with the Lagonda's restoration job. It felt as though I
would be doing at least something for Polly.

I bent over the rear seat.

I remember doing that but no more. It all happened so
quickly. A feeling of something wrong, a shape behind me, a
presence, a sense of danger – and then nothing. Blackness and
falling into infinity . . .

NINE

Polly was bending anxiously over me in some place I could
not define . . . I blanked out again, and when I next came
to I was in little doubt where I was. There was no Polly
and never would be. Instead I was in hospital, with a Formula
1 race going on inside my head and two old ladies, in beds
on either side of me, regarding me with great interest. What
came next? I wondered. In all the best films a ministering
angel would appear out of nowhere, exclaiming with relief
that I was conscious again. I clearly wasn't in a best film,
unfortunately, because no such apparition did. One of the old
ladies asked me what I'd ordered for lunch, but nothing came
to mind. The other one asked me if I was Bing Crosby, but
that didn't seem relevant either.

When my ministering angel did at last amble up, she was
not clad in pristine white, but in jeans and T-shirt and was
smelling of hand gel. It was Zoe, whose orange spikes of hair
were the object of rapt disapproval from one of the old ladies.

'Grapes?' I croaked. 'Chocs? Flowers?'

'Good. You're alive. We thought you were a goner yesterday.'

As greetings go, I felt Zoe was below form, but she did
look genuinely worried. 'I'm ace,' I assured her. 'What
happened?' There seemed a bit of a blank somewhere. I could
remember the Lagonda, and I had a hazy idea that I'd been
on my own.

'You tell us. When you didn't turn up, Bea and I eventually

wandered down to the Lagonda again to prise you away from
it and found you on the floor out for the count. Not what Bea
needed. She thought you were dead like Polly.'

There was reproach in her voice, and I scrabbled desperately
to think what had happened. My fault? I was penitent over
the shock to Bea, but still at sea. Then my memory obliged.
'Someone coshed me.' This came out so loudly that half the
ward looked at Zoe in pity at the maniac she was presumably
responsible for.

'You slipped and hit your head on the concrete,' Zoe
corrected me. 'Not a wise move.'

The Formula 1 race stepped up speed, but I was right at the
wheel now. 'I was coshed.'

'You're muzzy-headed.'

'Yes, but I was coshed. I'd checked the front end and was
leaning over into the rear seat. Then I was hit from behind. I
was *coshed*,' I repeated again to make my point.

Two brown eyes regarded me carefully. Hands on hips,
gimlet-eyed, and ready to pounce, Zoe gives no quarter unless
quarter is deserved. Thank heaven she decided it was on this
occasion. 'Who by?'

'Daft question.'

'Accepted. This Guy chap, maybe?'

'Who knows – but I'm going to find out. I'm leaving—'

One slim brown hand pushed me back to the horizontal as
I struggled to sit up. So far as I was concerned, the Formula
1 race was over and I was ready to depart even if a few cars
were still doing a lap of honour in my head. 'You're here for
at least another twenty-four hours, sweetheart, and no kidding.
I checked with the gaolers outside.'

'You're not my next of kin.'

'To them I'm your daughter.'

'That does a lot for my self-esteem.'

Banter is all very well to pass the time, but the V12s in my
head slowed sufficiently for me to think of the Lagonda, Polly
lying outside the barn, and how I'd been coshed. My tempera-
ture gauge instantly shot up, and I grabbed at Zoe's hand in
case she thought she was leaving. She wasn't. I needed her
like I'd never done before.

'Either I'm jumping ship now, or you have to be my
co-pilot.'

'What for?' I felt her hand tighten in mine. Action, she was thinking. Action. She was right.

'The Lagonda. Tell Bea we have to get it out of there faster than we reckoned. By fast I mean today, this morning, *now*.'

Zoe looked doubtful. 'She's got enough—'

'Tell her if she wants to find out who killed her mother, the Lagonda must hold the clue. Now the crime scene's lifted it won't be long before someone else is nosing around: either my cosher or someone else. Get it out before it goes up in flames. Get it to Frogs Hill *today*.' I was calculating rapidly that it would take some time before someone might get down there with a can or two of petrol. Night was more probable, when there would be little danger of interruption by farm workers or passers-by.

Once Zoe is convinced, she doesn't waste time. 'Drivable?'

'Precious little hope. I know it's a Sunday, but call Bea, tell her the need for speedy action and organize it.'

'Use Charlie?'

'Yes. And right now. Get hold of Len somehow, and join him at Greensand farm to move that car out.'

Our venerable ancient low-loader, affectionately called Charlie, is used for picking up classics that are either too spotless to risk getting mud on their paws on our less than perfect roads, or are such clapped-out wrecks that this is the only way the old codgers can be transported to car hospital – in the form of Frogs Hill Classic Car Restorations. Len loves Charlie and has a special rapport with him. He likes nothing better than charging along dusty old paths in Charlie like a knight of old on his way to rescue someone's beautiful classic in distress. If King Arthur had had a garage at Camelot, Sir Leonard would be supping at the Round Table waiting for the next quest.

'I'll be with you,' I said with some effort, 'as soon as I'm out of here. Tell Len to take the long road home, and it needs a twenty-four-hour guard.'

We have good security at Frogs Hill, with burglar alarms galore and heavy locking devices. We're deep in the country-side, however, so if the alarms went off tonight it was all too probable that no one would come to gallop to our rescue without special precautions. The 'long road home' was a security measure we'd set up but rarely used. It's a pretty simple one, and cheap, but one that in my car detective work I'd sometimes found useful. The Kentish lanes are narrow and twisting, and are a confusing complex until you know them. There's a particular combination of them round Piper's Green and Frogs Hill that's almost certain to throw off anyone in pursuit unless they know the area as well as we do, and even if they do they're unlikely to be as aware of every twist and turn as we are. The long road was designed for cars, but at a pinch Charlie could use it.

The race in my head had slowed to the point where I reasoned that if my cosher was anyone local they'd know all too well where the Lagonda would be heading. But, at the very least, it would be safer at Frogs Hill than in that field barn.

I watched Zoe's trim figure heading out of the ward with her usual terrier-like application now she had the scent of action in her nose. Cara, my true daughter, is in her twenties too, so Zoe could indeed qualify – odd, I'd never thought of her that way. The three of us – Len, my senior; Zoe, my junior; and me – make one of those triangles in which all three sides are equal. Age doesn't come into it, only cars.

I fretted once Zoe had left, especially when an official ministering angel turned up and briskly informed me I was to be transferred to another ward. A male ward, she emphasized, as though I'd been about to molest all the old ladies around me. 'How long?' I asked. It came out as another croak.

She decided on a joke. 'Oh, about another sixty years to go, I reckon.'

I tried a bit of banter too. 'I feel fine,' I lied, 'so I'll start them now. Can I go?'

'Not till doctor says so. Tomorrow, probably.' A bright smile full of promise.

'And when does doctor come?'

Tomorrow, it transpired. Hospitals are hospitals, and so it was another night's sleep for me right where I was. I tried to doze, I tried to ruminate. I trusted Len, and I needed to be in good shape once I did get back to Frogs Hill, so on the whole it seemed better to resist any macho impulse to rush out in my hospital pyjamas to hail a taxi to freedom. After all, I had one more card to play: Dave Jennings.

Gentle investigation every time I moved my head another inch, when a V12 started up inside it again, proved that my mobile had made it into the neat little locker at my side. Then I remembered no mobile calls in the hospital. Some hospitals have fancy machines for patients to phone from, but if this one had, somehow I'd been missed out on the fun. I'd have to get hold of a landline somehow, though. It took half the afternoon to accomplish it, and when I did, Dave was not on duty. I had his private number for emergencies, however, and this was one. He wasn't so sure.

'Your Zoe rang me too. The invisible Mason Trent after you, is he? Zoe said you were at death's door, Jack. Aren't you? I told Brandon you were attacked.'

We both knew that would go nowhere. 'Car crime,' I declared. 'Your territory. Unknown person after Lagonda.'

He saw where I was going. 'Can't guard it, but it's noted, Jack.'

I supposed that was something. If it was burned to bits or pinched, someone might get interested, especially if I were in it. Despite continuing to fret, I ate my healthy jacket potato, and even a rice pudding that evening. Then I conked out.

Next morning, being a bank holiday Monday, I was none too sure that any doctor would appear at all, but one did, and I was out of that bed and off immediately I had my marching orders. I took a taxi to Frogs Hill: an anxious journey since I'd heard no more from Zoe. The journey was punctuated only by the driver's moans that his Audi would need to go in for repairs if it went over any more of these bumps in Frogs Hill Lane, but once he was paid off and departed, I breathed the fresh May air, full of the fragrance of trees and flowers, the hum of bees and the incomparable smell of petrol and garages, with great satisfaction. Home again.

To my relief, Len strolled out of the farmhouse. No bank holidays for him then, bless him. He nodded at me on his way to the Pits, as if I'd just got back from the pub. I stood there a moment, rocking slightly as it occurred to me I wasn't quite so back to normal as I'd thought. He beckoned me towards the workshop, where the doors were closed, until they were dramatically opened from within, operated by Zoe. She was standing by the most glorious sight in the world. The Lagonda: blue, innocent, elegant and at present flying aloft on the lift.

'Just a car, Jack,' Zoe said, laughing, after my gurgle of delight.

'You got it here. Well done.'

Len gave something that might be a smile. 'Charlie did.'

'Any trouble?'

'Not a bit,' Zoe assured me. 'Bea thought you'd gone loopy after your bang on the head, but she was quite happy to go rushing around opening gates and so on.'

It was almost a let-down after my fears of conspiracies and arson attacks. 'Did you tell her to cover the traces?'

'She didn't need telling. She locked the barn up, and we removed all signs of Charlie's exit; he took a gate with him on the way out, but we've sorted that out too.'

'Anyone hanging around?'

'Passed a few people, but no one we recognized. Except for your Gorilla Guy, who wanted to know what the hell we were doing. Bea told him to mind his own business. He thought it was his business. Bea clarified the situation. Then Tomas turned up . . .'

'He had the nerve to come to see Bea with a possible murder charge looming?'

'Yup. He wasn't pleased to see me, and Bea made it clear she didn't much want to see him.'

'What did he want? As if I can't guess.'

'He was all charm. Realized that it was difficult for Bea and said he would keep out of her way for the time being, as the law had made this ridiculous mistake. Of course, Guy's workers would be in those fields all the time mowing and hoeing, so Tomas assured her he would be around if she needed him. You know, Jack –' Zoe changed course – 'I'm beginning to agree with you about this old banger.' She looked aloft at the Lagonda, but in the overall interest I ignored the slur. 'It's interesting.'

'Too kind of you,' I commented.

'Bea's overrun with caring relatives and whatnot, so I've become a good Number Two to keep them at bay. Or not. Harry Prince dropped by to see her yesterday afternoon.'

That did my head no good at all as my blood pressure shot up. 'Was Teresa with him?'

Zoe took my point. If his wife had gone with him it could have been a courtesy call. If not . . . it was business, however disguised. Harry was Harry. He didn't poke his nose in unless there was an angle that suited him.

'No,' she said.

OK. So we knew where we were on that one. 'What did he have to say apart from condolences?'

'From the sound of it, he was just oily old Harry Prince, oozing about poor old Jack, and was the Lagonda safe? Anything he could do to help, anything at all?'

'Like take it off her hands?' Surely even Harry wouldn't be that crass so soon.

Zoe grinned. 'How about: and if you need any help clearing up the farm, I might be able to help you out on any old cars around. After all, what's a pretty girl like you going to need an old wreck of a Lagonda for?'

I was lost in admiration for Harry's cheek. Or was there more to it?

'She turned him down.' Zoe hesitated. 'In case it's relevant, he said that after Mike's death there was a rumour flying around that Polly was worth more than a bob or two. Big money. It's died down now.'

'Any truth in it?' I was interested that this rumour had come to me from two directions, first Peter Winter and now from Harry Prince. And if it had reached *me*, was it also reaching other people – such as Tomas or Andy Wells?

'If so, Bea doesn't know about it. The way she talks she'll have to sell up to pay inheritance tax, but that wouldn't be too heavy anyway.'

'Polly had the money from Mike's business.'

'And was living on it, according to Bea. Picture framing and rent from Guy Williams didn't take her very far.'

I'd store this snippet away under the 'knowledge' category, I decided. 'Thanks, Zoe. Had a closer look at our beauty up there yet?'

'No. Len nobly decided to wait for you.'

The man himself looked modest.

'Let's go,' I said.

So what had Harry's call on Bea really been for? I wondered. Just neighbourly concern? No way. It was the Lagonda. Len, Zoe and I stared up her underside contemplatively – especially Len. In anyone else but him I'd have thought it sacrilege. A Lagonda has her pride and, unless in dire straits, doesn't need her innards and private parts exposed to gaze.

'Raring to get started, Len?' I called over to him cheerily.

A grunt was his only answer.

Together we gazed up at her, but nothing looked amiss other than the usual corroded exhaust system and brake lines. Len brought her safely to ground again, and then we considered the engine. It had presumably been unused for four years. If the engine had seized, of course, it would have to be disassembled so that Len could get to the pistons inside the engine block. That meant they'd have to be broken loose. Even if the engine hadn't seized, it would probably have to be rebuilt.

Len caught my eye. 'Tomorrow,' he decreed.

'Day after. There's that rush job, remember?'

Len and Zoe had an urgent date with a Porsche 356, and urgent in this case meant by the end of the next day, so there was no chance of getting to the Lagonda earlier. The Porsche was needed for a continental show and had to leave on Wednesday. I had no great hopes of finding anything more on the Lagonda, so whatever it was that my assailant thought was so important wasn't going to be obvious – even if it existed.

Len and Zoe reluctantly agreed that the Porsche had to come first, but that didn't stop us on our preliminary lustful examin- ation of the Lagonda.

'Headlights?' Zoe shot at me.

I did a few swift calculations on the bank balance and reckoned we could run to the real McCoy instead of these pre-war misfits. I handed over to Len the pleasurable task of consulting Brian Woollerton to see what he could dig out. I'd save my powder for the call about the Merc. Right now, there was something more important. I had a lady to attend to. I wondered where the number plates had got to, and, come to that, the tax disk. Why had Polly gone to the bother of taking them off?

Lady Lagonda's paint wasn't in too bad condition, and her interior would have to wait until the mechanical side was sorted. Certainly, the upholstery needed attention, once we'd sorted out the basics, and I'd have to report in to Bea at least on anything major that needed to be fixed.

I did remember the scrap of paper, however: the bill I had found in the car on that first occasion. The garage receipt was just a tankful of petrol, but it had been after I'd given the café bill to Polly that she had become so distracted, although perhaps that had been sheer coincidence. It was only for two coffees, and I couldn't even remember where they'd been drunk. Then I recalled how a mere 'scrap of paper', as the Kaiser had called it, had set World War One ablaze, so I decided to tuck the two coffees away in the back of my mind.

TEN

Bea sounded delighted when I called late that Monday afternoon to say the Lagonda was safe, and so was I, and that I'd like to come over. Discounting the possibility that a visit from me would really make her day, I guessed there was some reason for her delight. Her 'Do come, Jack. Straight away, if you like,' had the flavour of an ulterior motive.

When I hared up to Greensand Farm in my daily driver, the Alfa Sportwagon, I could understand what it was, even without entering the house. Parked in the forecourt was a familiar Bentley, which I recognized from the day of the art show. Either Rupert or Lorna Stack – or both – were laying siege to poor old Bea.

Forewarned is forearmed. Bea came to the door with an agonized expression and a whispered: 'Don't leave me alone with them, Jack. Get rid of them if you can.'

I'm glad she added the rider, because it became patently clear that one Stack at least would not be budged until a time of her choosing. All beams and smiles as I was ushered into the conservatory, Lorna promptly broke off her diatribe to Rupert to greet me. 'Why, darling, look. It's Jack Colby. You came to our art show, didn't you, Jack? You must be quite an art lover.' There was a little pause between the art and the lover, with a meaningful flutter of dark eyelashes.

Rupert politely stood up to shake hands. 'Of course. We didn't get a chance to talk much there, but Bea tells me you're being a great standby for her.'

'Not so much of a standby, as a falldown,' I murmured conversationally.

'I beg your pardon?' He looked bemused.

'Jack had an accident here on Saturday,' Bea explained. 'Hit his head and landed up in the hospital.'

'Oh Jack.' Lorna immediately leapt up to inspect the damage, which was now represented by a large plaster covering the wound and a shaved patch which had once been covered with hair. I felt her hand pressing my shoulder and her breath whispering past my ear. Another second and it would be in it. Sure enough, it was.

'I'm planning to set a new hairstyle trend,' I joked feebly, wondering where the vampire would attack next. My neck? Fortunately not, and having given me the message that she was available, Lorna sat down next to her husband, 'forgetting' to pull down that tight short skirt a modest inch further.

Having endured ordeal by Lorna, I chatted inanely while we all sized the situation up.

'Andy tells me you're checking over Polly's old Lagonda for her,' Rupert said, inadvertently launching the conversation in the right direction.

I gave Bea a slight nod as she turned to me. Better to get the news around that it was at Frogs Hill, rather than risk Bea being the next to be coshed if it was left in the barn.

'I wanted it out of the way for the time being,' Bea said brightly, 'and, as I told Andy, rather than sell it I thought I'd get it restored.'

'Darling, what a lovely idea,' Lorna cooed. 'A tribute to Polly. She loved it so much.'

Bea winced, and I winced for her.

'Your father did too,' Rupert added.

'Darling,' Lorna reproved him, 'that's rather tactless of you.' A glance between husband and wife declared some kind of stakes were up for grabs here. 'Bea went through a bad time when Mike died.'

He flushed. 'Sorry, Bea.' He sank back into his usual anonymity.

Bea was made of sterling stuff, luckily. 'No problem, Rupert. All I can grasp, Lorna, is Mum's death. Everything else sort of floats by me. The solicitors and police seem to be doing everything in the background of my mind. It's as much as I can do to remember to eat and drink now and then. So talk all you want about Dad and cars. It won't bother me.'

It was a long speech for Bea, and she looked a lonely and defiant figure as she sat on the sofa in her summery top and skirt,

which were made for happier times than she was going through
now. Polly would have been proud of her.

'You knew Mike well, then?' I asked the Stacks.

'Oh yes,' Lorna told me, heavy with emphasis that she had
known him *very* well. Perhaps I was imagining too much here,
and in any case, predator though she was, that had no bearing
on Polly's death.

Or did it? I thought of her genuine rage with Polly at the art
show – there was hatred there, I thought. Was that for some
reason that I hadn't yet fathomed out, or was it because she
really thought Rupert had something going with Polly? Or did
it go back further? Had Mike been a magnet for Lorna – and
had Polly then broken up the affair or possibility of having one?
Even if she had, it was a long way from that to Lorna wielding
a gun and shooting her, although I wouldn't yet rule it out. For
my money, that was more likely as a possibility than Tomas
deciding to take the quick way to a fortune. There *was* no
fortune, according to Zoe, but to a young man in Tomas's position the farm might look like one, especially if it was the way
to establish himself in lovely old Britain.

'Mike and Polly were good friends of ours.' Rupert gave a
nervous glance at his wife, obviously well used to mopping
up such situations. 'We arrived in Piper's Green within a year
or two of them, and Lorna and I bought our first Bentley from
them. We hit it off. Mike was certainly a rough diamond, but
a splendid friend, even if he didn't know a Bacon from a
Bellini.'

'Polly and I shared a love of art, so we got on very well.'
Lorna had clearly decided to go into feminine modest mode
and didn't even bat an eyelid at this lie, although she knew
all too well that I could have overheard her row with Polly.

With Bea present, I couldn't lead the conversation the way
I'd like to, but the telephone intervened, and for five minutes
I was blessedly alone with the couple from hell. Good friends
with Mike and Polly, eh? It seemed to me that the Davises
had had a lot of good friends – except when it had counted,
perhaps.

Nothing like a cliché to redirect conversational traffic.
'Dreadful thing, this murder,' I said.

'We're not over the shock yet,' Lorna promptly agreed. 'We
were so relieved that the police found the killer so soon, though

I hear he's out on bail. That's *terrible*. Poor, poor little Bea.'

'She'll get over him,' Rupert opined. 'It's his being out on the streets I don't like.'

Lorna shivered. 'Shocking. Bea will need protection.'

I'd had enough. 'Why?' I asked. 'She's surely safe. Why should Tomas Kasek kill her?'

Two pairs of hurt eyes fixed on me, although Lorna's managed to look triumphant as well. 'That's very cynical, Jack.'

'Rational,' I replied. 'Do you really think Kasek killed Polly?'

Rupert looked surprised. 'Who else would want to?'

The female of the species was getting the message that I wasn't going to fall for her. 'Guy Williams thinks *you* would, Jack. After all, you have succeeded in getting that car you were so keen on . . .'

Rupert looked bewildered at his wife's sudden thrust. 'Hope the restoration goes well, Jack.'

'So do I,' I said meaninglessly, and then, hearing Bea returning, began to talk cars. When my long and deliberately boring monologue on every classic I'd ever owned showed no signs of stopping, eventually Lorna unilaterally made signs that departure was essential.

'Thanks, Jack,' Bea said wearily after she closed the front door.

'I'll push off too. You need a break.'

'Don't I just. But I'm not going to get it. I'm glad Zoe's coming later. I just don't want to be got at by anyone else.'

It seemed Bea was doomed, however. Zoe was late, I had to leave and, as I opened the door of my Alfa, an Aston Martin swept in. Good old Andy Wells had turned up again. I watched as he cast a casual look at me and went up to the door. Whatever he said to Bea, she seemed willing enough to let him in, and the door closed behind them. I waited in case it opened again and there was a frantic signal for help from Bea, but none came, so I decided to leave. And then I saw Andy had a passenger sitting in the Aston. Well, well.

It was Slugger Sam, so nicknamed because of his strange reluctance to leave the pub at closing hours and his eagerness to take a swing at anyone. If one wanted a film extra to play the heavy, he would be your man. Now what was a nice guy like Sam doing with Andy Wells?

* * *

Like Schulz's Charlie Brown I could only cope with one worry at a time. Top of the next day's list for worrying was a feeling that I was merely floating over the core of the mystery of Polly's death, and the appearance of Slugger Sam on yesterday's scene had added one more dimension to it. Who was he working for and why? Slugger hadn't been around that long. He was born locally, but had only returned to this area a year or so ago, and even then he tended to disappear at intervals. So now he was back – with Andy Wells. Was it Slugger who had coshed me as a polite warning? Like DI Brandon, bless his iron heart, I couldn't see the wood for the trees. Andy, Guy, Dan Burgess, Harry Prince, Tomas and Slugger Sam made a fine array of the latter, but I couldn't see the whole picture.

Much as I would have liked the situation to be cut and dried, with Polly's death firmly marked down to Tomas, I had to admit that I couldn't see that scenario working. Polly had apparently gone down to the barn early that morning with a mission. What was it? To see Tomas, when she had already given him his comeuppance so far as Bea was concerned? No way. An equal mystery was what the police still had on Tomas that was keeping him in the frame. It was probably something to do with the car spotting, and the Lagonda had been one of his targets. There was only one way to find out: tackle it head on with Guy Williams.

I reckoned I had one ace in my hand: possession of the Lagonda. Whether or not it was connected to Polly's death, it was at least a temporary passport to my poking around on Polly and Bea's behalf. Today Len and Zoe would be heads down over the Porsche 356, so I decided not to interrupt them by prowling around the Lagonda and distracting their attention. There was nothing obviously amiss with the Lagonda anyway, which might suggest that its importance was symbolic rather than physical.

Nevertheless, symbolic wasn't a word that had the ring of credibility. I couldn't see the Andy Wells of this world going for it. Then I heard Zoe's voice calling me.

'Jack!'

'In the Glory Boot,' I shouted back.

I come in here sometimes when I want a quiet think. Surrounded by the peace and quiet of old car parts, ephemera,

and the smell of ancient leather, it's as good as a potting shed
to a gardener. I can still almost see Dad poking around in here
with his rolled up sleeves, pullover and slippers. 'What's on
the speedometer, Jack?' was his invariable reproof if I disturbed
him. It was his way of hinting that life is for reflection, not
forever speeding along motorways. Here, amid his Giovannis
and 1920s rally posters, was his chosen place for practising
what he preached. He'd left some of his peace behind him,
which is why I don't meddle with the place, in case it disturbs
the atmosphere by adding a layer of my own. Dad's is still
there – and Harry Prince won't be sharing it.

Zoe appeared in the doorway. 'What's with you? Head
still giving you gyp?'

'That's OK, thanks. I was thinking.'

'Takes time for you.'

I ignored this. 'What's your take on Tomas Kasek?'

'A lout with charm. Not good enough for Bea.'

I stored up those words to treasure for the next time Rob
was under discussion and I could remind her of them. 'Capable
of murder?' was all I asked now.

Zoe shrugged. 'We're thought all to be capable of that in
the right circumstances.'

'If right is the word. Charming louts wouldn't give Polly
an incentive to rush down to the barn. What would?'

'Broad spectrum there.'

Then Rob's familiar face loomed up behind her. 'The Old
Bill's money is still on Tomas,' he pronounced with authority.

I sighed. 'Good of you, Rob. How do you know?' I shouldn't
have asked. Of course Rob would know.

'My cousin's in the CPS – the Crown Prosecution Service,'
he kindly explained to us peasants. '*Entre nous*, Polly Davis
died about tennish, or so the thinking goes. The cleaner was
in the farmhouse and heard her take a phone call about nine
thirty, and after that she went straight out. Told the cleaner
she'd have to be back at eleven for another appointment, but
the cleaner left at ten. And no, they don't know who the call
was from. Couldn't be traced.'

I didn't care. Another appointment. Me! At least Polly had
remembered. I steeled myself to treat Rob as a reasonable
human being. 'But no clues at all to who rang? Was it a mobile
or landline?'

A pause and then rare words for Rob: 'Not sure.' He hastened to cover his lapse. 'The landline would be traceable, but with a pay-as-you-go probably not.'

'The cell site would be.'

This display of male jockeying for position obviously irritated Zoe. 'I've got a job to do.' She promptly turned on her heel and vanished, with Rob ambling after her.

It was time to get going, I decided. Polly's barn would be a natural meeting place to play my ace, if I could lure Guy Williams there. The trouble is that to play an ace successfully, it's preferable to be a Cool Hand Luke or Steve McQueen, and I am neither. I'm more of a dash-in idiot, usually failing to see that angels were fearing to tread there. I told myself I'd met bigger targets than Guy Williams in my oil roving days, but then in those days I'd had company bosses as background shadows, who would at least have followed up any sudden end I might have met. Now I was on my own – as my wounded head still reminded me. I changed my mind about the barn rendezvous. It would be too charged an experience for both of us. I'd pay him a visit – unannounced.

Guy's home, Friston House, was at the end of a long unclassified lane off the Charden to Little Chart road, which wound in the general direction of Ashford; it almost rivalled Frogs Hill Lane, but was a little more cared for. The house was modern, alarmed, tidy to a fault, and shouting money. The huge electric iron gates were firmly closed in my face, and I had to remind myself that I was Cool Hand Luke as I pressed the entryphone. A woman replied, rapidly replaced by Guy when I announced my identity.

'What the hell do you want?' was his welcome.

'We should talk.'

'What about?'

'Let's talk about that too. I'm unarmed,' I added placatingly. 'I'm here on Bea's behalf.'

Rather to my surprise, the gates slid open silently back into their sockets, and I was able to drive in with a flourish. Unfortunately, they closed behind me almost immediately, reminding me who held the advantage now.

Guy was waiting at the front door, but from the look of him not with eager anticipation. 'Come in,' he grunted.

'Thanks.'

I followed him into what in more gracious times would
have been a morning room and was now obviously his office.
It was big, practical, impersonal and atmospheric only of how
important he reckoned himself and his farm to be. Before I
could get a word in, he went on the attack.

'Just heard from Bea that you've got Polly's Lagonda tucked
up at your place. Your idea, I presume? *She* wouldn't have
suggested it.' He sat behind his desk as though it were only
that stopping him from hurling himself at me, fists flying.

'Words and Lagondas can travel fast,' I commented. I was
uneasy that everyone seemed to know about the car now, and
for all I knew Guy might be Polly's murderer. Why this great
interest in the Lagonda? I'd wanted to get it out of that barn
for Bea's safety, and not to be seen doing so. Such is my own
faith in Frogs Hill security that even though I'd believed the
car would be safe once we had got it there, somehow its
whereabouts had become general knowledge. I was by no
means sure that this was a good idea. Blame the state of my
head.

'The car's safe,' I continued confidently. 'Len Vickers will
do a great restoration job on it, and Bea can decide whether
she wants to keep it nor not.'

His eyes flickered, and he said nothing. I didn't like that.
I'd have to gun my engine. 'We didn't get off to a good start,
Guy,' I admitted. 'I was crazy to climb over that fence, but
now both of us have far worse things to think about than my
bad manners. There's Polly, Bea – and Tomas. I heard he's
out on police bail.'

Risky ploy, and Guy was still silent.

I pushed further. 'Bea's not up to much at present, as you
can imagine. If Tomas is back working for you it's going to
be difficult for her.'

He leaned forward across the desk. 'Not your business.'
Each word was rapped out with heavy emphasis in case I
missed the point.

'It *is* my business. Bea needs help. My mechanic Zoe Grant
is her best mate, and so I feel involved. Bea asked me to be.'

Perhaps some of my sincerity rubbed off on him, for it
seemed to me that the gorilla's guard was more relaxed, even
if he had an odd way of showing it. 'Don't you think I bloody
well feel *involved*?' he roared at me. 'I knew Polly and Mike

for over twelve years, and my wife even longer. She was at school with Mike. How do you think I feel, with Polly murdered and then a twerp like you storming in and telling me you feel *involved*?'

'Let's call it quits,' I retorted. 'We *both* feel involved. You don't like me, and I'm not crazy about you. We both want to help Bea over this. She doesn't want to see Tomas, whether innocent or guilty. And,' I added quickly, seeing hope of a ceasefire threatened, 'that's *her* business. Is Kasek still working here?'

A fist crashed on the table. 'He's not even been charged yet. He's out on police bail for four weeks from the nineteenth. That's three weeks still to go. He's a good worker. Bea will be all right either way. I'll see to that.'

'So he's still working for you.' I couldn't bring the car spotting angle into it, because that was between me and Dave Jennings only.

The eyes bored into me. Then the gorilla let me into his cage. 'I can watch him here. Better than letting him skip the country, isn't it?'

I saw his point. At last we had common ground, and I wasn't going to risk it by keeping Tomas on the agenda. 'Someone killed Polly, Guy, but for my money it wasn't Tomas.' I could see I had his attention at least. 'Next point: do you seriously think that *I* had anything do with Polly's murder, apart from finding her body?'

'Coincidence, wasn't it, you just happening to be there?'

'I had an appointment at eleven. She didn't turn up. I went to find her.'

'By jumping over the fence?'

So he'd spotted that. Why *had* I gone that way, when I'd had a legitimate reason for walking through the farm? I thought back to how I felt then, and told the truth. 'I was a new customer. I couldn't just stroll through her property without invitation – especially since she'd warned me off the Lagonda that first time.'

'Didn't realize you had so much tact.'

I wasn't off the hook, but he seemed somewhat less inimical, so I went on: 'So who killed her, Guy, if it wasn't Tomas or me?'

He still wasn't sure of me. 'Can't have been Tomas,' he

told me. 'He was nowhere near the barn. He was in Five Acre Field, a good way away.'

'You saw him there?'

The eyes narrowed again. 'There were witnesses, which is more than you have.'

He was hanging in there. But so was I. 'In that case, why are the police so convinced they've got their man?'

Guy struggled. 'Racist. He's Polish.'

'Not convincing. There has to be something. Same goes for me. You're my witness that I was a stranger to Polly that first time we met. Any reason I should take it into my head to kill her?'

'Depends.'

'For you too,' I whipped back. 'You've known her a long time. As wife *and* widow.'

He took the point. I thought I'd be right back outside the cage again, but oddly I wasn't. He considered me for a moment, then: 'OK, Colby. Quits – for the moment.'

No point quibbling, I decided. Take it. 'Do you know of any reason *anyone* would want to get rid of Polly?' Even now the idea seemed unimaginable. The waste. The senselessness. 'Omitting passing maniacs, of course.'

'Such as you.'

I gave him another chance. 'Was Polly having an affair and wanted to end it? Did the chap's wife or girlfriend object? Did she have money problems? Was jealousy at the root of it? Greed?' I rattled off as many deadly sins as I could think of, but he only picked up on one:

'Affair?' he echoed, and I could swear he looked astonished. 'She loved Mike.'

'It's four years since he died.'

'Who are you pointing fingers at? Me?'

I was caught off guard, particularly as there seemed no heavy meaning in the 'me'. 'Dan Burgess, Rupert Stack—' I stopped hastily as Gorilla Guy spluttered with laughter.

'That numbskull? You've been listening to the lovely Lorna. You're out of your depth, Jack. Way out.'

'Nothing in it?' I persisted.

He grew serious. 'Polly loved Mike. Get that into your head. As for me, if you're interested, ask my wife Sarah if it would have escaped her attention. She's a nose sharper than a bloodhound if I chat up anyone else, let alone take it further.'

'What's left then?'

He eyed me carefully again. 'I don't know, but I'm with you where Tomas Kasek is concerned. He's no angel, but if he's bent it's small time. Guns and murder are way out of his league.' A pause. 'That really was your first meeting with Polly?'

One up to Guy, for being smarter over Tomas than I'd given him credit for. 'Yes, and I only met her once after that.'

'She wasn't the person you might think she was.'

'Sexually?'

He flushed, but whether in anger or embarrassment, I wasn't sure. 'I haven't a clue. No one did with Polly.'

So where did that leave me? I wondered as I left and the black gates slid open again for my departure. He'd done a good job in convincing me he wasn't Polly's lover, but that didn't mean he hadn't *wanted* to be. It was on the cards. The trouble was that there were a lot of cards, and I didn't know which game was in progress. Poker came to mind, or Five Card Stud. All I knew was that I was going to have a place at the table, no matter what the game.

ELEVEN

I'd considered going on to see Harry Prince, as I wasn't far from where he lived, but decided against it. I felt I'd got somewhere with Guy Williams, and I might do better going one step at a time – not my usual four-wheeler in a china shop approach. He wasn't ruled out of the script, but he was a loner. He had his own agenda and, tough nut though he was, if push came to shove we could work from the common ground we had tentatively established. As for Harry, I wondered why his jovial red face was poking itself into this case. Was it just attraction to an expensive classic Lagonda? It was a reasonably rare car, but with Harry my guess was that there was more to it than that. And I had enough 'more to it' personnel involved already without adding Harry Prince to the mix unnecessarily.

Did I see him as a killer? I could hear his belly laugh in my imagination.

'Me, Jack? You know me. I'm far too wily an old bird.'

Did I know him? I wouldn't put him in prime place if a crime of passion was what we were dealing with, but a crime for money – maybe. I remembered the rumour that Polly had big money around and wondered whether there was any truth in it. Zoe said the rumours had died away, which seemed to answer the question. Coupled with what Guy had darkly hinted about Polly's unknown depths, however, I wasn't going to dismiss it out of hand. Nevertheless, it was hard to imagine what kind of big money could theoretically be involved, as her only apparent source in recent years would have been the sale of Mike's business to Andy Wells. Had Mike piled up a few million on the side? If so, why should Polly still be working for a living?

When I reached Frogs Hill, I saw we had visitors. That in itself was hardly unusual, but seeing the Aston Martin parked there and Slugger Sam loping around our forecourt looking for trouble was. I'd never rated a visit from Andy Wells before, so my stock might be going up. I wouldn't bank on it though. Approach with caution, I thought.

'Afternoon, Sam,' I called, more cheerily than I felt.

His large shaved head and upper body, clad in a beach T-shirt, were so tattooed where the skin was revealed that he made a formidable sight. Sam stopped his mooching, stared at me as though I were trespassing on his territory, then decided to nod. 'Good to see yer.'

It wasn't clear why it was good in Sam's book. Target practice? Or had he already practised on me? I wasn't in his league – thankfully, because he doesn't believe in rules. What on earth were Andy and his sidekick doing at Frogs Hill, and why had they been calling on Bea the night before? This great friendship between the two of them was a new one on me. I'd never linked them in my mind before, or to my knowledge seen them together, and I'm not sure it was a good move on Andy's part to deepen the relationship. If Sam walked into a downtown country saloon bar, everyone would dive under the tables without waiting for him to draw breath, let alone guns.

I could see Andy in the Pits, looking at the Lagonda in a thoughtful kind of way. She was not yet relegated back to her ignominious position aloft, but still lodged on the lift platform as if awaiting an imminent summons to the heavens. Len and Zoe were standing chatting to Andy, or rather Zoe was chatting. Len and Andy, both being taciturn by nature, were just nodding and grunting in time approved manner.

'How's the Porsche coming on?' I asked Len meaningfully, after exchanging nods with Andy.

He and Zoe looked surprised, as though no such car had ever appeared at Frogs Hill, even though I could see it over by the west wall and it was rapidly approaching its five o'clock deadline.

'OK,' Len replied. Well, that was something.

'Nice,' Andy commented, looking at the Lagonda, not the Porsche.

'All agreed on that then.' Maintain the small talk, I thought, and maybe someone would enlighten me as to the purpose of this visit by our car-dealer friend.

At last the reason emerged. 'Andy thinks he could have a good deal for Bea on this,' Zoe explained.

'Do you, Andy?' I tried to sound enthusiastic, but that's hard through clenched teeth.

'Chap out Lewisham way is interested,' Andy said, studying the floor with great interest. 'Dealer called Barry Pole.' Then, added as an afterthought, 'Dan Burgess might be too. Know him?'

'Yes.' Alarm bells were ringing everywhere. Barry Pole was the dodgy dealer running the car theft gang, and with whom Mason Trent used to be associated. Did a 'nasty piece of work' like that really want to *buy* the Lagonda? And Dan Burgess too? If Dan was so interested, why not talk to Bea direct? He must know her quite well at least. I decided to give him the benefit of the doubt. Transacting a sale through Andy and me might be less crass at this tough time for Bea, and also more professional, as I clearly had a restoration job in mind for the Lagonda.

'A popular car, it seems,' I commented.

'Got a deal going then?' Andy pushed harder than such a situation would normally warrant.

'Good grief no.' I tried to sound lightly amused. I was in a fix. If I said Bea was going to keep it, the locusts would home in on her in a trice. If I said it was up for sale, that would be worse. So I did the only thing I could do. I hummed and hawed. 'Long way to go before Len knows what this baby's about. When he does, that's the time to talk about its future.'

'You're giving it the works?' Andy said.

'Checking it out first,' I amended.

'Dan might take it unrestored.'

'Our prices are pretty reasonable.' I was even more suspicious. Delete the professional. The job was mine. Bea had commissioned a restoration. Dan was no car restorer, and Frogs Hill prices were indeed reasonable – and why should Dan want Andy Wells to fight a battle on his behalf?

Andy got itchy. 'Come on, Jack, let's give Bea a break and get rid of it for her. She'll do what you say.'

I noted that Slugger Sam was ambling up behind me, as if to ask if I'd like another cosh. What I felt like replying was, 'Get lost and take Dan Burgess with you,' but reason prevailed and I went with the casual approach. 'I'll have a word with Bea. I'm only the middleman. I'm seeing her tonight.' I glanced at my watch. 'Better get finished with the Porsche, Len. Time's passing.'

As hints go, it wasn't subtle, but Andy gave up the struggle more easily than I had feared, and even Sam backed off. 'Yeah. Talk to her,' he agreed in tones that suggested that gunfights at the OK Corral were outdated methods of settling disputes. Like hell they were. Seize the hour, as the Romans said. I could work out what Andy and Sam's game was later. Right now, there was work to do, and work today meant money. I watched Len and Zoe return to their Porsche job, and Andy's fair-haired truculent figure retreat to his Aston, with Sam at his side.

'Are they a regular team now?' I asked Len.

'Dunno,' Len said.

Zoe was more specific. 'Doubt it. Sam's his own man.'

So what job had Andy offered him? I wondered. And what could Barry Pole – and maybe even Mason Trent – be doing lurking in the shadows?

'Oh, and you've got another visitor, Jack,' Zoe threw at me offhandedly as she picked up her torque wrench.

I groaned. 'Where?'

'In the farmhouse.'

I rushed over immediately, envisaging Harry Prince set loose in the Glory Boot, but the front door opened as I reached it and Bea said rather sheepishly, 'Sorry, Jack, I've been skulking here and didn't fancy joining in the car talk. Mum found Andy hard going and so do I. Zoe said you wouldn't mind.'

'I don't.' It was a pleasure to see her, and quite apart from that it suited me nicely.

'I came to tell you Mum's barn was broken into last night.'

Just what I'd thought might happen. 'Are you OK?' When she nodded, I added, 'Thank heavens for that. Any damage?'

'Not that I could see. The lock was smashed again, the new one. At least it wasn't the Lagonda.'

Out in the nick of time, I thought, before someone who hadn't heard we'd removed it had a go at doing it himself. I wondered why Guy hadn't told me about the break-in. Perhaps he didn't know, or more likely he wasn't going to give me the satisfaction of knowing I'd done the right thing over the car. Another, less pleasant scenario, was that this might have been because Guy's own agenda had been kicking in.

Bea shivered. 'I'm glad you've got the car, Jack.'

'So am I. Has Dan Burgess been over to see you?'

'No. Why?'

'According to Andy, he's fuffing around saying he wants to buy the Lagonda.'

'Well, I'm not selling. I told Andy that last night.'

So that's why he'd paid his social call at Greensand Farm. Well done, Bea, I thought, for resisting the charms of Andy with Slugger Sam as company.

'Maybe Dan's keeping away deliberately,' Bea continued. 'He was close to Mum, and some people can't deal with it.'

'How close?'

Bea eyed me firmly. 'Not that close, so far as I know. She framed his ghastly pictures for him and was chummy with him because he was a friend of Mike's.'

'Like a son to her?'

'Wouldn't know. Friend, anyway. Are you making a suspect list, Jack?'

I liked her forthright approach. 'Have to. No one's going to roll over, put his paws in the air and 'fess up.'

She managed a giggle. 'I'd like to see Lorna do that. The rolling over, maybe, but the paws in the air? Not her style.'

She got serious again. 'I can't think of any reason Dan would want to kill Mum, but then—' She broke off and started again. 'He was around a lot in Dad's time, and when Dad died he gave Mum a lot of support over getting rid of the business to Andy and so on. There might have been a cooling off for a while, because I haven't seen much of him recently. That could just be because I've been living in Canterbury though. I'm out of touch with what goes on here. Gloria knows more than I do.'

'Gloria?'

'Mum's cleaner.'

'The one who heard the telephone call. Is she reliable?'

'As the proverbial rock. Come and meet her, if you like. She's going to keep coming in three days a week, as she did before. Drives me mad, but she needs the money and it's company of a sort while I'm living there. Though that won't be longer than necessary. My Canterbury flat seems a haven compared with Greensand Farm. Gloria wouldn't be privy to Mum's inner heart though. Mum wasn't like that. Strict boundaries had Mum.'

I could believe it. In her private life too. 'Is there any chance Lorna might have suspected an affair, even if there wasn't one?'

'Highly possible, but my guess is that it's just Lorna being dramatic. Rupert came up every so often, bringing pictures and so on, and even though Lorna was rarely with him it's a far cry from that to having a full blooded affair. After all, she's never accused the woman who does Rupert's secretarial work down here, and she's quite a looker.'

'Depends on the background,' I said, thinking this through.

'I don't follow.' Bea looked so bewildered that I wanted to hug her and tell her everything was going to be all right, but I resisted the impulse. I'd have to leave that to Zoe.

'I meant the Stacks were close friends with your father too. We don't know whether anything happened then that would lead Lorna to think there was an ongoing situation. Just speculation,' I added hastily. 'You've made it clear how unlikely it is.'

'It is,' Bea replied. 'Besides, neither Rupert nor Lorna could have shot Mum.'

'Why not?' I was shaken at this flat statement.

Her turn to look surprised. 'They're weekenders. They always go back to London on Sunday nights. Rupert has to be in the art gallery next morning. Sometimes he leaves a bit early on Fridays to get here, but Mondays are always spent in London. That's one of the reasons Mum never opened on a Monday. Last week Rupert was hosting a big gathering of dealers on the Tuesday morning, so there's no way he could have been here. And it would be a bit odd if Lorna had stayed behind after the weekend. They were only here yesterday because it was Bank Holiday Monday.'

So that was that. It seemed I was making excellent negative progress on Polly's behalf – hardly the direction I needed to go.

TWELVE

It was hard to tell what kept me from sleeping soundly that Tuesday night, but I'm glad it did: perhaps it had been the glow of satisfaction that I had indeed helped Bea a little by removing her Lagonda from danger. More probably, however, it was my underlying fear that I was missing a trick. A big one. There just had to be something about that car that I wasn't getting. The raid on Bea's barn could hardly have been a straightforward theft. No dodgy car dealer worth his salt would steal a car that now had so much public awareness focused on it, yet it had to be someone who hadn't got the news of its new temporary home early enough to prevent a wasted journey to Bea's barn. Was that the someone who had killed Polly, or was it an opportunist thief, now that the police scene had been lifted? I couldn't discount that possibility. Indeed, I hoped it was the right explanation, because the alternative was not welcome.

There could have been another reason for my restless sleeping. There was no one sleeping with me, and my hopes about Polly fulfilling that role had been cruelly dashed. I remembered the days of Liz's comfortable self tucked in beside me and for a moment or two missed her, until I also remembered the downside. It was a long time since I'd had regular company; or indeed any company, and so it was hardly surprising that when I had drifted off it was to dream of Polly in a Lagonda.

No – she was in a police car screaming along the M25, round and round and round and on and on – *and on.*

I was fully awake. It wasn't a police car; it was the burglar alarms going full tilt and the security lights blazing. Then I was at the window pulling back curtains with one hand and struggling into cords and T-shirt with the other. The Pits' lights were full on, and it was from there that the alarms were blaring out. Not just burglar alarms, but the *fire* alarms – in the Pits. I could see nothing – but I could hear and smell something. I didn't stop to reach the landline, but grabbed my mobile. One bit of me was telling me it was a false alarm, but the major bit knew it wasn't. I was calling in the big battalions even as I ran like hell towards my barn.

This was no accident, and it didn't occur to me then that whoever had caused this was probably still there, waiting for me to arrive so that he could dot me on the head again. All I could see as I drew nearer was flames at the side window, which had no doubt been smashed, as the doors still looked intact. The windows were the most vulnerable point, and the flames seemed to be mocking me, daring me to think I could win any kind of battle over them.

The Pits barn is a mix of centuries. The farmhouse was built sometime in the nineteenth century, but the barn's construction is much earlier, at least in part. There has been a farmhouse on this site since the Domesday Book, and the barn's foundations go back at least to the fourteenth century. A doodlebug had taken three-quarters of it out in World War Two, leaving only one wall shakily standing and the other three down to a few feet high. After the war, it had been securely patched up with no regard to style, leaving it with modern brick walls, a couple of windows in the east wall, and a corrugated iron roof. Not beautiful, but eminently practical for its use.

Frogs Hill is so remote that it was going to take forever for the fire engines to arrive, so I dived into my pocket for the keys, wrestling the doors open regardless of the extra impetus I might give the fire raging within. Thank heavens we'd had the wit to fit an outdoor fire extinguisher, so at least I could go in armed.

And then I saw it. Fire everywhere. The place was like a floodlit stadium, but these lights were moving and the heat was blasting into my face. Clasping my fire extinguisher I felt like David with a very small pebble to sling at Goliath. Thank heavens, the fire was still, I realized, on the eastern side, and someone – Len, Zoe? – had miraculously moved the Lagonda to where the Porsche had been before: thankfully, that had been collected yesterday evening. I didn't ask myself how they had managed to move the Lagonda or why. All I agonized over was whether I could get her out alone. I had only one small extinguisher and no protective clothing or even a mask against fumes. I'd have been crazy to risk dashing in. It might be macho, but I knew I'd be more use to Bea alive than dead. Which I soon would be, I thought, if I didn't use my head.

So I used it. Well, partly. I stayed outside, remembered an outside tap, fixed a makeshift mask, and dashed in, praying hard that the extinguisher worked. Someone up there aloft heard me, because it did, and I sprayed it all round the Lagonda and threw myself outside again. I was lucky to get out. Fire assaults everything, ears, eyes, nose, mouth, and it takes no prisoners. It kills by its fumes before it strikes. As I looked up, gasping for the night air, I could see the quiet sky above me, midnight blue and dotted with stars, and I wondered how we human beings could create such hell on this earth.

And then I heard the sound of an engine and bells ringing; help was on its way. Who otherwise would be driving along Frogs Lane at this time of night? Only the person who started this inferno, who was no doubt long vanished. As the sound grew closer, I could feel tears of relief, or perhaps they were of anger; with each second, more of my source of livelihood, and goodness know how much of the Pits, was succumbing to the ravages of the fire. We had other cars in there, tools . . . there was the insurance. I couldn't cope. Just let the Lagonda be safe, please, I asked the flames, the heavens, fate . . . anyone who might be listening.

My frustration at being virtually helpless sank into relief as two fire engines arrived, together with a police car, and the professionals took over. Figures leapt out of the two cabins, pipes were unrolled, water points established, a chain of command set up and I was answering the questions shot at me and not having to think for myself any more. It was out of my hands. I just directed them to this and that, and I waited, unable to waste their time by demanding to know if the Lagonda was safe, but equally unable to leave the scene until I knew. It was excruciating to watch what was happening, like a play being enacted before me in which I had no part.

And then Len appeared. He lives locally, but news travels fast in Piper's Green. Zoe was still sleeping at Greensand Farm, but then she, too, arrived, and Bea was with her. Both had that sleepy dishevelled look I love in women – and never more than at that moment.

Life seemed to take on a sort of normality with their arrival. Wasn't there usually a part of this procedure when tea and coffee were handed round? Zoe and Bea seemed to think so, because Zoe took one of my arms and Bea the other, and they frogmarched me into the farmhouse. I went like a lamb. It seemed perfectly normal for Bea to be handing out mugs of cocoa at two thirty in the morning.

She smiled at me. 'Don't worry, Jack. It's only a car.'

The Lagonda? Only a car? Still dazed, I couldn't believe she meant it. It was surely just a placebo. Even Zoe remained silent. It wasn't 'just a car' to us. Leaving Bea in charge of tea and comfort for whoever dropped in, Zoe and I went back to the scene. The professionals would clearly have preferred we stayed put, but we kept well back. I could see Len, who was obviously doing a good job liaising with the chief fireman and police, and I steeled myself to stay out of the way with Zoe. Neither of us spoke. What was there to say?

It took an hour before the fire was declared extinguished, and then the scene had to be assessed for safety and causes of fire. There seemed doubt about this – natural enough, I supposed, as Frogs Hill is a garage, but Len and I patiently explained that it was virtually impossible for any of the petrol in the tanks of the other two jobs we had in hand to have started this conflagration for us. That was finally agreed, when the seat of the fire was provisionally established – with the help of a sniffer dog, broken glass and charred woodwork – to have been by a side window. The police then started taking more interest. As they all finally trooped out to leave, the safety officer forbade us to enter, but Len, Zoe and I put on a united front. We had at least to peer in, we pointed out, so that we could contact the owners of any burnt-out vehicles (not a job I would relish).

The smell of extinguished fire is bad. It's depressing and somehow ominous, rather than a matter for rejoicing. We were allowed finally to stand at the doors and have a brief glimpse. The eastern side of the barn was gone, save for the fire-blackened walls. I could see the hulk of one of our two current jobs, an Austin 10. The other one didn't look too happy either. There were also all sorts of welding hoses, tanks and other tools and equipment in a charred mess. The workshop's centre had mostly disappeared too, and the roof looked as if it had taken a battering at least at the eastern end. But the west end had largely survived. The old brick wall had saved us, and it had saved the Lagonda. There she was, covered in what proved to be charred ash and made a paint job more of a priority than it had been. But she was safe.

Seldom had Frogs Hill had so many visitors: police, insurance, fire investigation officers, two furious car owners, Andy Wells, Dan Burgess, Liz Potter and Colin, and even a seemingly concerned Harry Prince. An endless stream trooped around in the hazy dawn and morning. Thoughtful though this was, all I wanted was time alone with Len and Zoe to sort ourselves out. We had genuine kind offers of workshop accommodation and help, so much that I left Len in charge of that side of things. Providentially, Frogs Hill did have a second barn, which was used chiefly to house Charlie and was completely unconverted for workshop use. But it had a roof. So our first job the next morning was to move the Lagonda there as secretly as possible – in-between visitors. That was vital. I didn't anyone spreading the word that the Lagonda was safe. If, and it seemed to me very probable, the car was the reason for this attack, then the fewer people who knew it had escaped the fire the better. So we swore Bea to secrecy and blandly lied to all (save the insurance assessor) that the Lagonda was a goner.

'Gone?' Andy Wells asked, horrified.

'Charred metal,' I told him.

'Burnt?' asked Dan, when he arrived.

'Charred metal.'

'Scrap?' Harry looked as if he'd burst into tears as he paid his visit.

'If anyone wants charred metal, yes.'

I took each of them as far as the Pits' doors only, claiming security problems, and pointed out the heaps of metal. No one was going to inspect such piles too closely. After suitable lamentations and offers of help they departed. Harry was the hardest to get rid of.

'You can trust me, Jack.'

Could I hell. 'Of course, Harry.'

'You're in a spot, old chap.'

'Agreed,' I said wryly.

'Bring any old bangers to me. I'll give you space and facilities.'

'Thanks, Harry. I'll see how things go.'

'And tell you what –' a burst of generosity – 'I won't charge you for a month.' He went off, no doubt chortling.

It wasn't until the late afternoon that Zoe, Len and I were able to pause. 'Time,' I said.

The auxiliary barn is a fair distance from the Pits, and on the other side of the house, so it was well positioned to escape notice from those who don't know Frogs Hill well. Even though it was only used for storage and Charlie, the Lagonda looked quite at home in her new accommodation, as though being on an earth floor with bits of old straw still lying around and a battered low-loader for company suited her very well.

I gave Charlie a pat to assure him he was doing a good job, and then we all gazed at the Lagonda. We'd already noticed as we brought her over that the fabric roof was not what it was. On the whole she'd come through her ordeal well, and then I got to the big question.

'There has to be something special about her,' I said. 'We're missing something.'

'Not necessarily,' Zoe objected. 'It could be something our chummy arsonist thought might have been left inside it.'

That 'scrap of paper' again. 'There was a café bill in it and a garage receipt. Nothing else,' I told them. 'I gave them to Polly.'

'No priceless jewels? No bundles of bank notes?'

'I'd have noticed.'

Len had been thinking. 'It's the car then.'

We are good, the three of us, at just standing and thinking about cars. Some people stand in front of an old-master oil painting for hours, just letting the atmosphere and meaning soak in. Len, Zoe and I do that with cars.

Someone had to make a start. I thought it might as well be me. 'There's the headlights, of course. We know they're wrong.'

'That's a given.' Zoe slapped me down.

'Anything behind them?' Len grunted. He grabbed a can of penetrating oil and set to work. Then we peered in.

'Nothing,' I declared.

'Inside them?' Zoe asked.

Len unscrewed them. 'Nope.'

So we went around the outside of the car, taking it little by little. Wheels, hubcaps, running boards, wing-mounted spare tyres. We all knew there was nothing underneath the lady, because the car had been on the lift, but nevertheless we lay flat on the floor; all I saw was the bit of straw that got up my nose.

'Inside then. Upholstery?'

'Doesn't look overstuffed to me,' Len declared. We poked at it, but nothing emerged, and short of ripping it all off we were stuck.

'Glove compartments?'

We delved into the lady's secret places, but she didn't oblige. They were empty.

'There has to be something,' Zoe said crossly. I agreed, but the engine compartment revealed nothing, and short of ripping up the carpets in the car even more than we had already, we were finished.

'Boot?' I said without hope since we'd already given it a quick look. We opened it, but only the carpet and tool kit greeted us, plus lights and triangle for continental travel. We even took out the carpet, but there was nothing but the board covering the petrol tank. We lifted that out, but only a petrol tank could be seen. The tool kit? Was the awl actually a Medici dagger? Or the spanner made from gold bullion? Nope, they weren't. The lights and triangle? Nothing there, and we already knew that Mike and Polly did the continental shows.

'Foiled,' Zoe muttered crossly. 'There must have been

something more left inside it, and it's gone. Or else the perp just thought it was there.' She and I gave up and began to leave, but Len didn't move. He had his thoughtful look on and was taking another overview of the car.

'Not right,' he said.

'What isn't?' I almost shouted at him.

'Don't know.'

My sudden hope vanished. If Len didn't know, how on earth could I? 'Do you think if you stood here for another twenty-four hours you could pin it down?' I asked ironically.

Len took me seriously. 'Doubt it, Jack. It either comes or it doesn't.'

Doesn't seemed to be the order of the day, but I have faith in Len. He'd smelled something, and if he could then there was no reason I couldn't have a go. I thought of all the Lagondas I'd ever known or seen. I prowled round her once again and stopped at the open boot. I looked inside and sniffed like I'd never sniffed before. Len was right. Something *was* out of kilter.

'Isn't it on the small side?' I ventured, staring into the boot.

My eyes met Len's, and with one accord we each had a door open and were scrabbling over the rear seat. With two pretty hefty guys in there we were stuck at the wrong angle though, so Len graciously got out again and hurried (yes, hurried) round to join Zoe by the open boot.

Then I realized what was odd. There might be a space, maybe two or three inches, between the rear seat upholstery and the closing panel. I could only be sure of this by pressing down on the upholstery that spread over to the panel from the rear seat. There *was* a gap there, because my fingers went down as I gently pushed.

'Got it!' I shouted to Len who was flashing his pocket tape measure.

Simultaneously, he cried, with what passed for excitement for him, 'Panel's been re-bracketed.'

And together we shouted: 'Why?'

Re-bracketing is not unknown, but usually there's a good reason for it, and there didn't seem to be one at hand over this Lagonda, unless Tim Beaumont, Spitfire pilot, had smuggled tobacco into the country. Or diamonds. Or maybe Polly was a champion smuggler in disguise. Or Mike. Having wiggled my hand as far as I could down the available space and finding nothing, however, I was no further forward.

'Someone,' I said rather obviously, 'didn't want us to find this.'

'A step too far, Sherlock,' Zoe whipped back promptly.

'Don't agree. Why make your boot smaller in order to have an empty space?'

'Maybe someone wanted to move the seats back, but gave the job up halfway.'

'And maybe Lagondas can fly,' I retorted rudely. 'Or they wanted to fix water wings to it.'

'Quite possible.' Zoe went into haughty mode.

'Perhaps they just thought they'd like a space of one foot high by three foot long and two and bit inches wide.' I was getting belligerent.

Len wasn't listening. 'What about the petrol tank?' he asked.

'What about it?' I was thrown.

Len wasn't into answering questions. He was levering off the boot carpet again. 'There's another space under here.'

'There always is, Len.' Zoe was getting cross too, so I called time.

'OK, that's it, folks. We've found something odd. Where now?'

That silenced them. Could an oddity like the rear seat space be the reason that someone had decided to burn down our Pits? And could it have anything to do with Polly's death? Or was it a red herring? All I had was a series of apparent coincidences: the fact that Polly was killed outside the barn housing the car; that Polly's barn had then been broken into; that my workshop was half burnt down – and that the Lagonda had something special about it. Even if it was only a gap.

THIRTEEN

'The Merc isn't that high priority,' Dave said mildly, when he arrived at the Chapter Arms a mile or so off the Canterbury road on Thursday morning. I had called more or less demanding a meeting.

I had the grace to blush – at least, I hope I did. 'It's not the Merc, it's the Lagonda.'

'Ah. Unofficial or official?'

'Whichever you think appropriate.' In view of what had happened, I needed to touch base with the police murder case, and I didn't feel Brandon would be the best choice. I proceeded to bring Dave up to date with events on the Lagonda front. He listened attentively, although his initial remark took me aback.

'Brandon hasn't lost interest in you. Thinks you and Tomas might have teamed up.'

'Thanks for the compliment.'

'Seriously, Jack, this cosh on the head, Polly Davis's barn break-in and now this arson attack. You may think they're connected, but Brandon is going to say you're inventing this so-called link to hide your own sins.'

I remained calm. 'What are you going to say? That I'm not so crazy as to set fire to my own barn?' The minute I said it, I saw that's exactly what Brandon *would* say. I groaned. 'I see; he'll think it an insurance fraud. If so, what would be the point of my having called the fire brigade so soon? I might as well have let the whole lot burn down if I was after insurance money. And I wouldn't have been so crass as to make the seat of the fire so obvious.'

'I see that, but Brandon could well not get excited about the idea of there being something fishy over the Lagonda. After all, why? A crazed collector risking all? I know there would be a lot who would give their eye teeth for a Lagonda belonging to a famous Spitfire pilot, although that doesn't fit with someone trying to burn your workshop down. And the technicalities of a panel of wood being shifted an inch or two would not weigh too heavily in favour of the theory either.'

'Do they weigh with you, Dave?'

A reluctant grin. 'I wouldn't put my whole unit on the job.'

'Any part of it? A junior cop?'

'Get it a stage further, and I could be interested.'

I took a deep breath. 'I can do that right now. This Lagonda must be really special. Your chum Barry Pole wants to buy it.'

Dave's sharp on the uptake. 'Wants?' he queried. 'Still going, is it?'

'Only to you, me and the team, Dave.'

He grunted. 'Hope you know what you're doing.'

So did I. 'Someone else is interested too. Dan Burgess.'

'Yeah?' Dave's attention was all on me. 'You know what, Jack? You really know how to stick your head into a can of worms, don't you? Pole, Burgess and, coming right along behind, maybe Mason Trent.'

In the early evening I gave in to the temptation to check on the Lagonda in her second home. Len had told me he'd disguised her as best he could with tarpaulins, and he'd rigged up a temporary alarm. I was torn between contemplating the Lagonda problem and wondering how we were going to keep the restoration business going. A little word called mortgage kept popping into my mind too. Len and Zoe would find a way to run the workshop, I told myself. I needed to concentrate on the other problems. We had only lost a few essential pieces of equipment, and Andy had offered to loan us replacements. He'd also offered space as well, which could be useful from several viewpoints in getting to grips with who'd burnt down the Pits in the first place. Slugger Sam? A bit too obvious, since he'd been there earlier in the day. But sometimes obvious is the answer, especially with chaps as thick as Slugger and Andy.

Maybe I should keep on the right side of Harry too, I thought. He was positively dripping with enthusiasm to help us out. He'd repeated his offer on the phone just before I'd come out to look at the Lagonda. 'As many of your old bangers as you like, Jack. I'll see you're all right.'

Old bangers? In Frogs Hill? No such thing. 'Thanks, Harry,' I'd said again, as cordially as I could manage. 'I'll be in touch.' When hell freezes, I thought as I put the phone down.

Next morning I found Len and Zoe taking care of the business by setting up a makeshift HQ in the garage where I keep the Gordon Keeble, Dad's old MG and my daily driver Sportwagon. First, I talked to Len, who, after consultation with me, decided to take up Andy's offer, rather than Harry's. Next, I rang Bea saying I'd like to meet the cleaner (and her), as she had suggested, and she was very keen.

I took the Gordon Keeble, thinking it might just be the kind of car Bea would like. I was beginning to feel Greensand Farm

was familiar territory, which made me uncomfortable. Polly
was as yet unburied, waiting for those who loved her (and that
included me) to sort out the mess surrounding her death, and
here was I popping in and out of her former home as if I had
some kind of right to do so. That could only be if I made
progress on finding her killer. I've a great respect for the police
– even for Brandon, though it might be possible to draw the
wrong conclusion from the way I've been writing about him
– and they seemed sure that Tomas was their man. Who was
I, a mere car detective, to contradict that?

Perhaps, I thought, I should concentrate on Tomas first. It
hadn't escaped my notice that, as Tomas was out on bail, he
was still around Guy's orchards and could have had ample
opportunity to break into Polly's barn and then dash over and
burn mine down. There was also the fact that he had deliberately cultivated Bea's acquaintance, possibly in the hope of
getting access to Polly's barn. It was unlikely, though, and I
knew I should stick to the more obvious reason he had for
killing Polly: that he wanted Bea and her supposed fortune
waiting to be inherited. Had he, too, heard the rumour about
the missing millions? Theoretically, he might also have some
line on the Lagonda. What, though? Always the little stumbling
block.

The police believed he had killed her, and therefore that he
had been at the barn that morning. They must have evidence
to that effect. Had he met her by chance, and they had then
had a row resulting in her death? No, back I came to the fact
that he wouldn't have been carrying a gun if it had been a
chance meeting. I needed to talk to cleaner Gloria and find
out more about this phone call.

Bea answered the door herself, to my pleasure. She was
looking more cheerful, and her face brightened when she
saw me.

'Come in, Jack. Gloria's here.'

I had pictured Gloria as one of the old school of cleaners,
not quite with overalls, hair tied up in a scarf and a fag hanging
out of her mouth, but at least someone of a certain age. No
way. Cleaners had changed in the time between my father's
housekeeper and this one. She was a lively twenty-something
with a bright professional manner and a determined way that
suggested no speck of dust would be safe from her eagle eye.

'Jack Colby.' I shook the extended hand.

The inevitable 'Hi Jack' came in response, but there was no giggle. Humour was out.

I decided on charm instead, but she seemed impervious to that too. 'I gather you gave the police very valuable evidence over Polly's death. Hope you won't mind if I ask you again?'

'Is that all right, Bea?' Gloria asked. I wondered what my father would have said if Mrs H. had addressed him as Tone. Then I decided I was getting old and stuffy.

'Go ahead,' Bea said cordially.

'I heard the phone ring. Polly always answered it herself, unless she wasn't here, so I didn't take any notice.'

'Not even of the time?'

'Oh yes. I just finishing off the kitchen worktops, so it would be about nine thirty. Polly went out a few minutes later and said she'd be back well before eleven if anyone called.'

Such as me, I thought, once more pleased. 'And you heard what she said on the phone?'

'Yes. And I heard her say that she'd come down straightaway.'

'Nothing else?'

'No. It was only short. There may have been a hello or something. I didn't know she was going to be killed.' Gloria suddenly looked much more like a human being.

'Did she sound nervous? Pleased? As if she were speaking to a friend, or to a colleague?'

I felt I was sounding like Hercule Poirot, but I needed to know.

'You could never tell with Polly. Very businesslike she was.'

I tried another tack. 'Did you know Mike?'

'No. I've only been with her two years.'

I could hardly ask her in front of Bea whether Polly had had overnight visitors, and I wasn't sure whether it was necessary anyway. If Polly had kept such secrets from Bea, she would have been just as careful in front of Gloria. I didn't seem to have taken things much further, and yet oddly I felt I was. Polly had sounded businesslike – didn't that at least tell me that whomever she'd met it was unlikely to have been Tomas Kasek?

*   *   *

When I returned to the farm, the smell of charred remains still hung heavily in the air, like the dull smell of ashes after a barbecue. Only, this one was a party I wouldn't have wished on anyone. It was a reminder that Tuesday night's conflagration had really happened, however much I longed to pretend that what was out of sight could temporarily be out of my mind too. I had to force myself to go into the farmhouse, where I knew reality would be waiting to greet me.

It was. Zoe and Len were working in my office. They'd given up on the initial HQ and decided on more comfort. The only consolation was that I didn't seem to be expected to take any part in what they were doing. They had apparently not regretted taking Andy up on his offer and declining Harry's, and nor had I. Accepting Harry's invitation into his parlour would be like three flies following a large spider into an unseen web. Len told me that Guy Williams had also offered space in one of his barns, which surprised and pleased me, but it would have been too ill-equipped to establish ourselves successfully, even temporarily. Andy's offer had the advantage of including equipment too. Len had apparently just returned from concluding negotiations. For negotiations read rent. Fair enough, of course, and Zoe was already installed at my desk, demanding from Len every detail of the figures he'd agreed – luckily, she has a gift for finances, as well as for things mechanical. Where Oxford University missed out, Frogs Hill farm cashed in.

After a while, hard at it, while they both shot rebuilding facts and figures at me, I began to reel, and so I took myself into the Glory Boot for a few minutes' breathing space. Even there I felt I wasn't offered escape, only reproach. Headlights stared at me accusingly, classic car posters of the forties and fifties pointed out to me that life could be joyous if only I didn't make such a hash of it, and Giovanni's pictures reminded me that the Glory Boot was a sacred trust and one that I seemed to be on the way to betraying. The name Harry Prince hovered over the whole Glory Boot like a sword of Damocles.

'Sorry, Dad, I've let you down,' I heard myself mumbling.

No reply. Naturally enough. Even when he was alive, he'd been inclined to answer with a look or grunt, rather than words, if he thought he could get away with it. What wouldn't I give for one of those grunts now?

Use your head, son.

So, with great effort, I tried. 'OK, Dad. Lagonda. An extra pocket carefully built in. Polly and Mike. What for? Dodgy car dealing? Money? Peter Winter told me there were rumours about missing money. What sort of money? Just missing – or dirty?' And suddenly I was there, able to raise my head in there without shame.

Dirty money, of course. *Money laundering.*

'Thanks, Dad,' I said gratefully, and I could have sworn I heard a grunt in reply. Now all I had to do was take the ball and run like hell with it. The first person to take it to was Peter Winter, who had first mentioned it to me, and a soft cushion to land on first.

'How's it going?' Peter asked, obviously thinking he knew exactly why I'd offered him lunch. With so much going on over the barn, I hadn't been at his disposal over his lost Merc and had even been forced to let the Lagonda question lie fallow until the next day so that I could pull my weight in the sorry mess of Frogs Farm.

I'd arranged to meet Peter in a pub near Holtham. It was crowded with Saturday drinkers and diners, but that helped in a way. No one would be listening to us when they had so much to say themselves.

'I've got a couple of leads,' I white-lied. 'Hope to have news soon.'

'I meant about your barn,' he said mildly.

I'd read him wrongly. 'Could be better.' I skated quickly over the rest of the dismal prospect before me and went on to talk about Andy Wells' offer of accommodation.

'Funny chap,' Peter said meditatively. 'I never took to him, but his heart seems to be in the right place.'

My own feelings exactly, although side by side with Andy's heart lay his self-interest. Ever since I'd seen him with Slugger Sam I'd been suspicious of him. As with the Lagonda, I felt there was something wrong, but I couldn't put my finger on exactly what it was.

'Did you lose much in the fire?' Peter continued.

'Bea's Lagonda, I'm afraid, and a couple of other casualties.'

He pulled a face. 'That's bad.' He asked me a few more

polite questions, and then added, 'Any more news to give me on my Mercedes? I'm holding back on the insurance just in case it comes back pristine. Not much chance of that, I suppose.'

'Unlikely, I'm afraid.' I waffled on about it probably being still in Britain, where cars were often stolen to order, given an innocent identity at a reception centre and then dispatched to a new owner either here or abroad. He didn't look happy, so I changed the subject hastily and went on to what really interested me. 'Incidentally, you mentioned rumours about Mike and missing money. Any chance he could have been involved with smuggling cash out or in?'

This was a leap from Peter's earlier stance that Mike was merely a lively entrepreneur who occasionally went astray, but he took it on the chin. 'Dirty or clean?'

'Either.'

'What makes you think the former?'

'Your comments about the rumours, plus the number of journeys I'm told the Lagonda used to make to continental car shows.'

'Why the Lagonda in particular?'

'That could have been the car he used to stash it in. Under the boot floor, perhaps.'

'It's possible.' He frowned. 'Risky though. But that might have appealed to Mike. It would have been one way of shifting large sums to somewhere where no questions would be asked. Bit obvious, though, don't you think, to use a Lagonda? A daily driver would be less conspicuous.'

'No,' I said flatly. 'He had the excuse of car shows, remember.'

He considered this. 'I could see him doing what you described just now – stealing cars to order. Not sure about the smuggling cash out.' He thought some more. 'Mike was a "live for the day" chap. That's why we got on, I suppose. I'm quite the opposite. Mike might not have seen smuggling cash as fraud or laundering, just as common sense. And Polly would have disapproved, that's for sure.'

That was a drawback, I admitted to myself. 'Perhaps she didn't know.'

'Polly *would* know. She wasn't into fraud or risks, any more than I am. You have to realize the kind of woman she was.

Straight as a die *and* observant. Mike wouldn't have got away with much under her eye – and nor, Jack, would Mike have wanted to. They were a team.'

FOURTEEN

Peter's words rang through my head as I drove back to Frogs Hill. *A team . . . The kind of woman Polly was . . .* Did I know what kind she was? But did Peter, come to that? Astute though he was, he was the kind of friend who would see no wrong, unless he elected to, particularly if the object was a woman. He clearly worshipped Polly. *The kind of woman Polly was . . .* From TV presenter to quiet country life as the wife of a classic car dealer, possibly dodgy, and then to picture framer. Did that add up to a *kind of woman*? No. So perhaps this case wasn't so much about Mike, as the sort of woman Polly was. There could be many interpretations of that, as everyone might know a different Polly. Nevertheless, try starting at the beginning, I told myself. Focus on Polly. I began to warm to this idea. Begin with her daughter. *Right now.* I promptly turned the car into a driveway and drove back to Greensand Farm, hoping that I'd find Bea in on a Saturday afternoon. I was in luck.

'Humour me.' I almost fell in the door in my haste as Bea opened it.

She looked, I flattered myself, pleased to see me. 'You're in luck. I'm in a humouring mood.'

I prowled around in that puzzle of a house. Could the Polly I'd assumed her to be have lived with that threadbare carpet, or with the print of an Ernest Shepherd Pooh illustration next to a fine original oil painting of what looked like Aigues-Mortes in the Camargue?

Bea took me to the living room this time, where a tabletop littered with bank papers and spreadsheets testified to the muddle she was still obviously in. 'Now, tell me what's bugging you,' she said. 'Not still the Lagonda, is it?'

Although I'd told Bea on the phone that the Lagonda was safe, I'd sworn her to secrecy. 'Yes and no,' I replied.

She grinned with some effort. 'It's not top of my conversational agenda at present.'

'Even if it's the way to find out why she was killed?' I asked gently. I wouldn't mention the secret pocket, not till I knew more about it. It could just have been fixed that way for safe carriage of something other than laundered money. Or maybe Polly's father had used it for smuggling drink or tobacco in his RAF days. A lot of that went on after the liberation of France towards the end of the war. Or perhaps Polly and Mike had simply used the pocket for extra cigarettes, when they were still dutiable in the heady days before the EU. I'd investigate money laundering first, however.

'But is it the way?' she asked bluntly. 'Does the Lagonda really have anything to do with her death?'

'I don't know, Bea. What I need to know before I go any further is what Polly was really like as a person, not just as a mother. I'm judging her from the couple of times I met her, and from what I've been told since. That makes her an enigma.'

'You make her sound like the Mona Lisa.' Bea began to look interested, to my relief.

'Yes,' I said in surprise. 'I suppose that's just it.' I remembered the cool smile in Leonardo's masterpiece. 'But although I don't know what Mona's life was like behind that smile, this house doesn't say Mona Lisa to me.'

'What does it say?'

'That I wish I'd known her better.'

She looked at me in silence and then gave a slight nod as if to say: 'OK. Acceptable.' 'As a TV presenter,' she pointed out, 'Mum was used to putting on the Mona Lisa grin.'

I thought back. 'In *Passing Through*?' That was Polly's famous chat programme about celebs passing through London, ranging from politicians to pop stars.

'A bit. But particularly in *I Know What I Like*, that art programme where she approached people in an art gallery and chatted to them about the pictures, especially the portraits. Mum was good at people. She'd find out why they liked such and such a picture, and she could worm reasons out of them that they didn't even realize themselves. I suppose that's why she took up framing in the end. The nearest she could get to *I Know What I Like*.'

'But why marry someone so completely different to herself?'

Bea frowned. 'Mum liked having fun. As a presenter you're hemmed in. With Dad she could relax, be herself, have fun, off to car shows and so on.'

'Was he a bit of a comic? Did they laugh a lot together?'

'Yes, but that wasn't the underlying link. They were just happy. Always let's do this or that. Something new and never something blue. See?' Bea looked up at me, and there were tears in her eyes.

'And after your father died?'

'That went. But it was slowly coming back. It *was*.'

I couldn't bear to look at her. I felt like crying myself. The waste, oh the waste.

I couldn't see Guy Williams moving me to tears, but he was my next port of call late that afternoon. I owed him a heart-felt thank you over the offer of his barn, anyway. He was working in his garden – somewhat of a busman's holiday, I thought. When I thanked him, he nodded, looking almost embarrassed.

'Sorry about the fire, Jack. Bad do.'

'Couldn't agree more.'

'You could still take my offer up. You wouldn't have Andy Wells breathing down your neck.'

'That's good of you.' I meant it. 'Hard decision, but Andy's closer to home and already fitted out.'

'Sensible of you, then.' A grin. 'Bet he's charging you. Get back to your own place soon though. Smells rub off.'

'That bad?' I was surprised. Firstly, Guy wasn't in the car business so he was theoretically a long way off from 'smells', and secondly, I hadn't thought Andy's reputation was that dubious.

'Where Mike left off, Andy took over, remember.'

'All legit business.'

There must have been a slight question mark at the end of my sentence because Guy replied, 'No smells without smoke, no smoke without fire.'

I took this seriously, coming from Guy. 'Personal experience?'

'Near enough.'

'Polly?'

'No, in fact, though she couldn't stand the chap.'

'He was calling on Bea the other day. He and Slugger Sam.'

He looked surprised. 'Weird, but Andy likes to know what's going on, especially where cash is concerned,' Guy commented. 'And cars,' he added. 'Still, hiring Slugger is stretching it a bit far.'

'Tomas Kasek knows Andy, doesn't he?'

Guy was on the defensive right away. 'Why should he?'

'That's what I wondered. Just rumours, maybe.'

'Tittle-tattle,' he snorted.

'As you say, no smells without smoke and so on.'

He flushed and surrendered. 'Andy's in the car business, and so is Tomas's brother. He's in Poland.'

Now we were getting somewhere. I couldn't reveal that I already knew about this brother. I could see Guy didn't like telling me, which sent up his credit rating with me. Then our eyes met, and I let him off the hook. 'Small world, eh?'

My mind was working overtime. Tomas, suspected spotter. Andy, with a question mark. Barry Pole, who knew Tomas's brother, thought to be a receiver. It looked as if Tomas was nicely tucked into a stolen to order chain, as Eastern Europe was a prime destination for stolen cars. He could even have spotted Peter Winter's Merc – and, more importantly, Polly's Lagonda. I thought I'd try one more name on Guy.

'Heard of a guy called Mason Trent?'

Guy shook his head without much interest – and I was glad. Trent's number was in Tomas Kasek's mobile, albeit a dead line, so it was a relief that Guy hadn't reacted to it.

Change of tack needed. 'I heard rumours about Mike having left big cash that never turned up after his death.'

He answered that one promptly. 'I heard them too.'

Too promptly? I wondered. 'Believe them?'

'Polly didn't.'

Second cue, and I switched direction again. Brake for the corner, Jack. This one could be tricky. 'I'm beginning to think I didn't know Polly well enough to help Bea. I need to get on her mother's wavelength, but I'm dodging between stations at present. How would you sum her up?'

Guy looked nonplussed. 'Could you describe your best friend if someone demanded an instant pen portrait?'

'No,' I admitted.

Guy grinned. 'Come with me.' He heaved himself to his

feet, and I followed him into the main house and through to a conservatory where the lady I had seen him with at the art show was in the throes of going through cookery books and composing lists. I had a sudden image of myself and Polly in later years sitting occupied in such a companionable job and had to swallow hard.

'Sarah, meet Jack Colby. Wants to know what Polly was like.'

If she thought this somewhat strange, she didn't show it. Sarah was a warmer version of Guy, large, somewhat intimidating and ultimately friendly – I hoped.

'So you're the desperado who threatened Polly, the hero who came to Bea's help, and the victim of a cosh on the head plus arson?' she welcomed me.

'That sums me up nicely,' I agreed. I took the offered seat. 'Do you feel up to talking about her?'

'Yes, if it helps. Guy and I liked her. And Mike. Both of us,' Sarah emphasized.

'But, as a person, how would you describe her?'

Sarah considered. 'I'd say she was rather lost, a bit sad.'

That startled me. 'You mean after Mike's death?'

'No, all the time we knew her. She seemed to be desperately looking for something and never quite appreciating she had it, if only she'd stop and look around her.'

'That's interesting. She did love Mike though?'

'Good grief, yes. No problem there. I remember her at school, though. She always wanted more. If we went on a school outing she couldn't believe that wherever we went was a goal in itself. There had to be a follow-up – something secret, something exciting – and it seemed like that with Mike too. But the odd thing is that she didn't approve of Tomas, who might have represented the same kind of excitement for Bea.'

Dead silence. Would she break it, or would Guy?

Guy did. He cleared his throat. 'Don't push it, Jack. Tomas was way out of order in going after Bea – I even had a word with him myself, and so did Polly – but he isn't a bad chap, in his way. Hot tempered, perhaps, and arrogant, but which of us wasn't at his age?'

I could think of quite a few who weren't, but I refrained from doing so. Interesting that 'the word' had been reported to me as a flaming row.

'He's already made one attempt to see Bea, but luckily she wasn't on her own,' I warned him.

Sarah looked appalled, and even Guy looked thrown for a moment or two. Then he rallied. 'He seems to be keeping to his bail conditions,' he said. 'And he's working well. But you can depend on it he won't be going within a mile of Bea from now on. *Or* Andy Wells. OK?'

I nodded. 'But there's a possible murder charge hanging over his head, so the police must have something on him.'

He snorted. 'They arrested a suspect, that's all. Something for the targets' list. It's up to them to find out who murdered Polly, not you, Jack.'

Was that a warning or a threat?

A lost sort of person, a happy person. How many other Pollys might there be? I'd keep on going. I wasn't sure I was on the right track, but I'd wait until proved wrong. The arson attack had had one good effect: I felt so hopping mad at the world that I had no compunction in doing my Poirot act. It would only be a matter of time, I reasoned, before the new home of the Lagonda was discovered and whoever disliked it so much would be after it – and probably me – again. I needed to work fast.

Not that fast, as it turned out, because the Stacks weren't in when I called. Not to be daunted, I presented myself unannounced on their doorstep on Sunday morning.

'How nice to see you, Jack.' Lorna's words belied her expression, which indicated that as I had so rudely rejected her earlier offers they were not going to be repeated, and that good though it might be to see me, the sooner she could slam the door in my face the better. 'We're just going to church. So sorry.'

Fortunately for me, Rupert appeared behind her and indicated that he at least would have time to see me. This could have had something to do with the fact that I'd said I was here on Bea's behalf.

He looked concerned, and for once brushed his wife aside, ushered me into the manor house and led me down a stately corridor into what was clearly his office. Lorna, having made it clear she wasn't wasting her valuable time on me, had left to go to church, and so fortunately we were alone together.

That suited me. There was something about Rupert and Polly that I wasn't getting. Was he friend? Customer? Lover? None of these, all of these?

'I hear you lost cars the other evening, as well as the damage to the barn,' Rupert said.

'Unfortunately, yes. Including Bea's Lagonda.'

'Irreplaceable,' he murmured.

'Except at a price.'

'But not that one. Mike and she loved it.'

'Then why didn't she still drive it?'

He looked at me in amazement. 'She couldn't bear to. She was sentimental about it.'

'Polly struck me as tough, as well – somebody who would feel deeply but tackle the problem, not ignore it.'

'But you, Jack, hardly knew her.'

Cue for question, especially with Lorna out of the room. 'Of course. I realize that. Which is why it's interesting to me to hear you talk about her. I get a better picture than if I talk to Bea, who sees her as a daughter would a mother.'

'Why should I want to talk about her to you?' His voice was mild, but it had steel in it, and I realized he would be a match for Lorna if pushed.

'Bea wants me to look into her death.'

He regarded me thoughtfully, and I decided I wouldn't like to be Lorna if he ever decided to take a stand against her flirtations, whether she carried them through or not. He was not quite the forbearing husband I had taken him for. 'Why you?' he shot at me.

I was ready for that. 'You might well ask. Because her chum Zoe knows I'm a car detective, I suppose.'

He made up his mind. 'Very well. I'll tell you what I thought of Polly. Just this. She was the nearest thing to a friend I had. I'm well aware that my wife sometimes gets carried away and accuses Polly and me of having been lovers. We spent time together. We had to; she did a lot of my framing for me. That's well known, and why not? Her service was far better and far cheaper than anything I would find in London. As for an affair, I'm a reasonably rich man, Mr Colby, and if I wanted an affair it wouldn't be difficult. But with Polly? Never. Firstly, Mike had a keen eye for any man other than himself who paid her attention, and secondly, I prized her far too much as a friend

and adviser. She had too good an eye for art to risk –' he
actually smiled – 'Lorna's wrath. Polly was all the things that
Lorna isn't. Steady, reliable, a good counsellor, she could step
back and make judgements. Very useful for my work.'

'So would you say she was cool-headed?'

'Very. But not cool-hearted.'

I liked that. 'Did she come up to London for your
exhibitions?'

'Nearly always. She was coming up for Giovanni's exhibition at my gallery.'

I did a double take, which amused him. 'Ah yes,' he added,
'you have a few of his early works, don't you? If ever you
decide to sell—'

'Unlikely.'

'Nevertheless, do come up to the exhibition. Come to the
private view next Friday evening. Giovanni will be there.
You're welcome.'

That sounded like an offer I couldn't refuse, and I didn't.
He said he'd send me an invitation. 'Security,' he murmured.

When I left, I discovered Lorna hadn't gone to church after
all. She was waiting for me, standing by her car, at the corner
of the drive. She put her head through my open window and
treated me to her no doubt expensive scent.

'Darling Polly,' she cooed. 'So she snared you too. I'm sure
Rupert has been treating you to the tale of what a sweetie she
was. So she was to anyone who could advance the cause of
Polly Davis. Which meant she wasn't sweet to me. She used
the same techniques as she did in her TV days to anyone who
didn't see her as an angel. You don't get to be a TV presenter
by being coy. Polly was devious, shallow and ruthless. And
that was before Rupert began his blasted affair with her.' She
fixed me with a glacial eye. 'And as for you, Jack—'

'I wait breathlessly,' I assured her.

'You're all beef and no balls.'

I returned to Frogs Hill not sure I had yet reached the heart
of Polly. She was happy, she was sad, she was devious, she
was straightforward, she was ruthless, she was a good chum.
All possible, and had it helped me at all? Curiously enough,
I thought it had. But even if Slugger Sam appeared with all
fists flying at that very moment, I couldn't have told him how

or why I felt that way. Somewhere in-between all these various attitudes lay the kernel that would provide the key to Polly's death.

FIFTEEN

When in a tizz, come to Liz – so she had idly joked once years ago, but on Monday morning it didn't seem a bad idea. There's something comforting about driving into a garden centre: plenty of parking space, the usual bags of soil piled up, the odd wheelbarrow and the promise of much more within – and we all know the verse that one is nearer to God in a garden than anywhere else on earth. Somewhere in the garden at Frogs Hill Dad even had a stone with that engraved on it – not that that had induced either of us to become Christopher Lloyds.

When I had reached home that Sunday evening, I'd felt frustrated and somewhat sorry for myself. By the following morning I felt worse. It was the first day of June, a month when most sensible people were out enjoying themselves – and I wouldn't be. It was then that the idea of popping down to Liz's garden centre came to me. Colin would be safely clad in his laboratory whites and poring over some inoffensive bug, and so Liz therefore might be relatively human. Busy perhaps, but equally perhaps not too busy to see me. I took the daily driver, my Alfa, not wishing to appear ostentatious (what me?), and as usual the sight of those bags of compost and the June roses and bedding plants all crying out to be bought cheered me up. There was an atmosphere about it that told me cars might come and cars might go, but gardens went on for ever.

Liz didn't seem to share my sudden enthusiasm for the eternity of gardens. I found her busy pushing a trolley-load of grit at the rear of the centre where all the plants were on sale.

'What do *you* want?' she asked.

'Your loving advice.'

A scornful glance. 'Advice doesn't make my tills ring.'

'Suppose I buy you a coffee?'

'And a bun?'

'Done.'

Liz has a small coffee shop at one end of the wooden building that houses the usual tills, seeds and paraphernalia necessary to make gardens grow and thrive. The coffee shop tables are gaily covered with red check tablecloths, and adorned with good crockery and cutlery. Mrs Greeve was on duty that day, which was good news for those who liked cakes because she is a dab hand at making them. It's not such good news for Liz, as Mrs Greeve is a talker par excellence, with the result that if you're in the queue behind her chosen target listener, customer satisfaction is not high.

That morning Mrs Greeve was doomed to disappointment, as Liz put paid to her hopes by retiring with me to an outside table, where she couldn't be either a listener or overheard, except to and by me. In her work clothes of jeans and a smock top, and with her short-cropped hair, she looked just as I remembered her nipping around her small garden in Pluckley where I often stayed with her.

No sentimentality was to be permitted, however. 'Sorry to hear the bad news, Jack,' she said briskly. 'Any problems Colin could help with?'

'Thanks,' I said hastily. The idea of Colin enjoying my misfortune was not a pleasant one. 'But I think I've got it sorted.'

'All that and a bang on the head too. You seem to be pushing your nose in somewhere it's not wanted.'

'Me? Never.'

She looked at me in that cynical way that used to entrance me. Now it just amused me, but I suppose that was good therapy in itself.

'Polly Davis,' I continued, pretending to be deeply interested in my cheese scone in order to avoid the snort of disapproval. 'I've had four different interpretations of the kind of woman she was. You said at the pub the other day that I should steer clear of her. Well, as you know, I never had the chance to steer in any direction – so tell me. Was she happy, was she sad, was she straightforward, was she devious? Did she like a quiet life, did she long for an adventurous one? Is it even fair to ask you?'

'Even if I said no, you'd still ask.' Liz thought for a moment

or two while I attacked the froth of cappuccino liberally
sprinkled with chocolate by Mrs Greeve. Eventually, Liz came
up with: 'I reckon she was all of those things, but none of
them drove her.'

'What did?' Could I be getting to the core of it at last?

'I didn't know her well—'

'Tell me what turned her on.'

'Danger.'

Of all the things, this I could not have foreseen. 'Danger
from what?' I repeated stupidly.

She considered this for so long that I had to grit my teeth
with frustration. Liz would pounce if I tried to hurry her
though. 'The spice of life. The edge. The darkness – oh, for
heaven's sake, Jack, you must know what I mean.'

Must I? I thought about Polly – the one I'd met, not the
one I'd been told about by various people including her
daughter. What had attracted me? The cool, calm lady? The
furious one? The controlled fury? All and none. Hopeless. One
can't define these things. All I remembered was Zoe telling
me I had a nose for trouble. Could I smell Polly's inclination
towards danger? Is that what had drawn me to her? For
chemistry read sex, but what are sex's components?

'Look at Mike,' I heard Liz say, and I realized I must have
missed a bit while I was musing. 'Why should the TV
presenter of a chatty art programme marry a second-hand
car dealer?'

'She had a classic car,' I reminded her.

'Whatever. He wasn't exactly her type. Not what she was
brought up to.'

'But perhaps the danger lay in dodgy car deals, so that
doesn't seem to fit either, Polly.'

'My name's not Polly, it's Liz.' Her hand crashed on the
table.

'I'm sorry – blame the bang on the head.' As contrition
went it was feeble. Nevertheless, Liz looked mollified, although
not completely.

I made it up to her by bringing her up to date. I could trust
her. 'I've been told there were rumours about missing millions
after Mike died. Any chance he was money laundering and
smuggling the loot overseas in the Lagonda? And that Polly
knew nothing about it?' I added hopefully. 'Or would you

come down on the side of her approving of it because of this
love of danger that you perceived in her?'

'I'm not coming down on any side, Jack. You asked my
opinion of Polly. You've got it. Now get the hell out of here.'

'Thanks, Liz. I mean it—'

'And another thing, Jack. I am not, repeat *not,* Mother Earth
for you to rest your head on my bosom any time you fancy
you're in trouble.'

I gave her a grin, aware that Mrs G. was listening with great
interest to our raised voices. 'This danger, Liz. Miss it yourself,
do you?'

The remains of the bun that she threw at me told me I'd
hit a nerve, and I laughed. Nevertheless, I went away in sober
mood. Did love of danger explain just why the spark had
ignited between Polly and me? If so, I was all the more
determined to track down who had snuffed it out for us.
Danger . . . Liz could be right. Bea wouldn't have seen that
side of Polly, nor would Peter Winter, nor Rupert – perhaps,
it occurred to me, Lorna had picked it up, however. That might
explain her impotent rage against Polly, even if misdirected
as to its cause. It might also explain Guy's protectiveness and
the way Tomas had managed to rub her up the wrong way.
What else might it explain?

It could indicate she was involved in the money laundering
– if there was any. That was an unpleasant thought.

I parked the Alfa back at Frogs Hill, but found the place
deserted. This was hardly surprising, as both Zoe and Len
were obviously installed at Andy Wells' garage – unless, of
course, they were at the rear of the farmhouse crawling over
the Lagonda. I doubted that, but nevertheless that seemed a
good place for me to go to meditate over what the hell was
happening to me and mine. In the 'mine', I realized that I
seemed to be including the Lagonda, not to mention her new
owner, both of whom I had taken under my protective wing.
I strolled round to have a look. From the outside the barn
looked well and truly secure, with no sign of Zoe or Len.
For a moment I had a sudden fright that the Lagonda might
already have been pinched, despite the closed doors. As I
had one of the three keys, I ran to the doors feeling stupid
even for being concerned over it. Of course she was
safe . . . or was she? I breathed again when I swung open

the door and saw her there, a bit of ancient hay sticking to her windscreen like a raised eyebrow. My very own classic in the barn.

'I have a song to sing, O . . .' I used to trill in my youth, when I was briefly in a Gilbert and Sullivan choir. The Lagonda had a tale to tell-O, as well, only unfortunately she wasn't as vocal as Jack Point. She had told me all she could, and now she seemed to be telling me it was up to me. Maybe it was, but how the hell could I delve back into her history without Mike and Polly's input?

That raised eyebrow still seemed to be sending me a message. Those blasted small headlights were winking at me like flashes on a camera . . . *Photographs*. I clutched at that inspiration in triumph. *That's* how I could view her history. All classic car owners take photos, and Mike and Polly had gone to hundreds of continental car shows. There would be dates, perhaps, and places, people. Bea must have some that would help rebuild the Lagonda's past history. Four years ago, when Mike had died, digital pix weren't so common, so with any luck there might be actual physical prints instead of my trying to beat a path into their computers, where most photos seem to prefer living nowadays.

'Thanks,' I told the headlights with deep gratitude. I almost offered them a reprieve on the spot, but common sense prevailed. I'd find another home for them when we replaced them with the proper ones. I still wondered why there were no number plates. The car was currently registered, so there was nothing to hide about it.

I couldn't get hold of Bea – I had forgotten that sensible people have jobs to go to and that her leave might be over – so I had to curb my impatience until she got back to Greensand Farm that evening. She told me to come up right away, which was noble of her. I offered to take her out to supper, but instead we settled for an Indian home delivery – for three, as she pointed out Zoe would be there.

'Rob too?' I asked with foreboding.

A gurgle of laughter at the end of the phone. 'No knowing, but maybe I'd better order for him too.'

In the end it was two. Zoe called to say she'd be late – something to do with cooking for Rob, Bea gathered, so it was just Bea, me, the prospect of an Indian home-delivery

– and several cupboardfuls of photographs. We gazed at the stuffed shelves in horror.

'Typical of Mum,' Bea said ruefully.

My first instinct was to plunge in, scattering pix in all directions, but I was sensible enough to let Bea make the running.

'We're looking for continental car shows, that right?' she asked. 'Here, you look through these, and I'll take the next one.'

She turned out the contents of a shelf on to a coffee table for herself and one for me on the other table. In grim silence we began our search. 'What are we hoping to find?'

'I don't know.'

She gazed at me as if I were mad – not unnaturally – so I hastily amended it to: 'Car shows that have the Lagonda in them.'

I searched through several hundred photos of Polly at dinner parties, Polly at dances, Polly in the garden, Mike here, there and everywhere, Bea at various stages of development, Polly laughing, Polly frowning, Polly looking beautiful and suave, Polly looking a mess and even Polly looking downright ugly, as we all can if the camera catches at the wrong moment. Forget about cameras never lying. They can lie all too often.

'Not doing well,' Bea announced sometime later. 'A couple of the Lagonda on a picnic, and a few with Grandpa in them, but that's all. I've put them on one side.' She patted a small heap on the table.

'No car pix at all?'

'Yes, but apart from these I can't see the Lagonda or any with Mum or Dad.'

'Snap,' I said in frustration. I'd had the same barren haul. I went over to sit next to Bea on the sofa, taking my own meagre pickings with me. 'The Wheatsheaf gatherings, Goodwood Revival Day, the Festival of Speed . . . But where are those continental car shows, Bea? I can't believe they didn't take any photos.' Even if Polly and Mike were up to no good, I thought, they'd be anxious to prove they weren't and therefore would take some happy holiday-mood snaps.

'I don't know.' Bea looked as puzzled as I felt. 'Perhaps she threw them away after Dad died.'

'Then why keep these?' I asked, indicating the British photos.

'I really don't know,' Bea said abruptly. 'You go on looking, Jack. I'll ring the order through. This job's making me feel sick.'

Me too, I thought, but I felt contrite at having put her through this ordeal. I was glad she'd left me alone to look through the remaining shelves, though. I'd begun to think the search was going nowhere until – wouldn't you know? – I reached the very last shelf. Right at the bottom of the last cupboard, a pile of loose photos was hiding two albums. There was something else too, nestling underneath them: two number plates. No ordinary plates – they were the Lagonda's, according to Swansea when we'd checked it out earlier. I took the albums out to Bea in the kitchen.

'Wedding album,' she said, not looking at them. 'I've seen it a million times.'

'Then look at the other one,' I said, feeling a heel. 'There are two.'

Reluctantly, she did so – and we struck gold. In fact, it declared itself twenty-four carat on the first page – it was a title page with a Lagonda photo posted beneath the legend: 'Continental Trips'. How much clearer could it be? Then a little voice inside me murmured: odd, isn't it? Especially since it was with those number plates.

Bea recovered immediately, and we rushed the album back to the table in the living room where we eagerly turned the pages. There they all were, neatly captioned. There were photos of the Lagonda, of Mike and Polly standing by them, photos of other cars too, though usually with the Lagonda somewhere in the background; cars, names and dates. What more could I want?

'What do they tell you?' Bea asked.

I hadn't the nerve to reply nothing, or even nothing yet. I could see this was getting to her, though, and so I gently took the album over and began to go through it again. It didn't tell me anything more than on my first look through. What had I expected? That Polly and Mike would be standing there waving piles of banknotes in high glee? Polly and Mike photographed nipping into a Swiss bank to open an account? Polly and Mike surreptitiously stowing banknotes under the boot floor? Hauling stuff out of that secret pocket?

Luckily for our morale, the home delivery arrived just as

we were both giving up, and so we left the rest of the album
to look at later. By the time we had slaked hunger with kormas,
poppadoms and vindaloo, and thirst with a beer, I had digested
more than curry. I suppose I'd been churning it over
subconsciously and reached a conclusion without even thinking
it through.

'You know, Bea, that album is like the Lagonda.'

'Meaning?' she asked wearily.

'Don't know. There's just something wrong about it. As
there was with the car.' Too late I remembered I hadn't told
her about the pocket and cursed myself. Well, I had to now
– and tell her where I'd found the number plates. She listened
and, to her credit, didn't cry out in horror: 'How dare you
imply there was any hanky-panky going on?'

Instead, full marks to her, she thought it through and said
at last, 'You know, Jack, you may be right. This album isn't
like Mum and Dad. The wedding album is one thing, but
it's not like them to do prissy little title pages to look pretty.
Is that the kind of thing you mean about the album? That
it's too tidy?'

'Yes, but it's more than that. It's the photos.' I was getting
there, albeit slowly.

'What about them?'

'They seem wrong.'

'How?' Bea began to look apprehensive. I could see that it
wasn't good for her to think that her parents were indulging
in something she couldn't explain, and I began to wish heartily
that I hadn't embarked on this. But I had, for better for worse.

'Look, would you prefer me to take it away and look at it
at home?'

'Not for my sake. I'd rather know *now* if there's anything
to find.'

I knew she was a brave lass, and this proved it. So we began
again. At first I thought we were getting nowhere, but then a
creepy feeling began to take me over. What had I been thinking
just now? That the camera could indeed lie, and here, I thought,
could be proof of that. Digital photos today can now lie to
their hearts' content owing to on-screen editing, but a few
years ago that was less common, especially back in the nine-
ties when some of those photos were taken.

Oh yes, the camera could lie – with man's help.

'Bea,' I said gently, 'I think some, perhaps all, of these photos are faked. There are perhaps one or two genuine ones put in, but a lot of them are definite fakes.'

She was gazing at me as if I were Merlin waving a magic want. 'Don't be daft – why on earth should they be?'

'I can't answer that, but look at this one. The Grand Prix Weekend show in Montreux, June 2001. That's genuine. Now look at this one. Look at the edges of the Lagonda, how sharp they are against the background. And look at this one. I'm pretty sure that's the same view of the Lagonda as in the other pic. *Exactly* the same.' Another aspect struck me. 'This claims to have been taken at the Antwerp Classic Salon in March 2003, but it's the same background as the April Techno Classica in Essen a year earlier, although the Lagonda's at a different angle. This one has Mike standing by it, but look at the sharp definition round his head.'

'But if you're right – if – why on earth bother? Why go to those lengths?'

'Because this is a showcase album, designed as such.'

'Why, why, why . . .'

I had no answer to that. How could I suggest money laundering to Bea? It was humming through my mind like an electric telegraph wire. Why fake car-show pictures if you were really there? Suppose you were actually at dirtier business than that? In Geneva, or Amsterdam . . . And was there a *fun* element too? I imagined Mike and Polly giggling together as they mocked up this album of their supposed lives together. Could I put that as a thesis to Bea – fun from which she had been excluded?

Bea poked agitatedly at the rest of the album, not really concentrating on what she was doing. The photos were mostly pasted in, but from between the last two pages a loose piece of paper slipped out. Automatically, I bent down to pick it up and handed it to her. But I could see what it was over her shoulder. 'It's that scrap of paper,' I cried.

'What scrap?'

'The one I found in the Lagonda.' A very cold feeling was creeping up my spine. 'It's the receipt for two cappuccinos, isn't it?' There was no sign of the garage receipt, so there must have been something special about this one to make her keep it.

'Yes.' She was staring at it.

'Why would Polly have kept it? And, moreover, kept it so carefully tucked away?'

'Perhaps,' she said with difficulty, 'because it's dated the day of Dad's death, four years ago, Wednesday tenth September.'

That did it. She burst into tears, and for a while it was me who played Mother Earth.

SIXTEEN

B ea had pushed the receipt into my hands in a frenzy as I left. 'Take it away, and that album. I don't want to know.'

'For better, for worse, Bea.'

'Yes, I know I wanted you to find out the truth. And I still do. But just tell me when you've found it. And make it quick, Jack. I don't know what's happening or why, but I want it over. I want Tomas nice and securely behind bars, or if he didn't kill Mum, whoever did do so. It's beginning to feel as if there's a very black pit out there and I'm heading straight for it.'

'I won't let you fall in, Bea. You know that.'

'Yes. I wish—' She didn't finish the sentence. Perhaps, considering the difference in our ages and the emotional state she was in, it was better for both of us that she didn't.

Next morning I decided I'd have to go over to Andy Wells' garage. It would take some doing, because all I wanted to do was look at that album, then look at the Lagonda and try to make sense of what I was seeing and wonder whether it would take me any further. Try as I might, I just could not see Polly mixed up in something so unsavoury as money laundering. Why bother? Just for the hell of it? Because she was so much in love with Mike that she'd agree to his every suggestion? Was she still at it when she died? No way. The Lagonda had been firmly under wraps, and so, I guessed, had that side of her life. Any new life would have been completely different.

So why had she died?

Conclusion: someone had known about the money laundering.

And with that in mind I took myself off to Andy Wells and what remained of Frogs Hill Classic Car Restorations. There was a sort of subsidiary garage at the side, an overflow, and I found Zoe and Len there looking as content as possible in reduced circumstances. Cramped though they were, I found them hard at work on a suspension overhaul badly needed by a Sunbeam Rapier, which had originally been booked in for Frogs Hill. As there was only room for one car at a time, the pressure was on for a quick turnaround. What Len thought of this is not recorded.

I went to see Andy first, out of politeness.

'How's Bea, Jack?' he asked.

'Doing OK. Glad when it's all over though.'

'You mean that Polish chap?'

'Yes. You knew him, didn't you?'

He struggled to think of an answer and finally came up with: 'Came in for a bit of work on his old Fiesta. So what? Is that all you want to know?' He wasn't exactly aggressive, but I wouldn't have wanted to see Slugger Sam walk in at that moment.

OK, I'd take this bull by its horns. 'No. Mike Davis's death, Andy.'

I could see him stiffen. 'What about it?' he shot back at me.

'I wasn't in England at the time. What exactly happened?'

'It was straightforward enough,' he muttered. 'The way I heard it he was on the track of some car in Canterbury, his dream car. A Riley, from what I remember, an RME. They don't come up often, and Polly would have seen that idea off right away if she'd known about it. Which she didn't. He never made it to the dealer. Slumped over the seats, dead. Heart.' He was getting definitely truculent now.

'He was on his own?'

He looked at me suspiciously. 'Yes.'

'In a daily driver?'

'No. The Lagonda.'

'Why the station car park?'

He shrugged. 'How should I know? On his way to see the car, most likely.' His eyes slid past me.

'Who'd you hear this tale from, Andy?'

'Inquest.' The reply came a bit too promptly, and I doubted very much whether a coroner would be gripped by the details of a dream RME.

'No doubts at the time that it was natural causes?'

'Ask the bloody police. I don't remember no talk though. Straight heart attack.'

'Could it have been induced?'

I thought he'd hit me; he didn't. Instead he went as white as the proverbial sheet. 'I'll tell you something, Jack. No one I knew of had an RME on the stocks around then. So don't go asking too many questions.' He wasn't smiling, and I knew it was time to stop. That receipt was for two cappuccinos. Mike could have drunk two cups. He could have treated a stranger. Or he could have paid for someone he knew.

Had Polly seen the date and realized it could mean something that had never occurred to her before? Something that had made her face very white and very abstracted . . . Had it suggested to her that Mike had not died of a straight heart attack, but could have been murdered? And had that sudden awareness led to her own death?

It seemed to me that, contrary to Andy's advice, asking questions was precisely what I should do. As soon as I got back to Frogs Hill, I put in my long overdue call to Brian Woollerton about the Merc and slid in the name of Mason Trent just on the off chance it produced something. Brian evidently thought I was ringing to follow up on the headlights, and the pause and heavy breathing that followed his discovery of what I really wanted was suggestive in itself. The Merc didn't make much impression on him; it was Mason's name that set the sparks flying.

'Sure you want me to?' he growled.

A nod's as good as a wink to a blind fool like me. 'Yes,' quoth I.

The frightening probability that Mike had been murdered was one subject I couldn't discuss with Bea – and yet who else? I was treading on scarily thin eggshells here, and if I wasn't careful I would end up as the omelette. There was no doubt I was putting myself in the frying pan with a vengeance; the problem was, when was it going to get too hot for my own good? It seemed a big jump from my 'evidence' to probable

murder, and yet it was a reasonable one – wasn't it? I mentally
ran through the list of people who might know more about
the circumstances of Mike's death than Andy Wells. There
would surely have been more gossip at the time . . . or would
there? Heart attacks happen. Maybe Mike had had known heart
problems. I could talk to Andy again, I could talk to Guy, I
could talk to Peter, Rupert, Lorna – even Slugger Sam – but
which of them could I trust? Guy or Peter would be my preference – apart from Bea, of course, as a last resort. She'd had
enough shocks already.

In the end the answer was simple enough. I needed a chat
with Dave, and when I rang him, the next day, for once he
was all for meeting. He had news for me and could I get my
butt over to his Charing office soonest? Provided Brandon
didn't reach out an arm and hoick me in as I passed his door,
I was only too happy. Dave then changed his mind and
suggested a pub in Charing. Charing is a pleasant village
drowning in history and on the A20 a few miles from Pluckley.
It's in the lea of the downs, and the short drive there was an
enjoyable one. On the North Downs our ancestors had clashed
with Romans, Anglo Saxons, and Normans all unsuccessfully
and more successfully with Napoleon and Hitler. Carbon footprints from all ages abound in one form or another, and for
me being there puts problems in perspective.

I found Dave sitting in the bar. He was looking more like
the Spirit of Ecstasy than ever, as he was hunched up over a
pint, looking grimly determined, his hair sleeked back as
though about to zoom across the room. I didn't even have time
to sit down before he fired up the engine.

'Another job for you, Jack. A BMW lifted from Wye
yesterday. Private residence.'

'What's so special you need me right away?'

His idea of an answer. 'Got anything on Winter's Merc?'

'Lines open, but nothing yet.' I'd tried, after all. 'So what
about this BMW?'

'Could be the same outfit as Winter's Merc.'

'With Kasek the spotter?'

'Possible.'

'Barry Pole?'

'Um,' said Dave. 'Possible.'

'Andy Wells?'

'Not so possible. Jury's out.'

I wasn't hitting the right buttons. 'OK, Dave. Tell me what this is all about.'

'Big art theft in Norfolk last week.'

That took me aback, though I don't know why, as stolen cars are often used for crimes, especially cloned ones. 'Yup. I remember.' It was at Talbot Place, a medium stately home with a fine collection of classic art. Not your Leonardos, but good: Watteau, Van Ruysdael, and many others, plus a first-class collection of old master drawings. If I remembered correctly, about half a dozen paintings and quite a few drawings had vanished in this theft.

I was losing the plot. 'The BMW's only just been nicked.'

Dave looked at me pityingly. 'Not the BMW, our Merc. It's turned up, abandoned four miles away. It was used for the getaway.'

'Cloned?'

'False plates, but the VIN number checked out. Keep this under wraps, Jack, till I give you the all-clear. It's being crawled over by the Serious Organized Crime Agency. It had one of the nicked drawings still in it.'

'Odd. They must have switched cars, but you'd think they'd have noticed something like that.'

'That's up to SOCA.'

'And our lot?' I enquired.

'We need a line on the car gang *and* on Mason Trent or whatever he's calling himself now.'

'I'm not with you.'

'That's fair enough. I'll fill you in. Our chum Mason Trent went behind bars for three years for cloning cars and theft. At roughly the same time a gent called Harry Smith went inside for art theft. The Met were pretty sure that the two were connected: Mason Trent cloned stolen cars with innocent identities and took commissions to supply them for getaway cars for the series of art thefts from stately homes; and Harry Smith was involved in the robberies themselves. After they went inside, the robberies continued, but not quite so many. Not until the last year, when they perked up again. Harry Smith was only one of at least three operatives, under a central godfather, who the Met think could be Mason Trent – who, coincidentally, has been out of jug for a year. He could be up to his old tricks and working with Pole again. Hence the eagerness to find Trent and, for good measure, his current cloning base.'

'Done by tomorrow,' I said sarcastically, but it wasn't taken that way. Dave just nodded approval.

It was my turn now. 'Talking about organized car theft, did you ever meet Mike Davis?'

Dave gave me what is known as a sideways glance. 'His website was clean.'

'One can have more than one site.'

'Sure. But we never found any links back to Mike on the dodgy ones.'

'Clever dealing?'

'Maybe. Spent fuel now though. Andy Wells has taken over, and before you ask, he's clean too, so far as we can see.'

'One last question.'

'Right, Columbo.'

'Any reason to think Mike's death was other than a straight heart attack?'

He sighed. 'In case you hadn't noticed, I run a car crime unit, not a murder squad.'

'Mike was a car dealer.'

He grudgingly conceded the point. 'I don't remember anything on it. I'll check.'

'Thanks, Dave.'

'Another for you, before you get too grateful. That other chum of yours.'

'Which?' I asked carefully.

'Dan Burgess. Lay off him.'

'So he's got the Met eye on him too?' As if Dave would come clean. He wouldn't, so I helped him out. 'Think he might be a classic car spotter?'

'Possible.'

I was about to say a classic car man wouldn't sully his hands with dirty trade, but held back. What the hell did I know what Dan Burgess might or might not do in his spare time? Apart from paint ghastly daubs of people's cars.

Which, come to think of it, my suspicious mind kicked in, would be a splendid way of getting to know who had what. 'Paint your car, mister? Bet you've got a treasure in that garage . . .'

Having earned my bread and butter by contributing my tuppence of knowledge about Dan's occupation to Dave's store, which interested him quite a lot, I assured him of my undivided attention to tracking down Mason Trent and departed to put this unwillingly into practice. I had to find out about the cloning centre quickly, if I was to keep my job with Dave. Try Andy Wells? I'd been warned off. Try Harry Prince? I'd been warned off. See if Brian had anything yet? Don't push your luck, I thought. But I had no choice. Brian it was.

'Double dosh, Brian,' I said cajolingly as I heard him breathing heavily at the other end of the line. I don't know why. This one, after all, was straight car and maybe art theft, not murder.

'Could go wrong,' he said. I could hear him gulping. 'You'll be hearing from me. OK?' If only I could rely on that, but I knew a put-off when I heard one.

With this possible breathing space, I began to think again about Mike's death. Heart problems cover a wide field, including the need for medication. At that insidious thought my heart sank. No one was going to know Mike's medical details apart from Mike himself, his doctor, Polly – and possibly Bea. The doctor was not going to be helpful to Private Investigator Jack Colby, so it was going to have to be Bea.

I invited her round that evening, cooked a thick tuna steak for each of us, made a salad, and fished some ice cream out of the freezer. She guessed what was coming next. 'OK,' she said. 'Now tell me what you want.'

She listened to me in silence, and I couldn't even begin to guess how much this was hurting her. 'Is it possible, Bea?' I finished. She was wearing a red dress, so if my psychological analysis of women was better than usual that might mean she was psyching herself up for an ordeal. Not me, personally, I hoped.

'Yes,' she said. 'Dad was on something . . . It could have happened any moment.'

'Suppose medication was withheld.'

'Ask a doctor. I doubt if it would have had such a sudden result though.'

'What about those pills that induce an attack, or whose symptoms are similar? Name like ten sixty-six, no, ten eighty.'

'Dope in the cappuccino?'

Bea was doing her best, but I could see it was time I stopped, and I told her so.

'Don't worry, Jack. I need to know what happened, and even this I can take if I have to. The trouble is that I can't remember. I wasn't here when he died. I was still at uni, on the point of graduating. Mum called me to tell me the news, and by the time I reached home all I could think of was how to deal with her, rather than how Dad actually died. We both knew he had problems, so we accepted a natural death without question.'

'Polly never suspected anything was wrong?'

'I think she'd have told me if so. She'd have needed to confide in someone, and I would have been the only one near enough. Telling Rupert, Peter or Guy might have begun unfounded rumours that could be taken as fact.'

'So is it possible that seeing a bill for two cappuccinos set her thinking? After all, he could have paid for two coffees for himself. No,' I corrected myself. 'There were two people there, that's what the bill said. Table 5, two persons, two times cappuccino. Some casual companion would have had no reason to hide the fact of their presence. First the date alarmed Polly, then she looked at the bill more carefully and put two and two together.'

'And made five.' Bea pulled a face, but I said nothing. 'No, it couldn't have been five,' she continued, 'if murder was the result, and the companion never came forward. Two and two make four. And that four could well have been the motive for Mum's death. After she saw that receipt you found, she might have got in touch with whoever she thought—' She broke off. 'I can't bear it, Jack. Get it over quickly.'

I moved in to comfort her, aware that I was still finding it hard to think of her as Polly's daughter. So I drew back. I've never been a baby snatcher, and I wasn't going to start with Bea, especially at such a vulnerable time. Tough though it was to think in such terms, Tomas was far more her age group than I was. I watched her trying to control her emotions and persuaded her to ring Zoe to see if she could put her up for the night. Zoe was back in her own flat now, but luckily Rob wasn't with her.

As she drove away, I felt I was no further forward than I was before, except that Mike's death being due to murder couldn't be ruled out. Brandon wasn't going to buy that theory though, and in his shoes I wouldn't have either.

SEVENTEEN

Next morning, I had a rude awakening to reality as I looked down from the bedroom window on to the forecourt of my beautiful house and battered barn, and at the track leading up to them. In years to come the major highway that Frogs Hill Lane could by then be might have a subsection called Burnt Farm Corner. Not if I could help it. The Pits was going to be rebuilt quicker than the barn-raising in *Seven Brides for Seven Brothers*. And it wouldn't have a canary-coloured horror in front of it, with Harry Prince patiently awaiting my appearance inside it. I don't like my breakfast being ruined, so I went down right away.

'Thought you'd flown the country, Jack.'

'Just working for my living, Harry.'

'That's good,' he said cheerily. 'I popped along to remind you of my offer, in view of this . . .' He waved a pudgy hand at the remains of the barn. 'Must be hard to keep going, waiting for the insurance and so on. You can bank on me to be generous when we talk terms.'

'*If* we talk terms, Harry,' I answered equally cheerily, 'we'll go on market value, shall we? Much the best way all round.' *If* was as far from the truth as *when*, so far as I was concerned, but there was no point getting on Harry's wrong side, and I'd already had to turn down his offer of space as gracefully as I could.

'Just selling me a couple of those Giovannis would set you up nicely. I could broker a deal—'

'You're a dealer in cars, Harry, not fine art.'

He wasn't offended. He even laughed. 'Where fine art concerns cars, I reckon I know my market.'

Did he indeed? I'd remember that in view of what Dave had told me. 'Mike Davis, Harry,' I said, anxious to change the subject in case I was forced to tell him point-blank that those Giovannis weren't coming his way.

'What about him?'

'Any gossip at the time of his death that it was no accident?'

The pause was a shade too long. 'Suicide, you mean? No way.'

'Come off it, Harry. Murder. Like Polly's.'

He emerged from the canary-coloured monster a trifle shakily and came right up to me to convey his message.

'Remember I told you to watch a few Ps and Qs? You've forgotten to watch, Jack.'

'Sometimes the Qs get a mite too interesting.'

'But the answer could be a lot hotter,' Harry said grimly.

'So there was gossip.'

Harry was white-faced now. 'Never reached Polly, I'll swear. Quiet corners only, and it died out. Leave it that way, Jack. I beg of you.'

I was shaken and dropped my guard, because he seemed genuinely worried. 'How can I?'

'Easily. What's the point of raking up Mike's death all over again?'

'There's a point if it's linked to Polly's.' I'd gone further than I meant to.

'Then I'd be very careful indeed, Jack.' There was no sign of a grin on his jovial face now. He was sweating with something that looked fear, not the last of the summer sun. 'Look,' he almost bleated, 'why would anyone have wanted to murder Mike? He was a greedy conniving rogue, but murder? No.'

The pot calling the kettle black? 'That's why, Harry. Mike *was* a rogue.'

'He wouldn't have double-crossed anyone.' He was getting defensive.

'There are rumours he left a stash of cash behind that Polly either didn't know about or didn't care to use.'

'Rumours,' he said uneasily, 'don't mean a thing.'

Not in my experience. 'Try this one, Harry,' I said without much hope. 'Car cloning.'

'What about it?' He looked very cautious, which was interesting. After all, everyone who has a TV knows about car cloning.

Where to go from there? I spoke without thinking twice. 'Heard of a chap called Mason Trent?'

This time I thought he'd pass out. When he recovered enough breath to speak, he was already running for his car. 'Get lost, Jack. You're not bad, but you're mad, and you're bloody dangerous to know.'

It was a good morning, as soon as Harry Prince had rushed for his canary monster and accelerated down Frogs Hill Lane. By good, I mean that not only did no one cosh me, but also that I had a call from Brian Woollerton. Not only had I not expected to hear from him at all, but it was also actually in the time limit I had mistakenly promised Dave.

I hardly recognized Brian's hoarse and nervous whisper. 'Barton Lamb, village off the A12, and you didn't hear it from me.' The phone was slammed down, but I didn't care. Brian had come up trumps.

Dave heard the news in minutes, as I risked Brian or his informant having pulled a fast one on me. I didn't have to wait long before he rang back with an invitation to join his team on the raid, but I turned it down as he had a better job for me. I could now collect Peter Winter's stolen Merc from a pound in south London and drive it back to him, with the proviso that I didn't mention where it had been found or why it was there. The fewer people who knew about a case in which Mason Trent was concerned the better, he told me. No problem. This job was much more to my taste, since I could take the glory and press Peter some more over Mike Davis.

I didn't warn him, and Peter goggled in amazement as early on Thursday evening I drew up in the Merc with a flourish at his door, complete with trade plates since his own were missing, having arranged with Zoe to drive over and pick me up. He recovered his savoir faire quickly and drove the Merc immediately into his garage as though the next car thief were lurking up in the nearest tree, checking the security three times and double-locking the garage doors. I told him as much of the story as Dave had permitted me to tell, and that didn't include ruining his day with stories about the nefarious purpose to which his beloved car had been put.

'Come in and have a drink,' he said, beaming. 'My wife's abroad, so it's a good opportunity to talk.'

I graciously accepted, as Zoe would be arriving shortly to drive me back. I was wondering how and when to broach the subject of Mike's death, when he gave me the perfect opportunity.

'Incidentally,' he said, 'I've been thinking further about the money Mike was rumoured to have had.'

This sounded good, and I put the matter of his possible murder on one side. 'So have I,' I said encouragingly.

'If there's anything to the story – and, of course, with stories of buried treasure there rarely is – have you given any consideration to where it might be?'

'Not in the bank, that's for sure. Not a British one, anyway.' I wasn't going to mention the Lagonda pocket. The Lagonda was a goner to anyone but Bea, Zoe, Len, Dave and myself. 'Bea would have found the loot if it was in the house.'

'I believe it would still be in England. Mike wasn't the type to invest in foreign banks. He was more the money under the mattress type. So I wondered if you'd searched the barn.'

For a moment I thought he meant mine, but then I realized he was back to Polly's barn again. 'Not specifically. But there was no sign of anything other than the car itself. Anyway, the police would have searched.'

'That's true, of course. All the same, I can't help feeling it's close at hand. Much as I dislike thinking of Mike as a casual crook, it would explain why someone would want Polly out of the way.'

My cue. 'Could it also imply that his death wasn't a natural one?'

This was clearly a shock to him. 'Surely there's no evidence to suggest that?'

'Some, and it might help explain Polly's death.'

He looked very distressed. 'I certainly never conceived the notion at the time, and nor did Polly.'

'But then it also didn't enter your head that he was a crook.'

'That's true, but murder . . .' He shook his head in disbelief. 'Who? Some gangster?'

The easiest answer was yes.

On the drive home, I thought over what he'd said. That barn . . . I knew I shouldn't put Bea through any more traumas, but I had at least to ring her to put her in the picture. There was a short pause as Bea took in what I proposed – even if not why I had this sudden desire to visit the barn – but she had no problem with my doing so. I even mentioned buried treasure to her, which greatly amused her.

'Dad? If he'd ever had two pennies to rub together, we'd have known about it, or at least Mum would. He'd have boasted to the skies about it, so it's unlikely there's anything to be found in the barn.'

'Someone thought there was,' I pointed out. 'They broke in.'

'For the Lagonda – no, you're right. It was afterwards. That's strange. Anyway, search all you like for the missing millions. I'll keep the line clear for the good news.'

It wasn't so good when I got there. The barn door was open, and Tomas Kasek was already inside. 'What the hell are you doing here?' I roared.

He flushed. 'Beatrice said—'

'No, she didn't. She's not given anyone but me permission to be here, and certainly not you. Get out.'

'Mr Williams said—'

'And he didn't either. What are you looking for, exactly?'

His mouth was set obstinately, and he was clearly weighing up the odds of punching me – or, a nastier thought, stabbing me. But he couldn't take the risk. On the one hand, I might be a lot older than him, but on the other, I was taller, sturdier and trained. I told him this, but he barely flinched.

'You touch me, and I say you attack me. Mr Williams believe me, not you.'

I had two options. I could turn the little pipsqueak round in an armlock and make him sorry he'd left home, or I could be sensible. With Bea in mind, I tried the latter for once. It was quite an effort. He's just the sort of cocky type I dislike.

'I'm actually on your side, Tomas.' I didn't coo, but I didn't do too badly at neutrality. 'At least I am if you're innocent of Polly Davis's murder. I'm trying to find out who really did kill Polly and why. Mr Williams thinks you're innocent and, believe it or not, I think so too – probably,' I added.

He looked doubtfully at me and said nothing.

I sighed. 'If I thought you were guilty, I could call my chum at police HQ right now and put you right back inside. Bet Mr Williams doesn't really know you're here.'

Bullseye.

'OK,' I continued, 'now tell me what you're doing here.'

'I – the car.'

'Gone. Burnt. You know that. Why come back here?'

'Business.'

'What business?'

'Something that might be here. Money. I need it.'

Progress at last. 'Whose money?'

'Andy Wells's,' he muttered. He looked at me defiantly, as though this ended the discussion.

For me it began it. I didn't trust him one inch. 'You're on bail for Mrs Davis's murder. If you're innocent, you'd better start talking. And talk the *truth*.'

Some hopes. There was silence, and I could see he was scared. But what could be scarier than the idea of serving life for murder? Only murder itself.

'Mason Trent?' I suggested.

His face was all the answer I needed.

'Where did you get the key?' I continued.

'In the lock.'

'Feeble, Tomas. I'll take it. Mr Williams' key, I presume?'

He handed it over so quickly, I guessed he'd copied it and no doubt had another one. Duly noted.

'Bea will get an alarm system and new locks put on it, just in case you decide to check this missing money out again.'

I watched him until he had disappeared well along the track, then went inside again myself. Tomas had obviously had a good look and found nothing, and my attempts achieved the same negative result. Even though Tomas had heard the same rumours of money as I had, it wasn't there.

What really gave me the jitters was that Tomas had had Mason Trent's number in his mobile, dead or not. My work for Dave could be heading on a collision course with the Lagonda and Polly's murder.

That night I was dreaming of racing round Brand's Hatch track in a Ferrari. I was humming away merrily, gunning the engine, passing Paddock Hill Bend, certain that I was going to win the race, despite the fact that I appeared to be the only car competing in it. I was vaguely aware of people waving furiously from the stands and urging me on – or so I assumed. I didn't appear to have a helmet on, but nevertheless the sun was out and I was doing 140. Then I cornered Druid's Bend

– only to see what appeared to be the entire line-up of a
Formula 1 race coming towards me. *Towards me?*

I woke up sweating in terror, wondering what on earth had
put that into my dreaming mind. I have no great ambitions to
be a Formula 1 driver or even Formula 3. What I like is the
whole motoring experience – without the bad bits, of course.
The halcyon days of yore as one gently motored through
villages able to explore interesting minor roads and stop at
pubs that took one's fancy are long since past, but nevertheless
on a good day one can recreate them very satisfactorily even
in overcrowded southern England.

I tried to put my dream-cum-nightmare behind me, had
some breakfast, and duly rang the security people about Bea's
barn, after having suggested this to her. I said it was urgent,
and for good measure, since I knew their rep well, I asked
him to come to Frogs Hill too, ostensibly to quote on the Pits'
refit, but actually to improve security on the barn that now
sheltered the Lagonda. We're so remote here that if there's no
answer to the doorbell anyone could all too easily wander
round the back of the establishment – and that went for anyone
with a particular interest in checking that the Lagonda really
had disappeared.

Then the nightmare resurrected itself. Dave rang.

'Barton Lamb, Jack. No go. Sure you got the right place?
There's only a garage right out of *Heartbeat*.'

He didn't sound pleased, and I could hardly blame him. It
wasn't like Brian to pass on duff info, however. His team
prides itself on its professionalism. 'Any chance they did a
runner?' I asked. 'That's Mason Trent's specialty.'

'Possible,' Dave said grudgingly.

The nightmare then continued when I began to open the
mail. My mortgage company was pointing out that I was in
arrears – only just, I yelled in silent indignation – and what
did I propose to do about payment? If their Customer Services
line could be of any help . . . The next piece of mail was
better: the promised invitation from Rupert Stack to the private
view of Giovanni's paintings. It was cutting it fine, as it was
taking place that evening. I'd intended to go anyway, and it
now seemed a sensible move. I remembered Harry's lustful
hopes of getting his hands on my Giovannis. No way. I'd
rather the paintings went on the open market. Nevertheless, I

had to face facts, and perhaps that was what my dream had been subtly reminding me. Stark reality was racing down the track towards me and about to obliterate me. Or rather obliterate Frogs Hill Classic Car Restorations.

With Mason Trent leering at me from all directions, not to mention the BMW job for Dave, plus avenging Polly's death, I'd need satnav to navigate through the next few weeks.

EIGHTEEN

I decided to postponc calling Brian on the Trent issue. He'd know by now the info he'd given me was duff and would be expecting my call, so I'd let him stew in his own juice for a while. I'd stick closer to home.

Dan Burgess, for example. Comic Cuts Hero Dan might not be so squeaky clean as his Superman profile and artistic lean-ings suggested. I just couldn't see him as a painter of quaint cottages and cars. It didn't fit. A classic car man, yes. Made for a Maserati, but watercolours for money? What was the logical conclusion to that? Was he up to something with Andy Wells, perhaps at Mike Davis's suggestion? Was he just Dan the Dirty Spotter or Dan the Dirty Money Launderer? Was there a pocket in the Maserati, just as there was in the Lagonda?

As he knew Rupert, it occurred to me that he might turn up at the private view this evening in his capacity as motoring artist, even though he was hardly in the same field as Giovanni. I began to look forward to the evening ahead. Not only would it be a good chance to meet Giovanni again, but I might be able to glean more about those art thefts in which Trent had been involved, and perhaps still was. All that, and checking out Dan too. What an evening it might prove to be. The draw-back was that Lorna would be there, but I could survive that.

I opted in favour of driving up to town, as with any luck the congestion charge would be over by the time I arrived and it would avoid the rush for last trains in the event that I picked up on anything interesting. Rupert's gallery was in St James's, and so rather than take my chances on parking there, I put my Alfa in a car park near the Royal Festival Hall on the South

Bank, gave her a pat, told her to ward off any marauders with
that nice big burglar alarm of hers, and set off to walk over
Westminster Bridge to the Embankment and wind my way up
to St James's. I found the gallery easily enough, and very nice
it was too. Emporiums with one object in the window carefully
positioned aren't my usual style, but they reek of money. Inside
I could see the merry hordes, and I braced myself for ordeal
by Lorna in case she felt that my appearance this evening was
due to contrition over my former coolness towards her charms.

I couldn't see her at first, although I knew she must be there
somewhere. Once inside, I remembered why I loved Frogs
Hill. I'd seen too much 'entertaining' like this in my oil days.
Fine for collecting names, but never count on it for collecting
friends. Even the former takes work, for working the room
takes skill, and I was out of practice. I could see my quarry
though – there was Dan Burgess, holding Giovanni in earnest
conversation. I thought Giovanni looked somewhat bemused,
but perhaps that was the champagne. I loved Giovanni best
when he, Dad and I used to slope off to the local trattoria to
while the hours away with wine and Giovanni's cheerful song
of rapture about every dame who walked by. When he tired
of that game, which was seldom, he'd start on the cars. What
Floyd was to cookery, Giovanni is to art; both treat their
specialty as illustrating the joys of life.

As Giovanni spotted me, something like life returned to his
eyes. He was outsmarted by Lorna, however, who slunk over
to me, dressed in silver like something out of an Art Deco
collection.

'Jack, darling, so glad you could make it.'

The slight pause before the 'make it' indicated she was still
furious at being turned down, but willing to overlook it if I
responded. Accordingly, I turned on what charm I could rustle
up to admire her, the gallery, the dress, Giovanni and so on.

'How's darling Bea?' she enquired anxiously.

'Doing fine,' I replied enthusiastically.

'Too young for you, Jack.'

Straight to the Achilles heel. I smiled, took a drink, told
her how *lovely* the party was, and moved away, followed, I
was sure, by very angry eyes. Rupert was easier going. He
greeted me as graciously as he would a multimillionaire about
to purchase half of Giovanni's work on show.

'My type of art,' I said. 'You should do well.'

He smiled. 'Giovanni has offered to put my Bentley into one of his masterpieces, but only if I sell all his paintings here. It's a great incentive.'

'How would he plan to use it?'

'He murmured something about the Bentley Boys.'

'All watching approvingly from the heavens?' The Bentley Boys, famous for their thirties' glamour and racing exploits, featured such legendary names as Woolf Barnato, son of the South African diamond millionaire, Barney. I couldn't quite see how Giovanni could fit real people into his usual fantasy background, but he is a law unto himself.

'*Ciao*, Jack.' With tears in his eyes, Giovanni embraced me like a long lost brother. He must be several years older than me, I suppose, certainly in his early fifties, but somehow one never thought of age in connection with Giovanni. He was just himself: tanned, wrinkled, blue-eyed, black-haired and as lithe as a lizard. I love watching him in his studio (a privilege granted to few, but luckily the few had included Dad, and therefore it was extended to his son). He nips around from canvas to canvas. Not for him, the dedication to one painting at a time.

'Like women, Jack. I tell your papa, one for sunny days, one for gloomy, one for laughing, one for crying, and one for *bambini*, yes?'

Hardly in line with today's thinking, but the twinkle in his eye always reminds me that back in his Tuscan home there is only ever one woman in sight. Pia, his wife, never travels with him. She knows nothing about art – only about Giovanni and the best Italian cooking I've ever tasted.

'What are you doing here? You come to buy?' he asked.

'Wish I could.'

'To sell?' he asked suspiciously.

'Not that either.'

'To see me?' His eyes lit up when I nodded. Well, it was partly true. So far I'd already picked up that selling just one of them would keep the mortgage happy for a year or two. 'We'll go drink, eh?'

He looked ready to leave straightaway, but I managed to persuade him this wasn't a good idea in the interests of good relations with Rupert.

'You are right,' he agreed. 'Someone might steal my paintings if I go drink.'

'Unlikely, wonderful though they are.'

'Yes. Wonderful,' he agreed. 'But much theft around. Big, expensive, good paintings. Almost as good as mine: Rembrandt, Rubens . . .'

Joking he might be, but the conversation was going in exactly the right direction. 'That's the problem with paintings. Just like classic cars, they can be stolen to order. Have any of yours been taken?'

'*Si*. But small ones, small time, you know. Now my paintings fetch more money, the insurance goes up, and up some more and more.' As did Giovanni's hand, managing to knock someone's glass over. When that was dealt with, he added, 'Especially insurance this year.'

'Why's that?'

'More theft.'

'Do the paintings go abroad or stay here, do you think?'

Giovanni looked mysterious. 'Don't know. Ask Mr Burgess.'

'Where is he?' I'd lost sight of him since my earlier spotting.

He inclined his head, and between a lot of bling and chiffon dresses I caught a glimpse of Dan, so I decided to seize the moment and go over to him. Giovanni seized another glass of champagne and stayed where he was. Celebs let people come to them; they don't do the going. I liked his style.

'Hi, Dan.' I reached Mr Superman. He really did look like it tonight. I almost expected him to dash into the loo and come out clad in dinky boots and blue and red tights. 'Giovanni tells me you're up to scratch with the stolen art scene,' I joked.

Dan blinked. 'I don't think so,' he informed me cautiously.

Just my luck. A serious type. 'Lot of art crime around now, I gather. You're an artist. Does it worry you?'

Very suspicious now. 'Yeah. Rupert, anyway. In the art business, you get used to being offered fakes too.'

'Interesting.' I might as well be polite.

'No one fakes mine.' Mighty chuckle from Superman, at which I did my best to double up with mirth. I was so successful that Rupert came over to share the fun.

'Just having a good laugh about art crime,' I told him merrily.

He gave me an odd look. 'A most amusing subject,' he managed. 'Except, of course, if you're the victim.'

'Not likely to be in that position.'

'You may be soon. Giovanni tells me you have several of his paintings.'

'Good news,' I said heartily, wishing I'd never started this conversation. I didn't want the art crime to include Frogs Hill, and I was none too sure of Rupert. '*Is* Giovanni right about theft increasing again?'

'Undoubtedly. There was the Rubens from Pulbright Hall a couple of weeks ago and a Constable.'

'And Talbot Place in Suffolk, of course,' I threw in knowledgeably. 'Looks like organized crime by the same operator.'

'Could be.' Dan put his oar in too. 'And that place in Sussex.'

'The same outfit, I would think,' Rupert said, going on to talk about the different levels of theft. The major works would be stolen for ransom, and the next level down would be sold abroad where they're not so well known. 'And of course,' he added, 'there are the maverick thefts stolen sometimes merely for the thief's desire to have something beautiful in his possession. If you can't afford to buy it and are keen enough, it's one option to pinch someone else's.'

I thought of the Lagonda, I thought of a Cord Beverley, I thought of a Porsche 356, translated their value as beautiful and desirable objects into art terms, and understood what he meant.

'Do you get approached with hot canvases?' I asked as casually as I could, but not sure where I was going with this.

The answer was quick in coming and very clipped. 'Stolen no, fakes yes.'

By the time I'd drunk my one ritual glass of champers and another to keep it company, I decided I would leave. There was no chance of a cosy dinner with Giovanni and/or Rupert, as the latter had made it clear that Giovanni was his property that evening. I wasn't sure that Giovanni was too keen on this outcome, but business is business, and he is the first person to agree with that. I was disappointed that not much seemed to have emerged from the evening other than getting me away from the problems of Frogs Hill. Except, perhaps, that I had been able to note that Dan and Rupert seemed on very good terms.

Taxi or foot? The long walk back to the car in the evening air would be good for me, so I chose that. Giovanni offered a last ditch attempt to accompany me, but Rupert scotched it, and indeed I did too. The rate he was drinking, I didn't want him falling down in the gutter, so we made arrangements to meet in Kent. He told me Rupert was holding an art show for charity in Kent tomorrow week, and he'd promised to attend with one or two of his paintings.

'I come to Frogs Hill and admire my pictures,' he informed me disarmingly. 'I tell you what a fortune you hold, Jack.'

I believed him. I'd just glimpsed the price list.

I like cities at night. They come to life in an entirely different way from their daytime personas. There's something about walking along darkened streets while lights are on in the houses and buildings around you, even if they're only business lights left burning for sales and security reasons. Even the cars going past look mysterious, and when one turns off along the minor roads and alleys one has the sense of walking through centuries of history, especially in London. In the past one wouldn't have dared to walk through alleys even in the West End without risking being garrotted or stabbed. Some things never change.

To avoid walking through the Park, I headed for Admiralty Arch and then down to Charing Cross and Hungerford Bridge. By the time I reached Villiers Street, however, I was beginning to have an uneasy feeling that I wasn't alone. Of course, I wasn't speaking literally. There were plenty of folk around, but as I went up the steps to the bridge, the prickle was still there. By walking alone, one's basic animal senses have a chance to speak for themselves, and mine were beginning to awaken. One is rarely alone in London at night, and yet it's amazing how suddenly one can find oneself deserted. As it was unlikely that someone was choosing exactly the same route as I was, at exactly the same pace, to get back across the river to the car park, I came to the reluctant conclusion that I should not be musing about the history abounding in Villiers Street but about my own safety in case Slugger Sam had fancied a day in London. The hairs on the back of my neck were definitely prickling, and it was nothing to do with my crew-cut hair. The river looked peaceful enough, but halfway across the bridge I stopped and looked round. Nothing untoward. A few people were strolling in the same direction as me, and several coming the other way, but no one I recognized.

Relief was followed by a slight regret that this wasn't going to be High Noon, with my enemy marching steadily towards me in the middle of the River Thames, in order to slug it out on Hungerford Bridge. That rang a faint bell in my mind, which I couldn't place. I didn't stop to write a sonnet on the beauties of the view, however, like dear old Wordsworth on the next bridge upriver. Instead I quickened my pace to the other side. There were still late concert-goers outside the Festival Hall, and looking down on them it could have been a scene from Lowry, pinhead figures scuttling away for trains and taxis.

Lowry. Art. *Stolen* art. Now that, I thought, was something that would have suited Polly down to the ground.

And then I did a double take. I'd been asleep at the starting switch. *It worked*! It fitted. It was the answer at last. Polly's love of art, her love of adventure . . . I'd leave the ethics out for the moment. So sure I was right, I stood stock still under the bridge. This was a different scene altogether, like walking into a dark El Greco, and I quickly moved on. Here one could all too easily have a rendezvous with a gun or destiny.

The bell rang in my mind again and this time sharply. Even I couldn't miss it.

My dream. The Formula 1 front line rushing towards me at Brand's Hatch. The people in the stands had not been waving but warning me. You're on the wrong track, they'd been yelling. And so I had been. The *Lagonda*. I'd been following will o' the wisp stories about buried cash and laundering money in the Lagonda. But those spaces in the car, the one behind the rear seat and even the one above the petrol tank. Not used for money. Used, surely, oh surely, for *canvases*.

And that was when it hit me. For real. From behind.

I hadn't been wrong. Someone had been following me. Someone had it in for me. It was not a cosh this time; it was an arm round my neck about to strangle me. Luckily, I was on firm ground here thanks to my oil days. A back kick, a thrust forward and a twist, and it was the other chap lying on firm ground. I hadn't laid him out though, and there'd be no ripping off the mask to reveal who it was. He was up immediately and had me again in his grip, but again I manoeuvred

my way out. This time he made off, as some brave folk were
coming to my aid. Panting and coughing, I supported myself
by the car-park fence, while solicitous people murmured about
muggers and gangs and ringing the police. No gang, this. Too
much of a coincidence. My attacker had been Dan Burgess's
height, but not his build. Not Slugger Sam's either. Nor Rupert
Stack's – though I played with the idea. I wasn't sure about
him.

Art, I said to myself as I sat in the car, wondering whether
I felt as good as I'd assured my rescuers I did. Art, and Polly.
Of course. But where did I go from here? And how hard would
someone try to stop me next time?

NINETEEN

I didn't waste time dreaming that night. I had to make
progress, and quick. I slept like the log my attacker had
done his best to make me into and arose on Saturday morning
knowing just where I was going and what I was after. There
was only a week to go before Rupert's art show on the thir-
teenth, and that seemed an unmissable opportunity to check
out my new lead on Polly's death – tentative lead, I reminded
myself, but it hadn't escaped me that wherever I turned I
eventually came back to Rupert Stack. Stolen art? He had a
golden alibi for the time of Polly's death. I had brooded over
this on my way home last evening, but I was forced to concede
that there was no way he could have hosted that meeting on
Tuesday morning and been down in Kent shooting Polly an
hour later. Theoretically possible, but the authorities aren't
keen on private jets taking off from Piccadilly.

A thousand questions popped up. Was Polly still involved
in the business when she died? If, that is, she ever was. Once
again I seemed to be jumping so speedily from one leaf to
another that Frogs Hill could have been named after me.

Could that pocket at the rear of the Lagonda really have
held masterpieces of art? Again, theoretically possible, and if
Polly were involved it would be much more likely than its
having been used for money laundering.

First port of call was the Lagonda. Cursing the time it took to negotiate all my new security measures, I opened the barn doors and found her safely inside gazing out at me with those mournfully inadequate eyes. No doubt about it, this lady deserved something classier than laundered money inside her. Nevertheless, she looked as if butter wouldn't melt in her engine, let alone have canvases illicitly behind her rear seat and on top of her petrol tank.

Seeing the Lagonda there steadied me for some reason. Fantasy began to dissolve and a more chilling picture arose. The more I looked at that so innocent-looking seat, the more I could picture Polly and Mike's lives – and perhaps deaths – as they had really been. Polly, lacking adventure after her former high profile job, and Mike, game for risk at any cost, could well have been smuggling stolen canvasses or drawings across the Channel. Their frequent trips to continental car shows would hide the rare trips on less innocent pleasures, although visits to receivers could also have coincided with the shows. The game, as they saw it, would have extra spice as they faked the photos for that make-believe album to prove their presence at these innocuous events. If this were not just a scenario but fact, would it make me think the less of Polly? My bones were telling me that it was indeed fact. That made me all the more frustrated because, having been deprived of Mike, she had been killed when her love of life might, just might, be returning.

But there lay the nub of it. Did she die because she was still playing Mrs Art Thief, or was it because of what she might have discovered about Mike's death? I remembered yet again that look she had given the car when I had first met her. Of course she had loved that Lagonda. Of course she didn't want to get rid of it; for her it conjured up her whole marriage to Mike and all they had been through together. She would still keep it registered in order not to draw attention to a sudden disappearance, but she removed the number plates and logbooks from the car itself in case of unwelcome visitors. Such as me. That made me gulp, and it took a moment or two to see the Lagonda clearly again. There seemed to be some kind of mist over my eyes.

Forward, I told myself. I played with the notion that there might be or had been a Leonardo or Van Gogh hidden in

Polly's barn, and that, not a pile of banknotes, was what the rumours of missing money were all about. Money would tie with an art racket, of course – all too well. The downside was that in that case Polly must have known about it. I couldn't wait to get to Greensand Farm and back to the barn.

I gave the Lagonda a last loving pat. No doubt DI Brandon's forensic lab could find proof of presence of canvas or paint in the car, but even without that I was increasingly sure of what it had been used for. Next stage, if she and Mike were the brains behind the thefts, there must still have been – and still be – others involved. After all, Mike was undoubtedly a car dealer, and Polly lived in Kent, not London. Neither of them could physically have shimmied through windows at dead of night to carry out the actual thefts. It was possible, therefore, that they'd conducted the whole operation from Greensand Farm, although unlikely. Polly might still have been running it, but I was inclined to think not. I couldn't see her dealing in getaway cars and the likes of Mason Trent. And the last question, and perhaps the most important: did Bea know anything about her mother's involvement? I couldn't believe she did.

Nevertheless, I ought to ring her right away to make sure her barn was secure, so I turned to go.

The first thing I saw was a pair of smart leather boots.

There were on two sturdy legs planted outside blocking my exit. My eyes travelled up. I didn't know those boots – or the grinning face above them. Swarthy, longish black hair with occasional curls, black shirt, jeans and a chain round the neck. Thirties. Tall. Straight out of Hollywood? Doctor Who?

Neither.

'Mason Trent,' announced the boot-owner. 'Jack Colby, I presume. Heard you been asking about me.'

Now that I knew what I was dealing with, I recovered quickly. 'We've met. Last night, I believe.'

His eyes slid over me. 'Maybe.' Then they slid past me. 'Nice car.'

The Lagonda. I went cold. There was nothing I could do, but brazen it out – if he gave me the chance. He wasn't going to risk another flooring from me, so the odds were that he was armed. I couldn't see any obvious signs, but he hadn't come bearing goodwill.

'Heard you lost the little darling in a fire,' he continued chattily.

Who from? Harry, Andy, Tomas – did it matter? Not just as that moment, no. 'Forgot where I left it,' I said casually. Keep the cool going. 'What can I do for you?'

'Not a lot. Car detective, you call yourself, don't you? Police work?'

Corner this carefully, I warned myself. 'Work where I can get it.' Nice, I thought. Imply I'm anybody's for a fiver.

'Right.'

I saw his hand go to a pocket. So this was it. I stiffened. Perhaps I could somersault myself at his feet – stupid, stupid . . . I didn't move.

The hand emerged again, and it wasn't holding a gun. The hand stretched out towards me.

'Here's my card, mate.'

I stared at the revoltingly bright-pink object announcing Smiths' Restorations and Repair Shop with an address in Barton Lamb.

'Very funny,' I observed.

'Yeah. Used to know Mike Davis. Nice chap,' he informed me. 'Pity he went the way he did.'

Play this up front, I told myself. Taking a deep breath, I became matey. 'Never knew him myself, but I liked Polly. You heard she was murdered too?'

That did it. He hadn't missed the 'too', not Mr Mason Trent. 'Yeah,' he remarked, and the atmosphere grew chillier. He didn't say or do anything. He was waiting for me to make the running. OK, I could take a hint.

'Thanks for the card,' I said politely. 'What would I want to talk to you about?'

'Mike owed me.'

'Money?'

'Yeah.'

'Art money?'

A long pause now. 'If you were to stumble across it, Jack, let me have it, eh?'

To my amazement – and relief – he began to stroll back towards his car. No bright-pink flashy job here, a modest Ford. The window was down, and he leaned out for a farewell word:

'Oh, and, Jack, tell your chum Dave sorry we had to move

out.' I looked at the pink card – and he grinned. 'We won't be back.'

I tried: 'So if I want to get in touch with you?'

'Whistle and I'll come to you. Just whistle, Jack.' He drove off laughing, but I was under no illusions. I was on probation. One more move he didn't like, and the laughing would stop.

I felt as if I was watching the Tardis pull out, but there was no benevolent Doctor inside. There was an urgent job for me to do. Trent wasn't going to wait for me to hunt for that money – he'd be off to do it himself. And Bea might be on her own. I whipped my mobile out quicker than Clint Eastwood.

'*Bea*!' I almost yelled down the phone, relieved to find her in, but terrified for her safety at the same time. 'I'm on my way. Don't open the door to *anyone* except me.'

'OK.' Bea sounded as though she had this command thrust at her every day. 'Rob and Zoe are here though.'

I never thought I'd be glad to hear of Rob's presence anywhere. 'Great,' I said.

Even so, I leapt into the Alfa feeling like Doctor Who myself, and when I arrived at Greensand Farm, I dashed for the front door. At least there was no Ford in the forecourt. Nevertheless, I fell in the door – opened by Rob.

'Bea's OK, is she?'

'Mind telling us what this is about?' asked the supercilious little twit.

'Chap called Mason Trent. On the hunt for missing money.'

'Aren't we all?' Rob drawled as Zoe and Bea emerged from the kitchen. At least they had the decency to look anxious.

'Are you all right, Jack?' Bea asked.

She was actually worried about me, bless her. I gave them an edited account of my morning so far and the advisability of our getting down to the barn soonest.

'Why?' Zoe asked practically. 'This Mason Trent might be hiding behind the door.'

'But he might find—' I began. 'Stupid of me. We know there's nothing there.'

'And even if the dosh is somewhere around,' Rob said languidly, 'I'd sooner be here than there if he does show up.'

I longed to say I'd protect him, the little darling, but for Zoe's sake held back. I'd not been thinking straight, of course.

There was no ring at the doorbell for the next few hours,

and by the afternoon Zoe and Rob decided they had a mission elsewhere, but said they would be back later and stay on for supper. I pointed out that no way could Bea stay here tonight alone, so I'd sleep over here again. This caused a raised eyebrow from Rob, which surprised me until I thought it through. The trouble was that this place was beginning to seem much like home, and Bea such a fixture that I almost wished she wasn't too young for me. Grow up, Jack, I told myself as I looked at her slumped in the garden – in Polly's garden. I still thought of it that way, and I began to realize it wasn't Bea so much as Polly for whom I was still hankering. Bea was the closest I could get to the dream, but she dwelt in another country, one which was twenty years younger than mine.

'What's that bruise?' she asked curiously, when Rob and Zoe left. She was carefully inspecting my face. 'I've been dying to ask you, but thought you might not want to make a public confession. Another cosh on the head?'

'A mere tussle, and I won. Not serious.'

She looked relieved, which was pleasing.

'Bea,' I continued, 'I've a theory to put to you. You won't like it.'

'Try me.'

'How about art theft? Big time.'

She looked blank to my relief. 'What about it?'

'Smuggling paintings through customs in the Lagonda.'

She was there in a flash. 'No money laundering then? Mum and Dad together?'

'Right first time.' I proceeded to explain, almost forgetting that it was her parents we were talking about, but luckily she seemed to take it with the same attitude.

'What about after Dad died?' she asked. 'Mum did travel occasionally, but not in the Lagonda. I truly didn't know she still had it.'

'I believe she would have given up after your father died. No fun without him.'

Bea went very pale. 'Then she must have been killed because she realized he'd been murdered too, just as you suggested. It's still one big guess though.'

'But tenable, and it implies that there were other people involved in the art operation. Maybe your parents were just cogs in the wheel.'

'Must have been quite big cogs,' Bea said bravely. 'My father wouldn't stand for being a lowly cog. He thought big.' She paused. 'Does this mean there would be no buried treasure after all, or that it's more likely?'

'I don't know.' The unpleasant thought occurred to me that Mike and Polly might have been responsible for bringing back the cash for the stolen paintings. Smuggling art out and money in. Handing the cash over – minus a bit. Perhaps not handing any cash over . . . Arguments over the cash. A hundred scenarios, but they all came down to the fact that only Mike and Polly would know where the loot was, and therefore murder would seem an inappropriate route to take.

'If there really is buried treasure,' Bea said with a wobbly voice, 'I don't think Mum knew about it. Fiddling the till might have been Dad's private venture. He saw that kind of thing as exciting, but Mum didn't. Not where money was concerned. So it's all too possible he never told her.'

'If you're right, Bea, I need to check the barn again.'

'I'll come with you.'

'No way,' I said firmly. 'And I'll wait till Rob and Zoe are back here before I go dashing down there. That's if you don't mind my poking around?'

'Be my guest.' She made an attempt at humour. 'Don't run off with the loot, though.'

I promised her that after the British Museum she would be the first to hear about it.

TWENTY

For all my brave words, I was not hopeful of finding anything buried in that barn, however hard I looked. The only thing that decided me on this venture was that I wasn't the only person interested in it, although it was probable that by now they'd come to the same conclusion as I had. It was worth a second go, however, so I left my car outside the farm – as a subtle hint to Mason Trent that I was around if he wanted a repeat match after last night's – and walked through the farm to the barn.

As I did so, smelling the earth and trees around me, I wondered how many times Polly and Mike must have made this journey. They almost seemed ahead of me as I went through the kissing gate. I imagined them playing around there and laughing at the 'game'. I began to feel less confident that I was going to achieve anything at the barn. I was a mere intruder into what was *their* secret. I began to wish I'd taken Rob up on his half-hearted offer to come with me. Especially as I felt my stomach muscles tighten. I could see what lay ahead of me – or rather who.

I wasn't going to be alone at the barn. Big chap though I am, I felt the chill of fear strike again. Then I relaxed a little as I saw it was not Mason Trent but Guy Williams, and unpleasant words would be the worst that could pass between us. As I drew nearer, however, I sensed there was something strange going on. He wasn't looking at me, though my arrival must by that time have been obvious. He was standing quite still, looking at the ground or something lying at his feet. He didn't even look up as I approached and called out to him. It was almost as though he had been expecting me.

He was not far from where Polly had lain. And then I saw what he was looking at. Another dead body, more blood, more brains spilling out over the dry ground.

'Tomas,' Guy said to me matter-of-factly, as I felt my stomach heave. 'He's been shot.'

He must be in shock, I realized, and I must be too. I swallowed hard and tried to discipline myself into calm. 'Have you called the police?'

'No.'

'I'll do it.'

My oil business days had taught me it's wise never to be far from a phone, and I had my mobile in my pocket. My mouth felt dry. Should I ask Guy outright if he'd killed him? He didn't look like Guy the Gorilla any more; he was out of his depth, struggling to communicate, only able to jerk out the words:

'Gun's over there. Not mine.'

He was right. Tomas Kasek's body was hunched up on its side and the gun tucked into its curve.

'Did you use it?'

He looked at me as if I were mad. 'He was dead when I got here. I didn't touch it.'

I believed him. We were communicating OK now. On the same side. At least I hoped we were.

I made the call, and we retreated to the same tree trunk I'd sat on before. Correction, *I* retreated there, but it was only with difficulty that I persuaded Guy to move. He remained gazing down at the body, and I had to return, grab him and drag him back with me. Then he began to go to pieces. He clasped his trembling hands, as though that would stop them. But it didn't, and talking was only going to make it worse. I reckoned I had to push it though. No time would be wasted once Brandon got the message, as he undoubtedly would.

'OK,' I said to Guy gently. 'Tell me. Before the police get here.'

It took him a while, but he managed to speak. 'He was dead. Killed hours ago, I reckon. I came to see where he'd got to. I touched him.'

I wondered whether the irony of the situation had occurred to him. Our roles were reversed from the day he and Polly had found me apparently looting the barn. If so, he didn't comment. Everything served to confirm my impression that he was innocent. What on earth would Guy want to kill Tomas for? Guy had been his main supporter, and one of the few who believed him innocent.

'Any sign of anyone else around when you arrived?'

It couldn't have been coincidence that Mason Trent had appeared at Frogs Hill that morning. No sign of a gun, but that was no proof. Would he have been fool enough to come to see me, however, if he'd had every intention of meeting and killing Tomas? Or had that been mere chance, because Tomas and he had arrived at the same time on the same quest: buried treasure.

I glanced across at the barn, trying to avoid looking at the body lying outside it. I couldn't be sure from this distance, but it looked as though the door was still locked. The security system was in place, and Bea would have heard if there was an intruder.

'No.'

'He was here the day before yesterday too. I saw him off, and Bea got a new security system fitted. I told him I'd throw the book at him if he came again – yet he obviously did.'

'There's no current maintenance work in this field,' Guy

told me. 'There's no legitimate reason for his presence. I came because someone told me they'd seen Tomas heading this way, so I hoofed it up here.'

A crazy idea came to me. 'Listen, Guy, we've about two minutes before the police arrive. I've got the keys, and I'd like to go into that barn to look for something before they get here. Will you bear witness that that's all I'm doing?'

A return of his old spirit, hardly surprisingly. 'No, I bloody won't. We'll wait for the police.'

He was right, and I told him so – reluctantly. If Tomas was so determined, there was a strong chance there *was* something in that barn. The initial attraction must have been the Lagonda, perhaps in his role as spotter for his Polish brother's network. But that didn't explain why he'd kept returning to the barn when it no longer housed the Lagonda. Maybe he was working for someone else too? Someone who didn't want that secret pocket found, and who had gone to the lengths of trying to burn Frogs Hill down in order to be sure the Lagonda vanished for good – and who had commissioned Tomas to search the barn thoroughly after the car had departed. If I needed more evidence that Polly and Mike weren't the only players in their game this could be it. It surely showed that they couldn't have been the Mister Bigs of the organization. Which brought me back to buried treasure.

It might seem heartless for me to have been thinking about buried treasure, but it served the purpose of taking my mind off Tomas's body and the memories it raised of Polly. Tomas's face was half hidden from me, but it didn't take much imagination to think what the shot had done to him.

The usual routine of a couple of constables arriving first to assess the situation didn't apply in this case. Brandon arrived with the whole caboodle, so eager was he to nab me. He looked most pleased to see me, as though it made his job all the easier for him and he could arrest me right away. Fortunately, Guy confirmed my story that he was here first this time, to Brandon's disappointment. No doubt he was wondering whether I shot poor Tomas, hid in a nearby tree and then returned, but if so he didn't bother to waste his breath.

I waited to give my evidence, bore the removal of my shoes patiently, and Guy and I sat side by side on our tree trunk, donning our crime scene shoes.

We were then left on our perch to await Brandon's pleasure, and Guy grew surprisingly chatty after his former reticence. 'Tomas has been strange recently, Jack. Not surprising, I suppose, with a murder charge hanging over his head. Not that he seemed worried, more . . .'

I helped him out. 'Belligerent?'

He thought about this carefully. 'Smug's more the word. The sort of "I know more than you do, mate" look.'

I hadn't taken to Tomas, but he was young and he probably merely suffered from the arrogance of youth; he was brash and self centred rather than evil, and money was a high priority. I wondered whether, baulked of finding his crock of cash gold at the end of this rainbow, he'd been daft enough to look for it in other directions. Such as from Mason Trent.

I felt honour bound to suggest this to Brandon when he marched over to us, but he forestalled me with the usual: 'And what were you doing down here again, Mr Colby?'

'I came to look for something in the barn on Bea Davis's account – you can check with her.'

'We'll do that. What's the something?'

'Money.' I had hesitated whether to tell him, but the police would have to know sooner or later, so there was no sense in holding it back. I decided what I would hold back, however, was any mention of Mr Trent or art theft until I'd consulted Dave. I'd no proof that Trent had been planning to visit this barn.

'What money?'

'Cash left by Mike Davis.' How honest can one get?

Brandon just grunted though. 'Keys?' he barked.

I handed Bea's set over. 'Does Tomas – the victim – have keys on him?'

A scathing look. 'Yes. They're evidence.'

'Of course,' I said meekly. 'Thought it might provide a motive.'

'How?'

'Money always does.'

Brandon just grunted again and said grandly he'd bear it in mind.

It was well into the evening by the time Brandon said we could go. Sarah had come down to join Guy, after he had rung her, but there was no sign of Bea. Nor could I bear to ring

her. She must have wondered where I was, and I just hope
she hadn't heard the sirens and connected me to them. Instead
I asked permission to go with a PC if necessary to break the
news to her myself. Permission was grudgingly given.

All the way back to the farm I rehearsed what to say.
Everything seemed wrong, but I couldn't leave it to the PC
to do, even though Zoe and Rob would be there as extra
support. In the end my telling her came out naturally. Bea
looked alarmed, but that was partly seeing me arrive with the
law.

'Sweetie, there's a problem,' I told her as gently as I could,
glad she had come to the door by herself. 'You don't have to
come back with me, but you do need to know what's happened.'

'What? Who?' She looked almost paralysed with fear.

'It's Tomas. I'm afraid he's dead. Guy found him.'

I'd hoped to get away with not telling her where he was
found, but I was unlucky. The PC saw his chance of importance. 'I understand it's your barn, Miss Davis.'

'That's where . . .' Bea swayed on her feet, and I had to
remember that she and Tomas had been lovers, even if the
relationship had been a short one. 'I'm coming with you,' she
managed to say. 'I'll get a coat.'

'What's up?' Rob the Rabbit was scuttling out of the kitchen
and on the scent, and in the end he and Zoe came with Bea and
myself, PC still in tow, as we went back to the barn.

The coat Bea had grabbed must have been Polly's because
I recognized it. That sent a shiver through me. Apart from the
PC telling Bea a few things about Tomas that she didn't need
to know, we walked in silence. I took Bea's hand in token
support, for which she seemed grateful.

As we walked along the track, we had to stand aside for
the mortuary van to pass us. I was relieved – at least there
was one ordeal she didn't have go undergo, and she didn't
seem to realize that's what the van was.

So far as I could tell from the perch to which all of us
except for Bea were promptly banished again, Brandon went
gently with her, and when she returned to us, Guy, too, was
in comforting mode. Luckily, Sarah homed in as chief
comforter together with Zoe, which kept Rob out of the picture.
It hadn't escaped either Guy's or my attention, however, that
Bea was bound to be a suspect. Tomas was her former lover,

there'd been a first-class family row over him – all on record – and worst of all Brandon might come up with the idea that she could have shot him in revenge for his killing her mother. I knew none of these scenarios would get past first base, but Bea could do without them.

'Mr Colby –' Brandon summoned me as daylight faded – 'you might like to know there's nothing in that barn. It's been checked. If Kasek did have plans to break in, whoever murdered him got him first, as the alarms didn't go off. But who, Jack?'

For a moment, Brandon looked almost human.

I could have murmured Mason Trent, I could have told him about the possible stolen art connection, but that wasn't possible without Dave's permission. Anyway, I was still trying to get my head round what the hell was happening.

It took until Tuesday for the crime scene to be lifted, and time seemed to pass in interminable interviews and talking to everyone under the sun. Guy seemed to have become a bosom friend of mine, so had Sarah – and as for Bea, hats off to her. She and Guy dealt with the police, and I rang Brian, assuring him that there were no hard feelings over Barton Lamb, and in gratitude he said he'd come up with the goods on Dave's missing BMW. I rang Dave about this and about Tomas's death – he'd already heard about it, of course, and he told me that the gun was unregistered and offered little in the way of prints, which didn't surprise me. I brought him up to speed with my run-in with Mason Trent and passed on his cheery message.

Dave sounded fairly friendly about it, so I launched into the magic words: 'Art theft? Could the Davises have been mixed up with it?'

Funny how you can sense reactions over a phone line. Even from the silence I instantly knew just how unhappy Dave was over this. All he said was: 'Not your job, Jack.'

'My job too now, Dave. Believe me. Mason Trent had a special message for me too – my neck in particular – only I floored him first.'

Pause. 'Convince me.'

I spent some time doing just that, ending up with: 'Trouble is, I don't see Trent as a godfather in the art world, Dave. A Spanish master to him would be a man with a whip and a girl in a frilly dress doing the fandango.'

'Right.' He was making me work for it. 'Who then?'
'Give me a few days and I'll tell you.'

'Dave, you said Mason Trent ran the cloned getaway cars for the Talbot Place job.'

'Maybe I did.' Dave was still playing cautious. Then he opened up a crack. 'That Merc we got back was another of Trent's teasers to make us think he had us on the run. Which he has. Call in whatever favours you can, Jack, from whoever you have to. We've no line on Trent, and we need one.'

He told me to steer clear of art theft where Brandon was concerned – that was *his* business, not mine – and rang off, leaving me to puzzle a way through this quagmire. Mason Trent was thought still to be running a cloning business. Mike probably owed him money. Which presumed he could have been working with Mike over the art thefts. Mike was not an art expert, but Polly was. Was the reason for Mike's death the money? If so, how did Tomas's death fit in with Polly's and Mike's? Money again, or had it been coincidence that Tomas's body was found in exactly the same place? Tomas knew the Lagonda was no longer inside the barn, so the attraction had to be money – or canvases.

Whichever way I looked at it, I realized that the sooner I had another look there myself the better. I didn't believe that I was any cleverer than Brandon's team, but I had the advantage of knowing that the likelihood was that there was something *somewhere* in that barn. Stolen art, stolen money, whatever.

When Bea rang me that afternoon to say that the barn was now accessible, I was over at Greensand Farm like a shot. She told me she had pleaded for more time off work to cope with this emergency. 'Want to come with me this time, Bea?' I asked doubtfully. I was in two minds because the chain round Trent's neck might still be jingling with thoughts of that barn.

'Yes,' she said immediately. 'Dad used to say that if you can't find something, go to the place you've already searched and check it again. So I'm coming. I'll be OK if you're there.'

I swelled with pride. I felt like a million bucks – and I might even be going to find them.

It was raining, which was hardly auspicious, but we went anyway. Entering the barn was an ordeal for both of us, but I fixed my mind on buried treasure and hoped Bea was doing the same. We were faced with three bare walls, another with a door in it. It looked innocent of anything but piles of hay pushed to the sides and its iron roof. I examined the hay hopefully. Nothing. I gazed at the walls in despair, but there were no disguised holes to be found, no hollowed out bricks, and the roof was clear of secret pockets.

'It must be the floor,' I said. My only excitement so far had been seeing something that looked like a crack in it, but it had been a false start. There were plenty of cracks because the floor had been constructed in concrete squares like pavement slabs. My mind wasn't working fast enough, because it was Bea who queried this.

'Why?' she asked.

I stared at her, I stared at the floor. Where do you hide a body? Amongst other bodies. How do you hide a crack? Surround it with other cracks. Could that be why it was in squares? 'Perhaps one of them's loose,' I said, ever hopeful. None of them looked loose, and only logic made me give them a careful going over.

'How do we get it up when we've found it?' Bea asked as she watched me doing so. It sounds a silly question, but she was right.

'Crowbars?'

'Not for the first heave. Too fat. Call the Gorilla,' I ordered her. 'Got your mobile?'

She nodded.

'Tell him we want the digger.'

Bea giggled, but did as I suggested. I went on staring at that floor. 'That one?' I pointed at one that looked out of kilter. It was at the rear, where the backside of our Lady Lagonda had been swathed in hay. 'No.' I changed my mind. 'The one next to it. Look. It's not as flush as the others.'

Mere fingers achieved nothing, nor the nail file Bea found in Polly's coat pocket, nor the screwdriver I carry with me. We waited impatiently for Guy, and when he at last strode in, he didn't so much as blink at seeing me. 'What's this about a floor?'

I explained there might be something hidden underneath, and he blenched.

'Not another body,' I said hastily, following his thoughts, and he looked happier. 'Money.' When I told him my theory about Mike as a courier of stolen art, he looked less than convinced, however.

'*Mike*? Are you sure?'

'No, but we might be if we're right about that slab.'

We weren't – not the one I'd picked out, anyway. Guy nobly went outside and drove in the digger, but we had to work our way right round the barn until we were fairly sure we were on the right track. With enormous self control I let Guy make the discovery though – just in time, as my credibility was getting very thin indeed. He still thought I was barking mad. But once we'd found the right slab, it was relatively easy going because the concrete was thin at that point, as it had been used only to disguise what lay beneath. That was a thick iron lid and under that—

'A hole,' I cried in triumph.

'Buried treasure?' Bea said. Her voice wobbled, but this time it was with excitement. Even Guy got interested, and as I saved my macho image by heaving up the iron lid myself, we realized that the hole was bigger than we'd thought, and moreover had something in it: a metal box about a foot deep and three feet long, purpose built, it seemed, for this very special hole. It had been provided with straps to help heave it out, but even so Guy and I had a tough struggle. When at last we managed it, we placed it at Bea's feet, and watched her as she squatted down to try to open it.

'It's not even locked,' she said in disappointment. 'It's probably empty.'

But it wasn't. It was packed solid with used fifty-pound notes and hundred-dollar bills.

There was a stunned silence. I don't think any of us had really expected cash treasure like that. Guy cleared his throat. 'That should take us all to the Caribbean for a week or two.'

An underestimate. There must have been at least a million there.

'Money,' Bea said in awe, and she burst into tears. Through relief? Through despair that her parents weren't as she had assumed them to be? Or because this was one more step towards a solution to Polly's killer. A step that was going to take us I knew not where.

TWENTY-ONE

'**B**ut why didn't they tell me?' Bea had seemed annoyed rather than upset at the confirmation of her parents' secret life. So much had happened, perhaps her emotions had been put on hold. Between us, we had thrashed over the subject of Polly and Mike's choice of fun to the point of exhaustion after we returned from the barn. It still didn't seem to be taking us forward, so Zoe had answered a three-line whip to join us, and she had her own answer for the question.

'Generation gap,' she answered briefly. 'Don't worry the children with matters that don't concern them.'

Guy and Sarah had also been included in our council of war and didn't depart until well after midnight. Zoe and I had stayed over, but the night had brought only fitful sleep to me. It still felt odd to be sleeping in Polly's house, especially as I seemed to be making a pretty poor fist of finding her killer. A box of buried treasure was a step in the right direction but not nearly far enough.

Tomas's death had changed the perspective. From Brandon's viewpoint, he would have to consider the possibility that Tomas's death was a revenge killing by Bea, Guy or even me. The discovery of the money opened up a whole new dimension. When morning came, we dutifully rang the police, and Brandon raced hotfoot up to view the evidence and interview us one by one. I was reasonably sure that even Brandon couldn't think I was cuckoo enough to kill not once but twice for a woman I'd only met a couple of times. But doubt is an obstinate beast, and he could well suspect I'd been after the money the whole time. Nevertheless, he and his gang departed without slapping handcuffs on any of us – and without the money. Brandon had no mandate to take it, as evidence in connection with Polly's or Tomas's death, but I suspected he might be taking advice on the issue right now.

Scenarios flashed through my mind. First, would there be fingerprints or DNA on the notes? Could be. So Brandon might be back. Or was this ball in Dave's court under its car theft implications? Or the Met's remit under art theft? I was getting out of my depth, and the way Zoe and Bea looked, so were they. In the end it was solved. Guy was summoned once more, and later that morning he and Bea drove off to her solicitors' office in Ashford, complete with the loot. Zoe and I went over to Frogs Hill to check on the Lagonda and discuss exciting things like insurance.

Lunch at the Black Lion in Pluckley proved the balm we all needed, and Bea joined us once she had dropped Guy off at Greensand Farm where he'd parked his own car.

'Mr Brandon kept asking me if I was *sure* my parents never mentioned that money,' Bea said desolately. 'I told them yes I was, and that I was certain Mum didn't know about it.'

'How can you be certain, Bea?' I asked. I'd love it to be so, but it seemed doubtful.

'Because she wouldn't have left it hidden there. She'd have turned it in when Dad died.'

'Even if it incriminated herself?'

'She wouldn't have cared by that time.'

'It's more likely she did know, Bea.'

'Can you prove it?' she shot back at me furiously.

'Only by common sense coupled with the Lagonda pocket.'

'You mean that's how the money travelled back?'

'It adds up. The painting would travel out, the cash would come back; it was hidden away in the barn until it was handed over to a Mister Big. For some reason the last batch stayed where it was, probably because of your father's death.'

'Fault, Jack. I knew you were wrong,' Bea promptly said. 'I don't see Dad getting a digger in every time one of these handovers took place.'

Then Zoe pitched into me. 'You're up a gum tree there, Jack. You think Mike was murdered, but no one would do that without finding out where the loot was hidden.'

I could deal with that one, but not in front of Bea. If we accepted that Mike and Polly were the Mister Bigs of the operation, together with Mason Trent, then only Trent would have had reason to kill Mike. If Mike was a number two, however, he could have become too big for his boots and decided to blackmail this Mister Big for a bigger share of the booty. If so, his permanent disappearance might have been more desirable than the cash. It's true, however, that the million or so quid that we estimated was in the box was one helluva lump sum to give up lightly, the kind of oversight that Mason Trent was unlikely to make.

I wondered if Mike had been involved in some very private enterprise of his own, perhaps cutting Mr Big out so that he wasn't aware of the fortune he was bypassing. But that scenario wouldn't work unless that private enterprise consisted of cash for items unknown to Mr Big. Now that, I thought, was a possibility – especially as the art Mike would have been shifting would probably be from the next rank down, the relatively lesser known paintings and drawings. If one or two extra of those slipped into the Lagonda, Mr Big might not necessarily know about it. But if he found out . . .

'OK.' I made up my mind with great relief. 'I accept Polly might not have known about the cash.'

Zoe looked at me curiously. It wasn't like me to backtrack, but this time I was willing to do so. 'So all we have to do is find Mr Big, is it? Who is he?'

We all knew the answer, but none of us wanted to be first. We held back, and it was Bea who bravely broke cover.

'Rupert was hosting some meeting or other in London.'

'Rupert was,' I said. 'Was Lorna though? She and Rupert had left Piper's Green together on Sunday evening, but Lorna could have stayed in easy reach of their target.'

Could I really see Lorna facing Polly with a gun? Yes, but not pulling the trigger. Could I see her organizing major art thefts? No. She was too volatile. Rupert was a different kettle of fish – a cold one. I could see a partnership between the two working, though. Rupert opens the gallery for the meeting, rings Polly on an untraceable mobile, arranges to meet her at the barn, on some made-up reason, but it's Lorna who turns up to do the job.

In theory it was possible, but I *still* couldn't see her pulling that trigger. Rupert must somehow have been involved more actively.

'Not Lorna's style.' Zoe confirmed my thoughts. 'Rupert took all his framing to Polly though. Good cover.'

It was, but I still couldn't see how he could have killed Polly.

'Dan Burgess took his daubs to her too, but that doesn't mean—' Zoe stopped short at the sight of Bea's and my faces.

'Dan Burgess.' My turn to be triumphant. 'Rupert delivered

the stolen paintings to Greensand Farm for Polly and Mike to take them over to the continent, and then after Mike died, Dan took that job over.' For the first time pieces were falling into place. I'd forgotten Bea, however.

'I don't think,' she said abruptly, 'that I fancy this pizza much.' She pushed her Margarita aside.

'You're out of order, Jack,' Zoe said angrily. 'Bea's had enough.'

'Only of this pizza,' Bea managed to joke. 'Go on, Jack. *Go on.*'

I took her at her word. 'Polly wouldn't have wanted to continue taking paintings across the Channel after Mike died. That adventure was over. But another one opened up. Polly began the framing business as cover for Rupert to bring the hot stuff down to Greensand Farm, where the switchover took place. Dan would pick it up when he dropped off his next masterpiece. How's that for a scenario?'

I had Zoe and Bea's full attention. No one shouted me down this time. 'As Professor Higgins so memorably said, I think I've got it,' I concluded.

We fell on this meaty bone, dissected it, and it still proved edible. 'So what now?' Zoe asked. 'March along to DI Brandon and tell him we've cracked the case? He *will* be impressed.'

'No. He might ask for something called evidence.'

'There's the pocket in the Lagonda.'

'Even if it had bits of paint from the Mona Lisa still attached, it doesn't prove who put them there and why – and neither will it show who killed Polly, Tomas and possibly Mike.' My confidence began to ebb away – but then cautiously flowed back. I still couldn't see how Rupert could have killed Polly, but Tomas was a different matter. He was killed on a Saturday, when the Stacks would be at Hurst Manor.

There's a limit to how much even very stiff upper lips can take, and I could see that Bea had reached it. Zoe could too. 'Tonight, Bea, you're coming home with me,' she said firmly.

'I can cope—'

'No, you can't.'

I caught Zoe's eye – and agreed with the message it was sending me. Three people close to Bea had been murdered. Neither Zoe nor I would let Bea be the fourth.

* * *

I knew I should take this to Brandon, but something still held me back. I was well used to showdowns in the oil business – but I was sensible enough to know that this was not the oil business, and if I was to tackle the Stacks, I had to be much surer of my ground.

The needle that was irritating me took the shape of Slugger Sam. Daft though it sounded, I just couldn't see him fitting into this pattern. He was a straightforward villain, and Rupert and Lorna played cards close to their chests. Very close, in Lorna's case. Sam and Andy Wells fitted together like a pair of gloves, but I couldn't see either of them having a major role in a sophisticated art racket. I had two days left before Rupert's charity art show on Saturday, and I had to work quickly if I was going to make the most of it. Again, I wasn't sure what I expected to happen there. Just something to set me on the right track – and preferably not another attempt on my life.

There were two other unknown factors in this puzzle – excluding Guy, who now seemed to have entered the stakes as Good Guy. When I reached Frogs Hill, averting my eyes from the desolation of the Pits, there was a message to ring him. He was out, but whatever he was doing he stopped it immediately when I rang his mobile.

'Thanks for ringing, Jack.' A change to the old days indeed, I thought at this courtesy. 'Thought you should know,' he continued, 'that Tomas's brother hit town today. He's breathing fire.'

'At you?'

'No. Andy Wells.'

'Thanks, Guy. Is this confidential or can I share it with the law?'

'Don't give a damn who you tell. I want that lad's killer found.'

I switched off, feeling I'd been headbutted, but in the right direction. Not Andy's – Dave's. I needed to bypass the small fry.

I fumed until Dave returned my call several hours later.

'Mason Trent, Dave.' I launched straight into it when he'd finished chuckling at the idea of my finding a million and not making a buck out of it. 'Permission to personally hunt him down and steam ahead?'

Guarded answer. 'What tracks?'

'Relationship with Mike Davis on private art theft deals, as a sideline to working with the godfather.'

He considered this. 'Approach with extreme caution, and keep me in the picture. OK?'

'Agreed. What about car cloning ops? Both modern and classics to order.'

'Mine, all mine. Keep to specific jobs for which he might have supplied cloned getaways in the *past*. Got it?'

'Got it. Got his mobile number?'

A snort. 'As if. You're the car detective. You find out.'

Great. All I needed, when every hour counted. I took out the dog-eared pink business card with its Barton Lamb address – it wasn't lamb, but dead mutton. Instead of panicking, I tried a spot of psychology. Did Mason Trent want to keep tabs on me, or did he not? He did. He usually operated in south London, and Barry Pole was in the Lewisham area. I have a gift that's useful in my trade – I can remember number plates, and I remembered that Ford's, so it wasn't rocket science to get the owner's address. Mason Trent was good, but even Homer nods, as they say. Not altogether to my surprise the search produced an address in Lewisham. It was worth a go.

'Impressed, that's what I am.' Mason Trent wasn't even barring my passage the next day. In fact he ushered me in with a lordly sweep of the arm, although lordly was at odds with the style of the small and anonymous terraced house where the Ford was registered. Wherever Mrs Trent and family (assuming Mason had these assets) were, it wasn't here, however, which was hardly surprising in his line of business. Nor was it much of a home. It looked barely furnished apart from the one office he showed me into. I walked into this 'parlour' like the proverbial fly into the spider's web. I'd seen his eyes giving me the once-over as I came in, and I obligingly lifted up my arms to reassure him I was unarmed.

'Been expecting you,' he began the proceedings. 'Heard you went over to that barn where the stiff was found. Find the loot, did you?'

'No, but I found Tomas Kasek. The same day you paid me a visit.'

'Yeah.'

'Your doing?'

'Now would I, Jack? You insult me, you really do. We done the place already.'

'Wrong. We had new security put in.'

'I should know. One of my lads was on the team. Reported nothing there.'

I wasn't going to disillusion him. 'My turn to be impressed, Mason. Let's start by saying you never came to Kent to see me, and in return you tell me about Mike Davis. Before you went inside, you worked with him.'

'Good old Mike.' He was watching me carefully, lolling back in his black leather chair as though he ran a bank. He looked amused too, which could mean he was ready to be pally or could mean I wasn't getting out of here, whatever he told me. I decided to be optimistic.

'In the *past* did you organize the art thefts or just the getaways?'

'Something like that. Tell me more, Jack.'

'The way I see it good old Mike was double-crossing you.'

'Could be. Always been a victim, I have.'

'And you reckoned he had the proceeds tucked away, some at least of which were yours.'

'Maybe.'

'Let's assume you provided the getaway cars. You had,' I explained delicately, 'access to clones of expensive cars. In the past, Mason, in the past. I'm not interested in the present situation.'

'Just as well, Jack.'

'You have a partner, who organizes the actual art thefts.'

'*Did* have.' He looked hurt.

'Maybe you double-crossed him through your private arrangement with Mike?'

'Now that's a word I don't like. Double-crossed. We parted ways, that's all. A business arrangement.'

'Who?'

'I don't think you'd like to know, Jack. You really wouldn't. And nor,' he added, 'can I remember, come to that.'

'There was a chap who went down for art theft around the same time as you.'

'Small fry. Always whining about not being treated fair.'

'Tell me.'

'As if.'

Well, it had been worth a go. 'So to tie down what your memory does recall, Mike got more money than reached your former partner, and he split it with you.'

'I don't think my partner would have liked that. Jack. Not at all.'

I saw him grin and knew I was on the wrong track. I switched over. 'Of course, pinch one more painting or drawing than the organizer ordered, but nothing too grand, so that the subsequent publicity would concentrate on the big stuff. But your partner found out.'

The grin disappeared. 'Not quite right, Jackie boy. Mike was a greedy lad, wanted more pie than Mummy served him with, started banging his spoon on the table making threats, and Big Daddy had to put him to bed, like you said. But Big Daddy found out there were a few more pies cooked than he'd known about.'

'So it just depends who Big Daddy is. You?'

The atmosphere cooled considerably. 'Now, Jack, you go too far. You really do. Me kill Mike? You're way out. Mike and me were mates. Understood each other – most of the time. You know what you're doing here?'

'I traced your number plate. You forgot that.'

A leer more than a grin. 'I don't forget, Jack. Not ever. I knew you'd need me sometime – had to leave a way open. I heard you'd been adding two and two over Mike, and I reckon you can make four. Good enough for me. And his killer's going to pay. Done and dusted. Understood?'

I nodded. 'Big Daddy?'

'Oh yes, this time. No choice.'

I was looking at the real Mason Trent: ugly, powerful and in deadly earnest.

'Each to his own, Jack. I do cars, not art,' he continued. 'He did all that side of it himself: the hired hands, the mark and the hit. Big Daddy and I parted on bad terms. Him and another chum of mine got me banged up. Would you believe it? Me. I've gone straight ever since I got out. Honest.' The grin was back.

'You're being remarkably helpful.'

'Ain't I just. And I'll tell you why, Jack. I want him behind

bars, without me being wiped out first. Or you,' he added
considerately.

I was going to ask him why in that case he wasn't worried
about telling me so much (if it was pukka, of course). But
then I saw several piles of pink cards on the table and noticed
each pile had a different name and address. I was aware that
he saw me looking at them.

'Yeah,' he said. 'And tell Dave Jennings I'm moving on
today. Address unknown. I got twenty more piles of them
cards tucked away, all different.'

I'd been expecting to hear from Giovanni, but by Friday afternoon there had been no word. But to my pleasure he arrived
that evening. I did have a call of sorts first:

'Jack, I come. We drink.'

'Great. In an hour?'

'I come *now*.'

And he came, bless him.

The charity art show was going to be a big do for Piper's
Green. I'd been seeing posters everywhere advertising that
proceeds would be divided between the local hospice and a
charity for gifted art students. It was going to be more than
just an exhibition. There would be drink, food, 'how to paint'
displays, children's corners and other attractions. One of the
latter was Giovanni's presence; another was that owners
attending in their classic cars could receive the privilege of
Dan Burgess's offer to paint them outside the manor house
(for a price). So Dan would be most certainly be present. He
couldn't miss a chance like that.

'Ah, Jack,' Giovanni murmured as I took him into the Glory
Boot. 'Antonio, dear Antonio, how I miss him.'

'Me too.' Being here with Giovanni made me even more
conscious that it wasn't the same without Dad.

With some trepidation I showed him round, fearing that he
would not approve of Dad's arrangements for his precious
paintings. Fortunately, the idea of one of his masterpieces
flying from the ceiling appealed to Giovanni, as did the posi-
tioning of one of them inside Dad's old picnic basket. The
silence was so long that I was sure an explosion was on its
way. Instead, there was a gentle sigh.

'Ah yes, I am good.'

'Very,' I agreed. 'The best.'

That settled, I decided to tell him about Polly, the Lagonda and my theory about how the art thefts were arranged. I didn't mention Rupert and Lorna, but Giovanni is quick-witted and grew very interested.

'You think Rupert is a big thief?'

Not politic to answer that. 'I've no proof of anything like that.' True enough.

'Ah,' said Giovanni. 'He is a clever man that Rupert, and so is his wife.'

I'd love to have asked him whether he was one of Lorna's targets, but as so often Giovanni read my mind. 'Good thing I have my Pia, yes?'

I agreed. I could do with a Pia of my own. Then I took him outside to show him the Lagonda – under strict rules of secrecy, I explained. He thought this very amusing, but the laughter stopped when I opened the barn doors and he saw the Lagonda. He put his head on one side, with that abstracted look in his eye that I connected with planning a new painting.

'Nice, Jack. Not a Monet, not a Turner for this beauty. I think a Vermeer, but better a Giovanni, yes?'

'If only,' I agreed fervently.

'So you show me this pocket, Jack.'

I led him round, and he squeezed into the rear seat to have a closer look. 'Small, Jack, for big works of art. You sure that he smuggle the Leonardos out this way?'

'Not Leonardos, but less well-known paintings. Still make a mint, but not so much hue and cry about them.'

'And drawings,' he said immediately.

'That's what the thinking is.'

'Smaller. Fit in very nicely. A Reynolds, a Constable, even a Rubens, all sorts.'

He was so spot on that I almost wondered whether he knew about Mike's little game on the side.

'You check it out more, Jack.'

'I'll do that. But now I feel like checking out a bottle. How about it?'

'Jack, I love bottle. I love two bottles.'

The rest of the evening passed in a haze, before he returned to the manor. By mutual agreement, he took a taxi. We agreed to do the same on the morrow.

But a lot of water could have passed under the bridge by then.

TWENTY-TWO

'd decided to go in style – to Hurst Manor, that is. I'd no intention of heading for the great hereafter just yet. On Saturday morning, I strode out of Frogs Hill farm, told the Gordon Keeble it was lucky to have me and tried to look 'monied'. No casual cords for a Gordon Keeble. Nonchalant and relaxed should be my approach. It didn't bode well that the familiar image of High Noon refused to disengage from my mind, despite the fact that I was not going to walk towards my enemy down a dusty empty street and beat him (or not) to the draw. I was going to an art exhibition in an English house on an English June weekend. Noon for me would find me sipping my first bubbly of the day, not at a shoot-out.

Signs pointed classic cars towards a field at the side of the house, whereas the hoi polloi were being directed further down the road. This was no mere local show. This was money, and it flaunted itself. The array of expensive cars took me aback. Classic car owners are no respecters of class. I prefer the class mix where they are concerned: there are rich aristocratic owners born with or without silver spoons in their mouths; and there are also poor owners, who in their lovingly restored classics – often picked up surprisingly cheaply – see their dreams amply fulfilled without parting with much money. Others part with every penny they've got in the great cause. Days like this are the reward for all of them.

However, I reminded myself, I wasn't here for the art or even for a classic cause. I was sniffing Polly's killer out, and he could be close. I wasn't going to be deflected even by the sight of that slinky E-type Jaguar I spotted in the car park set aside for the classics.

The exhibition was in the manor house, and the lowly barn, where the art show had been, was devoted to refreshments including the bar. The rear lawns boasted two huge marquees, and I could see the gathering was in full flow. So was Lorna.

Clad in leather miniskirt and jacket, she looked formidable. For a moment I thought I saw a whip in her hand, but it turned out to be a fly swat. No flies on that lady. I could see familiar faces all round. I glimpsed Guy and Sarah, Liz and her ghastly consort, Peter and Jill Winter, and Harry was there with Teresa, though I hadn't put them down as ardent art lovers. I even thought I saw Andy Wells, though mercifully without Slugger. It only needed Mason Trent to show up and the party would be pretty well complete.

Rupert must be inside the house, and perhaps Dan was already at work painting his masterpieces. Giovanni would be in the barn sitting at the bar. It was time to start gunning my engine. But then Rob strolled into my path with Zoe, who was clad in a skirt, I noticed. This must be a posh do indeed. The lemon-coloured skirt and top suited the orange spikes of her hair well, and I stopped my headlong rush to destiny to tell her so. Rob looked hurt at being ignored, but I had bigger fish than him to fry that day.

'Bea's here somewhere,' Zoe told me. 'Gotta plan, gov?' she asked mockingly.

Any semblance of one promptly vanished, not least because I'd forgotten Bea might be there, and I didn't want her caught up in any possible trouble. When I saw Rupert and Dan walking into the house, however, I forgot even Bea. High Noon had arrived.

I tried to slow my impulse to run into a saunter, and as I reached the door into the manor I could see them going into Rupert's office, the room he'd taken me to before. I could hardly follow them in. Besides, I wanted to tackle them singly. That way I stood more chance of success. I could have listened at the keyhole, but that didn't appeal to me. I have *some* pride. So I just hung about in the corridor, admiring some ghastly racing prints on the wall. I was therefore taken by surprise when Dan emerged almost immediately. He didn't notice me at first. He was looking grim and clutching a piece of paper, as though it contained the winning line for this week's lottery.

'Morning, Dan.'

He looked as startled to see me as I had at his reappearance.

'Looking for the loo,' I explained feebly. Well done, Jack. Really original.

'Back the way you've come,' he said politely. 'On the left.'

Dan's face is chiefly set for only one reading; he's too keen on the superhero one to switch his expression unnecessarily.

'Care for a drink?' I asked, planning my strategy carefully.

'No need, Jack. Everything you need is here.' He proudly waved the bit of paper in front of me.

I'd lost the plot before page one. Was he about to cosh me? Had he mistaken who I was? Had I a role in one of the special 'attractions' today?

He pressed the precious paper into my hand and grinned cheerfully. Next move mine. I glanced at it, but saw only a list of names and places, none of which made any sense. Maybe it was written in some kind of Enigma code, but I didn't have Bletchley Park at my disposal.

Dan looked surprised at my inaction. 'Rupert's waiting for you,' he explained – or thought he did.

Waiting with what? I wondered. A hand grenade? A Smith & Wesson?

I remembered the loo I'd claimed to be seeking and retreated there for recuperation. Dan kindly said he'd wait. I looked at the list again and this time I took in that there were two English stately homes and a list of people's names, some of which I recognized as artists. Grant Wood was one. And another American artist, Jack Levine, and the Mexican Diego Rivera. My ex-wife Eva was addicted to American and Mexican art and thought it most unfair if any of their work found its way to Britain, instead of their native lands, but I could hardly see her behind this racket. What did this list imply? Targets for the next art raid, or that their paintings were already winging their way across the Channel to a new owner courtesy of Dan?

He was lolling around in the corridor when I emerged, and so there was no retreat – even if I'd wanted one. This was what I'd come for, but I preferred to go in fully armed with a few clues as to why I'd been presented with this. Was I in the gang now? Or did Rupert only want to discuss buying my Giovannis, and Dan had given me the wrong bit of paper? He left me at the door, which encouraged me into thinking that at least this was not High Noon, but only coffee time.

It wasn't. Rupert was sitting behind his desk looking businesslike; party host mode was non-existent. Even his voice seemed brisker than the Rupert I was expecting.

'Good to see you here, Jack. I wanted a word with you. Have a seat.'

'Thanks,' I said cautiously.

'I hear you've been getting too interested in major art theft. You might need that list for starters.'

'Thanks.' What game we were playing? I hadn't a clue. Who had his information come from? Giovanni? Bea? Mason? Whatever the game was, Rupert had won the toss.

'Your theory about Mike and Polly,' he began.

This was looking bad. I said nothing.

'And the Lagonda,' he added, watching me like a particularly steely-eyed hawk. 'You still have it, don't you?'

Getting worse. 'What theory?' I countered, then cursed myself. I was following when I needed to lead if I was going to stand a chance of getting out of this labyrinth.

'Come off it, Jack. Continental car shows, my foot. Smuggling art.'

The script wasn't getting any simpler. He was luring me on. I'd stop in my tracks, I decided. He'd overreach himself, he had to.

He sighed. 'I suspect you have me down as major art thief and double murderer, of Polly and Tomas.'

Time to play my hand. 'And Mike. It fits. That's why Polly died. She realized you'd killed him.'

He took this in his stride. 'The pronoun's wrong, Jack. Not "you", but "someone".'

'No point, I've evidence, starting with the coffee bill.'

'Coffee bill?' He lost his cool. He looked completely shaken. Of course he would. He'd have forgotten that long ago. 'What bill?'

'Two cappuccinos on the day Mike died supposedly alone in Canterbury. Polly told you it had been found.' Bluff, but it sounded OK.

'I wish she had.'

There was emotion in his voice now. I saw his hand go to the drawer in his desk, and my heart went into overdrive. What to do? Dive for the floor, run – I stayed where I was, with a vague thought that Gary Cooper would be proud of me. And then the drawer shot open.

Even an old hand like me can be surprised by events. No

gun. Instead, Rupert took out an old-fashioned box file, which he handed to me.

'If you look inside, Jack, even you might realize that we're fighting on the same side. Law and order. More specifically the police's.'

I was stupefied. A bluff? A trick? Memories of medieval Medici cunning in the way of hidden poisoned daggers flashed through my mind. I opened it and glanced down. I was greeted by the sight of CD disks, official badges and ID cards. Fakes? No, this was the real McCoy, and I was out for the count.

Rupert was watching me with amusement. 'Sorry, Jack. I thought you'd cottoned on to me. Some years ago the London Stolen Arts Database approached me to work for them, just as you do on cars for the police, and I'm now working with the Specialist Crime Directorate. There has been a series of major art thefts over the years, too infrequent to draw conclusions, but enough to get them interested in the idea that there was one brain behind it. They were kind enough to tell me they'd checked me out and were satisfied I wasn't involved, even though my country home was conveniently near the Channel. It didn't take me too long to realize that there was a pattern to these thefts; the major losses seemed always to be accompanied by less valuable paintings or drawings, but unfortunately one name on their list of those to be watched was someone I knew in Piper's Green. Someone I liked, in fact. Mike Davis, so it was a tough assignment. As you know, he died, but the thefts are still ongoing.'

I felt as though Slugger Sam had kicked me senseless. There was no doubt about the credentials I was looking at. So much for my detection abilities.

He must have read my expression correctly. 'Don't blame yourself, Jack. In your position I'd have thought Rupert Stack was suspect number one for chief villain.'

'Then who is the chief villain, if it wasn't Mike? Can you tell me? Not Dan?'

'Hands tied, Jack. I can only tell you who it's not, and it's not Dan. He's been working for me since Mike died. So far the police haven't been linking Polly's murder with the Specialist Crime Directorate investigation, but with Tomas Kasek's death to take into account it's a different matter.'

He paused. 'You believe Mike was murdered too. Take care, Jack, at *all* times.'

'Should Bea take care as well?'

The pause was too long. 'Let's hope she knew nothing of what her parents were up to.'

'I don't think she did, but she does now.' Just in time I pulled back from mentioning the cash – to be on the safe side. He might, or might not, have known about it yet, but it wasn't my job to tell him. 'What about Polly? Was she in this up to her neck?'

'She was heavily involved, and possibly it was even her idea.'

Instinctively, I still drew back from believing this credible. My brain told me one thing, my heart another. What Rupert said made sense when I thought of her giving up TV, going in with Mike, taking on the game . . . But my heart still could not accept it. 'So who's the big cheese who decided to kill her? Mason Trent?'

'That's who your chum Dave Jennings favours.'

I had to think this through, after I left Rupert. I'd been so sure, and I needed time. That wasn't like me, but I wanted air and space to think, not have to face chatty crowds. Did I trust Rupert? I was still in two minds. There are plenty of double agents in the world. I even had a fleeting doubt about Bea. Could she have known all along about her parents? Or Andy? Was he really the 'everyone's favourite garage man' that he appeared? Was Guy a gorilla after all, not a pussy cat? Had Tomas found out about the money and killed Polly for it? If so, who killed *him*? Was Mason Trent even now stalking me? A thousand questions were racing round the Brands Hatch of my mind, and none of them reached the chequered flag. Something else burnt into my mind as well. Rupert's 'Take care, Jack, at *all* times.' He must know something I didn't, because it wasn't a platitude.

Until I'd reasoned my way through this quagmire, I didn't want company, so I drifted into the garden, avoided the crowds and marquees, and made towards the less frequented part. Then I saw Lorna making straight for me. The last person I wanted to see, but luckily I still had time to casually turn away and stroll (stop myself running!) towards the wild area of the garden. To my relief I could see she'd been accosted by Peter and Jill Winter, and I managed to disappear out of her sight, screened by trees and bushes.

Hurst Manor overlooks a heavily wooded valley, which is all part of the estate. In the spring, the Stacks allow the peasants in for the bluebell season, but there were no bluebells now, just undergrowth, a few ill-defined paths, and green, green trees. It felt daft taking cover there, but at least Lorna wouldn't follow me, and the cool calm of the woods was a refuge until I could decide what came next.

One thing was clear. I had been bang on target with the general background of Polly and Mike's life. Where I'd gone wrong was in misconstruing the structure, and in that lay the clue to what was happening. My head felt like a low-energy light bulb. Light was there, but it was taking longer to come on.

There had to be an answer. Did I really see Polly as a master art-gang organizer? Part of an international art racket? Away with logic, follow instinct. No, I didn't. She would have had to have been ruthless to carry out such a job, and the Polly I had longed to hold in my arms wasn't. There was someone else. Someone close.

I stood listening to the sounds in the wood. I'd thought I was alone there, but I wasn't. A primitive instinct warned me of danger. Those prickles stung me again, and I felt my muscles tightening as they hadn't since I was faced with a maniac with a machete in the oilfields. I could see nothing, hear nothing, but that was immaterial. I had company.

'You got too close, Jack.'

When I spun round at the familiar voice, I saw who was blocking the path back.

Peter Winter.

Forward? Plunge off through the bushes? The path was petering out, and anyway, guns are quicker than men at covering distance. I couldn't see one, but he had one all right.

Odd that I'd once thought he had a pleasant face. It wasn't. It was mean, it was ugly, it was ruthless, and if I couldn't think fast enough it would be the last one I saw.

'Brought your toy gun with you, Jack?' He sounded so jolly that for a moment I thought I'd got it all wrong again. Still no sign of a gun in his hand, nor any overt sign of menace either. But I could feel it all around me.

'No.'

'We'll make it quick then.'

Was he bluffing? Still no gun in his hand, but I was in no doubt that facing me was Mister Big – Polly's killer, Mike's killer and probably Tomas's; he or his chum Slugger. Slugger must have been Peter's man, not Andy's. I tried desperately to debate my options, while somewhere in the background Gary Cooper cheered me on.

'Too many people around, Peter.' How odd that my voice sounded so calm.

'All the best killers use silencers. Pity, I liked you, Jack – and you did get my Merc back. Unfortunately, you worked out what happened to Mike, just as Polly did. The big mistake.'

Then his hand was in his pocket and a gun was pointing right at me. Forget about previous life flashing before you – what was whizzing through mine was a plan, but it whizzed too fast. I couldn't catch it before there was a loud trampling behind Peter that unbelievably assumed a familiar shape. Slugger Sam. Sheer shock at a new arrival made Winter hesitate a second too long, and Slugger's famous cosh felled him, not me, to the ground.

That should have been it, but it wasn't.

Slugger and I made the same mistake. We both dived for the gun and collided – result? Winter was up and away, while we recovered from our head-on engagement. He ran surprisingly quickly for an out of condition middle-aged man and was in open ground long before we were. I realized as we staggered after him that he was heading for the classic car park.

You have to think in these situations, but sometimes, believe me, you're not thinking straight. Did I think: no point trying to stop him now; he'll deny everything; grab your phone and hand it over to the professionals?

I did not.

Instead I went right back to oil days' mode and raced after him. Slugger was no cleverer; he was still panting along at my side when we reached the car park field. Somehow when I saw Peter Winter climbing into that fifties Lagonda he didn't deserve, reason deserted me. It seemed to have deserted Slugger as well. He headed straight for the Lagonda, waving his arms, but Peter was in it with the door slammed before he got there. Slugger promptly dashed round to its bonnet as if about to lie down in front of the wheels to prevent its leaving. Luckily

– as I could envisage the Lagonda making straight for the exit unimpeded by mashed Slugger – he must have thought better of it.

I wish I'd done the same. I leapt for my Gordon Keeble, parked near the exit and was driving my proud beauty across it with some damn-fool notion that the Lagonda would stop. Instead it came straight for me, crashing into the side of the Gordon Keeble and skewing it into the gateposts. The impact did, however, halt the Lagonda long enough for Rupert's pre-arranged cavalry to arrive.

It stopped me for rather longer.

TWENTY-THREE

I woke up in hospital once again. The first time I came to, Bea was cooing over me. I think I smiled and passed out again. I must have repeated this procedure several times because I have vague memories of seeing Zoe, Len, Guy, Rupert, Lorna (I only pretended to fall asleep that time), and even Slugger. He brought my memory back with a vengeance, although not quite accurately, as I squeaked: 'You can't cosh me here.'

Slugger actually grinned. 'Sorry, mate. Trent's orders.'

I couldn't make head or tail of this. Next time I woke up – after a poke in the ribs – I saw that damned chain round a swarthy neck again. Mason Trent was leering over me.

'I'm not dead yet,' I managed to say this time.

He, too, looked apologetically at me. 'Sorry, Jack.'

Everyone seemed to be sorry. What for? Mason, it seemed, was only too happy to tell me. 'Had a side deal going, see, with Mike, like you said. He reckoned Winter was taking too much of the cash, so we'd add a few bits and pieces to the shopping menu Winter issued us with. I'd drive the goods down to Kent, Mike would whip them across the Channel and we'd split the cash three ways: me, him, and the small fry who did the nicking. But Mike went a step too far, like I told you, so he went and got murdered. I never got my rights in the cash line, especially as Winter got me locked up, courtesy of my former chum Barry Pole. All because I'd had this sideline going with Mike, and Winter thought he was being left out in the cold. As if. So I had three years to think of a nice way to thank both Winter and Pole for grassing.'

'Not my fault,' I managed to say.

'You got yourself interested in a Lagonda.'

'Andy Wells told you,' I said resignedly.

'Andy's a good guy,' Mason said indignantly. 'Real worried about you, he was. Him and Harry Prince look out for you.'

I decided silence was best.

'Polly went to him,' Mason continued, 'about Mike's death after your little escapade with the Lagonda. When she was hit, Andy got scared, knowing I had an interest, as they say. Quite right too. I reckoned that was where my cash might be stashed, and I didn't want no busybodies like you sniffing around.'

'So you coshed me.'

'Sorry, Jack. Slugger feels bad about that.'

'So did I.'

'He made it up to you. Saved your life, didn't he?'

'And my barn?' I managed to squeak.

'Not me, mate. Winter hired one of Slugger's mates because he didn't want people nosing round that car and maybe seeing what it was used for. That's what I reckon. He's a right villain, Winter is.'

'But you and Slugger have morals?'

Another leer. 'Sure, Jack. Slugger was all for a nasty end for Winter over what he did to me. He's my man, you see. Loyal. But I'm smarter. I thought of a scheme with no pain for us and a dozen years inside for Winter over the art jobs. So I sort of leaned on my former chum Pole to put Winter's Merc on his list in April and get young Tomas to do the nicking. Tomas was one of Pole's spotters.'

'What did you want the Merc for?'

'Patience, Jack lad, patience. You're not a well man. It was like this: Winter was carrying on his business under a new team, but Barry's still doing the getaways. So under one of my pink card names I'd promised Barry I'd do the cloning for the next big do at Talbot Place in May; persuaded him he needed two, not just one, clones on this job, and I drove the Merc meself. I took the stuff to begin with, and the lads

switched over to number two with the stuff after a mile or
two; I left the Merc nice and noticeable, with a drawing inside
to show where it had been, and went back in the number two
with the lads.'

'So what was the plan?' I murmured feebly.

A chuckle. 'The car I drove there was Winter's Merc, but
I didn't exactly clone it.'

'You used his own plates?' I began to see. Or did I? What
message would that send the cops except that a stolen car had
been used? It had been reported in April, and the art theft at
Talbot Place was in May.

'In a way, mate.' Mason looked smug. 'See, I nipped down
here in April and paid young Tomas quite a bit of cash to get
the identity details of Winter's Lagonda while he was busy
nicking the Merc for Pole. Then I used the Lagonda numbers
for the Merc.'

I had to struggle with this. 'You put the Lagonda DB plates
on the Merc? Why?'

He shook his head sadly. 'You disappoint me, Jack, you
really do. And you calling yourself a car detective.'

I struggled some more. 'So the police are left with the right
car – VIN number checks out – but the wrong plates, all
belonging to the same man.' I began to see it, and it was clever.
'So the Norfolk police think there's something odd going on
here. Car stolen in April, reappears weeks later cloned to his
own second car number. They think: could be a nutter, could
be something rather more interesting. Better look into this
chap Peter Winter.'

I began to laugh. It hurt, but it was worth it.

'Right, Jack.' Mason looked pleased. 'Then enter your
chums: Dave Jennings on law and order for cars, Rupert Stack
on the art side. Not a word to Winter though. Result: bingo,
Peter Winter appears bang in the middle of the frame – just
what he don't want. He likes to keep even his own team at
arm's length. Works through a middle man, but suddenly, little
does he know, but the whole of the Met plus the Kent car
crime chaps are looking into him very carefully indeed. They're
just waiting for him to put a foot wrong.'

The laugh went on – until I realized that it was me who'd
sprung the trap. 'So I was the foot! Thanks a lot.'

Mason looked embarrassed. 'Yeah. Well, wasn't meant to

happen like that. I was right suspicious of you, when you went shouting your head off about a Lagonda. I just made a little mistake like we all do, not knowing Polly still had her Lagonda. I thought you were asking round after mine.'

'By which you mean Winter's DB,' I commented.

'Yeah, and after Polly got knocked off I decided you were getting too interested in Mike Davis's affairs. You might have done it, after all, and grabbed my cash into the bargain,' Mason explained virtuously. 'Still, I sorted it out after Slugger coshed you. Can't blame me for giving you a bit of a hint that messing with me wasn't wise.'

'Sorry about that,' I said sarcastically.

'OK, Jack. That's OK,' he reassured me. 'Mind you, I got a bit upset, like, when you told me Mike was bumped off. Hurried things along a bit.'

I remembered Polly, and Tomas too, and grew very quiet. 'Winter killed Polly?'

'I reckon so. She was asking too many questions about Mike. After Andy, she must have realized who done Mike in and went to see Winter. He couldn't risk it. She might not have been able to prove he done Mike in, but she could prove he'd been running the art racket and probably still was. She'd kept that doctored Lagonda.'

Oh my brave Polly. I felt tears forming and could see Mason looking curiously at me. He didn't say anything. He's a good guy is Mason, I thought idiotically. 'And Tomas?' I managed to say. 'Or was that you?'

'Me? No, mate. I don't do killings, unless I have to. That lad got a bit too big for his boots, I reckon, like Mike. You don't do that with Peter Winter or Barry Pole, who isn't such a nice gent as I am. When I popped down here and explained to young Tomas how he could earn a lot extra by adding on that Lagonda job for me, he went round boasting to the likes of Andy and Harry that he was working for me. They knew nothing about Winter, but they did know about me. I've got a bit of a reputation – don't know why. I'm a gentle sort of chap, as you know. The kid must have wormed the story about me and Mike and Winter out of Pole, put two and two together over the Lagonda in the Davises' barn, and went shouting the odds at Winter asking for a cut and banging on about the missing cash. Winter then would have hired young Tomas to look for it, but no way would he take a kid like that as a partner, so he would have arranged to meet him and shot the poor blighter.' He eyed me thoughtfully. 'Funny choosing the barn though. Almost as though my cash was really there.'

I made a strategic decision to close my eyes.

A day or two later I got much the same story from Dave, who seemed to be handing out pats on the back – apparently, he got one himself from the Met over the way he'd cooperated to trap Peter Winter. He had the grace to blush. 'We were all waiting there,' he assured me anxiously. 'Rupert was waiting for his boss to get there, but he was worried about you. Told his wife Lorna to stick with you throughout.'

I groaned.

'Sorry, Jack. Couldn't put you right in the picture.'

'What about Brandon?'

'He's waiting outside. Thinks he's got some kind of DNA match to nail Winter for Kasek and for Polly.'

'And Mike?'

'So far as the record's concerned, you're raving. He died of a heart attack. Too many cappuccinos.'

And my Gordon Keeble? That took a lot longer to repair than I did, but it's now safely retired to a special barn at Frogs Farm. I don't drive it any more, because it's fragile after its brush with the criminal world.

So what do I drive on special occasions? What makes me the pride of the car shows? What gives me a glow every time I climb into it?

Bea's present to me: the 1938 drophead Lagonda.

'It's my thank you, Jack,' she told me, handing me the keys after Rupert Stack's art chaps from the Met had finished crawling over it for trace evidence. And then she kissed me. A real kiss, not a thank-you kiss, but one with sadness in it. For our different reasons we were bidding our farewells to what might-have-been and saying hello to friendship.

I watched Bea drive out of Frogs Hill Farm and turned back to *my* Lagonda. And just for one glorious moment, by some trick of the light on the front passenger seat, I thought I saw Polly smiling.

THE CAR'S
THE STAR

James Myers

Mike and Polly Davis's 1938 Lagonda V12 Drophead

The Lagonda company won its attractive name from a creek near the home of its American-born founder Wilbur Gunn in Springfield, Ohio. The name given to it by the American Indians was Ough Ohonda. The V12 drophead was a car to compete with the very best in the world, with a sporting 12-cylinder engine which would power the two 1939 Le Mans cars. Its designer was the famous W.O. Bentley. Sadly many fine pre-war saloons have been cut down to look like Le Mans replicas. The V12 cars are very similar externally to the earlier 6-cylinder versions; both types were available with open or closed bodywork in a number of different styles.

Jack Colby's daily driver: Alfa Romeo 156 Sportwagon

The 156 Sportwagon is a 'lifestyle estate', which means that it's trendy and respectable to have on the drive, although it lacks the interior space of a traditional load-lugger. For those who value individuality, its subtle and pure styling gives it the edge over rivals such as the BMW 3-Series. It gives a lot of driving pleasure even with the smaller engines.

Jack Colby's 1965 Gordon Keeble

One hundred of these fabulous supercars were built between 1963 and 66 with over ninety units surviving around the globe, mostly in the UK. Designed by John Gordon and Jim Keeble using current racing car principles, with the bodyshell designed by twenty-one-year-old Giorgetto Giugiaro at Bertone, the cars were an instant success, but the company was ruined by supply-side industrial action. Ultimately, only ninety-nine units were completed, even after the company was relaunched in May 1965, as Keeble Cars Ltd. Final closure came in February 1966 when the factory at Sholing closed and Jim Keeble moved to Keewest. The 100th car was completed in 1971 with leftover components. Its emblem is a yellow and green tortoise.

Dan Burgess's Maserati Mexico

The Mexico, intended eventually as a replacement for the 5000GT, arose following the development of a customer car by

Italian design studio Vignale, which was built as a 2+2 with a 4.9 litre V8 and appeared at the Turin Auto Show in 1965. The following year the definitive version of the car was presented at the 1966 Paris show with a 4.7 litre V8. Somewhat uniquely, the car was offered with the 4.2 litre motor from 1969.

Rupert and Lorna Stack's Bentley Mulsanne Turbo

A new level of achievement was represented by the Bentley Mulsanne Turbo. The Bentley Mulsanne Turbo offered really crisp acceleration. Driver and passengers were catered for in a unique environment dominated by a highly polished walnut veneered fascia, blemish-free leather and carpets, and head-lining of pure wool. A radiator shell painted in the car's colour, light alloy wheels and 'Turbo' labels attached to boot and front wing flanks distinguished the Bentley Mulsanne Turbo from the Bentley Mulsanne.

Peter Winter's daily driver: Mercedes Benz S500

The Mercedes-Benz S-Class is a series of the largest sedans produced by Mercedes-Benz, a division of Daimler AG. The S-Class, a product of nine lines of Mercedes-Benz models dating since the mid-1950s, has ranked as the world's best-selling luxury flagship sedan. As the foremost model in the Mercedes-Benz line-up, the S-Class has debuted many of the company's latest innovations, including drivetrain technologies, interior features, and safety systems (such as the first seat-belt pre-tensioners).

Peter Winter's 1950 Lagonda DB 2.6

The first new automobile produced by Lagonda after its purchase by David Brown in 1947 was the 2.6-litre. It was named for the new high-tech straight-6 engine which debuted with the car. The so-called Lagonda Straight-6 engine was designed by Walter Owen Bentley and would propel Lagonda's new parent company, Aston Martin, to fame. The 2.6-Litre was a larger car than the Aston Martins and was available as either a four-door closed car or, from 1949, a two-door convert-ible drophead coupé, both with four seats.

For more discussion of classic cars, see Jack Colby's blog at jackcolby.co.uk/classiccars.